VEGAS TABLOID

BRAD -
HOWEVER !

ALSO BY P MOSS

<u>**fiction**</u>

BLUE VEGAS
VEGAS KNOCKOUT

<u>**non-fiction**</u>

LIQUID VACATION

VEGAS TABLOID

a novel

P Moss

Squidhat Press • Las Vegas, Nevada

Editor: Scott Dickensheets
Designer: Sue Campbell
Author Photo: Square Shooting

First Edition

ISBN: 978-0-9989872-0-0
ISBN: 978-0-9989872-1-7

Published by:

Squidhat Press
848 N. Rainbow Blvd. #889
Las Vegas, Nevada 89107

Printed in the United States of America

For Velvet

Las Vegas is a sudden town ...

THE FABULOUS. SPORTS BOOK.
WEDNESDAY 3:07 PM

Bill Revson had crossed the country to stop the most dangerous mass murderer in American history, yet all the chain-smoking scientist cared about at the moment was the outrageous bet proposed by the man in the orange Hawaiian shirt seated beside him.

"If I win you'll pay me $10,000, and if I lose I buy you a hot dog?"

"That's the bet," agreed gravel-voiced Jimmy Dot, fireplug stocky with a fuzzy-bald head and dark whiskers that kept the barber shop on its toes twice a day.

"It's a bet you can't possibly win."

"Just keep thinking that," smirked Dot as he took a hit of his dark Robusto cigar, the aroma of rich tobacco pleasing him.

As the men shook hands to confirm the bet, the slender middle-aged lab geek was unaware that this was just the first in a long string of absurdities in which he would play a starring role during his brief stay at The Fabulous, a gleaming shard of ice soaring seventy-seven stories into the desert sky above the Las Vegas Strip. A hotel/casino renown for stimulating every one of the senses. A futuristic orgy of recreational debauchery where the most unbelievable fantasies could come true, and often did.

Jimmy Dot looked a decade older than his thirty-eight years and had a different orange floral-print shirt for every day of the week, which he wore over black slacks and army boots. Hung out at the sports book most afternoons doing both the *Los Angeles Times* and *New York Times* crosswords, enjoying the pride of accomplishment on days he was able to complete the latter. Garnering inspiration from being around suckers who bet the rent on other peoples' ability to accomplish something. Life and death with every bounce of a ball. Yelling at the gigantic ultra HD televisions as if the players could hear them.

Bill Revson comprehended the greed that drove the crazed gamblers in the sports book to vigorously cheer on their teams, just as he comprehended the greed that motivated the killer he had followed across the country. But he did not for one second understand Jimmy Dot.

"Why a hot dog?" Revson hated how cigar smokers fouled the air of those around them, coughing loudly to make his displeasure clear. "Why not a steak? Or cash? Why would you risk so much money on a bet you can't possibly win? It doesn't make any sense."

"Not to a Poindexter like you," Dot told the bookish sucker who refused to allow greed to blur his curiosity. "You could never understand because it's not the kind of thing they teach in school."

"Then why don't you explain it to me," demanded Revson, as he pushed back wire-rimmed glasses and lit another cigarette.

His analytical mind trying to scratch an itch it couldn't quite reach.

Jimmy Dot eyed the juicy foot long dogs percolating in the pushcart near the entrance of the sports book. "All you need to concern yourself with is making sure your ass is here Saturday night to settle up."

"You're worried that I'm going to stiff you for a one dollar a hot dog?"

"I wouldn't advise it."

"What if I win?"

"You got a better chance of growing tits and winning Miss America," cracked Dot as he got up and walked out of the sports book. Tossed his completed crosswords into the trash, and disappeared into the dazzling multi-tiered casino that revolved above a white sand pool where guests could swim with mermaids 24/7.

The man wearing Wednesday orange had not gotten more than a few steps into his getaway when a rube with an insurance convention laminate hanging from his neck excitedly dashed up to him. Face to face quick as a hiccup.

"Jimmy Dot! Can I get a picture?"

Dot flung his arm around the delighted tourist. Smiled as the picture was taken, then extended a hearty two-handed handshake and sent the man on his way to text the photo to everybody in the office back at Indiana Corn & Casualty. Then Dot relaxed the fingers of his clenched fist and checked out the watch he had deftly liberated from the tourist's wrist. Rolex. Not gold, but not bad. Then he stopped a passing scuffler who looked like he had just gambled away his last dollar.

"Excuse me, pal." Dot showed him the Rolex. "You lose this?"

Before you could say Merry Christmas, the scuffler was out the door in the direction of the nearest pawnshop.

THE FABULOUS. WHITE BAR.
WEDNESDAY 3:54 PM

Like everything else in the futuristic hotel, this uber-hip lounge was sleek in design and texture. Everything white, from furniture and carpet to the ashtrays and swizzle sticks. Technetronic ear candy complementing disconnected blips of spirituous color exposed through cocktail glasses made the lounge an ever-changing work of art. And despite the seven-foot Albino at the threshold enforcing the policy of all-white attire required for admittance, afternoon business was brisk.

A midget in a white Elvis jumpsuit sketched on a bar napkin as he goggled two girls drinking exotic cocktails on a white sofa. Pretty girls in short white dresses, one he recognized from a TV show he used to watch. He elbowed the man on the barstool next to him. "The one on the left. Wanna know what her pussy looks like?"

"How could you possibly know that?" laughed the thirtyish man with close-cropped blond hair whose name was Howard.

"Eyebrows, texture of the hair, skin tone, contour of her thighs." Sparkle showed him the napkin on which he had sketched a detailed rendering of what he calculated to be the landscape between the girl's legs, while at the same time lifting a twenty from his new pal's change on the bar. "I got a gift for it, and I'm never wrong."

Howard turned to get a better angle on the girl. He looked at the sketch, then back at the girl.

"How do you know you're never wrong?" He nudged his stool backward to keep from gagging on the cheap cologne and B.O. that made the midget with the oily black pompadour smell like a flocked Christmas tree. "Do you ever have sex with any of these girls?"

"Sometimes. When you're three feet tall, charm only gets you so far. I need a gimmick and this is it."

Sparkle's gift of insight into the feminine arts began when he was eleven years old. His devoutly religious parents viewed their midget progeny as punishment from above for sins that could not be clean-slated in the collection plate on Sunday mornings. But eleven years was a long time and they finally decided that they had been punished enough, so they aimed their pickup toward the Devil's backyard, where they discarded their pint-sized burden in a casino parking lot, then headed back home to claim that clean slate. Confident that in Las Vegas their mutant spawn could secure asylum in a freak show or at the zoo.

Instead, Sparkle found shelter by crawling through the doggy door of a house whose occupants were away, and for the next decade used that method of entrance to make himself comfortable in the upscale homes of vacationing families. He ate their food, drank their booze and watched their porn. Lots of porn. Eventually he graduated to ordering hookers.

Lots of hookers when he was lucky enough to find the home-owners' credit card information. His first pro was an Elvis Presley fanatic who called her pussy Sparkle, and from that moment on his life had direction.

He was living the dream, until one day when he discovered the joy of a well-stocked medicine cabinet and woke up facing a laundry list of criminal charges including credit card fraud. The top count of the indictment earning him three years in a place where there was no booze, no porn and no hookers. The goal of the prison system being rehabilitation instead of punishment, Sparkle learned a trade. Upon graduation he was a skilled thief.

"You two peeping Toms want a better look?" snapped the girl from the white sofa who now stood before them, then focused her anger at Sparkle. "And you, of all people, should know how uncomfortable it is to be stared at."

Howard was mortified and began to assemble an apology, but instead found himself taking that better look. Fair complexion. Light brown hair and eyebrows that were naturally fine. He could not help but wonder.

But the midget didn't wonder. He knew. Showed her the drawing. "This look familiar?"

The girl tried her best to appear offended, but was unconvincing. Maybe that's why she was no longer on TV. But after awarding style points for creativity and sheer audacity, she couldn't keep herself from laughing.

Ice broken. Smiles all around.

"I'm Sparkle," said the midget, bursting with lecherous confidence.

"You're cute. I'm Madison." Then she turned to Howard who could not believe Sparkle's crude gimmick was actually working. "What's your story?"

"Owen Howard." He set down his beer and shook her hand. "I'm an investigative journalist."

"Working or on holiday?

"I'm here to interview Preston Bond."

"I saw him a little while ago. He was having lunch at Bacon&Beer with Jimmy Hoffa," Madison told him, then burst out laughing.

Such derision was to be expected, as Preston Bond was the world's biggest movie star when, two years before, on the way home from a fishing trip, he died in a plane crash in the Grand Teton mountains of Wyoming. Young. Handsome. Rich. Life in the fast lane with an adoring public at his feet. Then all of a sudden he was gone.

Media coverage dwarfed wars and elections and still hadn't eased up much. And because Bond's body was never found, it wasn't long before he was spotted behind the counter of a 7-Eleven in Tennessee, pumping gas in Florida and on a bus in downtown Sacramento. Such rumors were routinely presented and debunked. But the one rumor that had legs was that Bond lived reclusively in a secret penthouse atop The Fabulous, and that he often wandered the casino in disguise late at night. A rumor the hotel did nothing to discourage as it had tripled graveyard business.

Preston Bond was an even more dominant presence dead than he was alive, but Sparkle was not about to be cock blocked by a ghost. He leered at Madison. No x-ray vision

required to describe tits that pushed invitingly against the delicate fabric of her dress.

"How about we have our next drink upstairs?"

"Slow down, Cutie. A girl likes a little sweet talk first."

"Tell her she has nice eyes," whispered Howard, noticing that she did.

"What kind of fag bullshit is that?" sneered the midget, giving Owen Howard a reassessing look.

"He's right, Cutie. Eyes are the gateway to the heart."

"So you're sayin' I got a better chance of getting laid if a draw a picture of your eyes?" He turned the napkin sideways and thought about a Chinese hooker he knew.

"A girl never forgets the eyes," said Madison, looking at the bartender whose white shirt and white tie set off radiant baby blues. Familiar blue eyes, but she couldn't place them. Then she turned her back to Sparkle and asked, "What color are my eyes?"

The midget consulted the drawing. "According to this it doesn't much matter."

It didn't much matter.

Howard had seen stranger things, but not many, as he looked across the lounge as the malodorous midget Elvis now snuggled between two pretty girls on the white sofa.

"Forget about trying to find Preston Bond," said Bill Revson as he walked toward Howard, limping from the pain of an injured right knee. "I can give you a much bigger story."

"Assuming there is a bigger story anywhere in the world than finding Preston Bond, which I guarantee you there is not, why tell me?"

"I overheard you tell the girl you were an investigative journalist, so I Googled you. The exposé you wrote about elder
abuse in *Harper's* last year got you nominated for a Pulitzer
Prize."

"I don't have to be much of an investigator to see that you've
gone to a bit of expense to get past the abominable snowman
at the door," said Howard as he looked at Revson's wrinkled
white short-sleeve dress shirt topping neatly pressed white
slacks still sporting the price tag from one of the casino shops.

"Please, Mr. Howard. I'm only asking for a few minutes of
your time."

The journalist finished his beer and licked foam from his
upper lip. Signaled the bartender for another. Took a closer
look at the man with hair that used to be on his head now
growing out of his ears and deep gashes on his arm that had
just begun to scab. A washed out geezer pushing retirement
age who still wore his Dartmouth class ring.

"Whatever your problem is, pal ..."

"Bill Revson." He set his gin and tonic on the bar, taking
weight off his injured knee by propping himself on a stool that
retained an olfactory suggestion of Christmas on Skid Row.
Fired up a cigarette as his analytical mind demanded to know
if after work the bartender watched his white television on his
white couch in his white boxers. Then he checked out Owen
Howard's white jeans and tight white T-shirt that accentuated
a fit upper body. "You don't look much like your picture online.
Been working out?"

The bartender poured a Budweiser into a frosted pilsner glass and served it to Howard. The first icy sip refreshing him as it went down. Enough cat and mouse.

"I don't believe you just happened to run into me, Revson. How did you know I was here?" Howard fanned away cigarette smoke then slid his phone from the front pocket of his jeans. "And what would I find if I Googled you?"

"That I was a research chemist at EcoGreen Pharmaceuticals who helped develop a drug called ZeeFil that cures the common cold. It doesn't just mask the symptoms, you take one pill and in thirty minutes the virus is completely gone from your system. It's an actual cure and it goes on sale to the public Monday."

"It's a miracle drug and everybody in America will buy it." Howard pushed away Revson's ashtray. "Old news."

"What if I told you that a side effect of this miracle drug is that it causes pancreatic cancer?"

"Keep talking."

"I was the chemist who perfected the key component of the formula. When I later discovered the potentially lethal side effect and alerted my supervisors, I was called on the carpet by the company's top lawyer and reminded of the non-disclosure clause in my employment contract. And that if I knew what was good for me and my family, I would keep my mouth shut about anything having to do with ZeeFil. When I refused, I was fired and blackballed in the scientific community."

"Why would the Food and Drug Administration approve a drug that kills people?"

"Because the drug is such a medical breakthrough the FDA fast-tracked the process. Their official findings from clinical trials concluded that 2.4 percent of the people who take it will experience dry mouth, 3.7 percent will suffer itchy eyes and 8.6 percent will develop a mild rash. But not one word in the final report about the side effect that causes pancreatic cancer. I went to them and explained that the drug needed to be retested and told them what to look for. But because EcoGreen had poisoned my reputation, they refused, dismissing me as a disgruntled former employee. So I went to the media, but EcoGreen used their power to destroy my credibility there as well."

"Quite a conspiracy," smirked Howard.

"This drug is going to kill people!" Color flushed the scientist's face.

"Lower your voice." Howard paused a moment until white on white eavesdroppers returned to their own white on white prattle. "Look, Revson. If I find Preston Bond, no reputable news outlet will run the story without verifiable evidence and video of me having a beer with the guy. So they sure as hell aren't going to run with an unsubstantiated crackpot fairy tale as ridiculous as yours."

"EcoGreen CEO Randy Leeds will do anything, and I mean anything, to make sure his tainted drug goes on the market as scheduled. I've tried everything I possibly can to call the public's attention to this so the FDA will be forced to pull the drug for retesting, but absolutely no one will listen to me. My last chance is to try to crash the annual EcoGreen shareholders meeting on Saturday."

"You're saying that Randy Leeds, CEO of the world's largest pharmaceutical company, knows the drug will kill people and still plans to sell it to the public? That's not possible."

The beleaguered scientist pressed the palm of his hand against his knee, trying without success to subdue a stabbing pain courtesy of a beating twenty hours and two thousand miles ago.

"If ZeeFil is allowed to go on the market, every man, woman and child in America will be exposed to pancreatic cancer. Thousands, maybe millions of people will suffer and die in the name of greed." Revson, weary from stress and lack of sleep, was braced by the truth. "Please, Mr. Howard. You're a respected journalist with a reputation of digging for the truth wherever you believe there is truth to be found. Help me expose this horror before it's too late."

THE FABULOUS. SHOESHINE STAND.
WEDNESDAY 4:11 PM

As Jimmy Dot made his way toward the shoeshine stand near the light-streaked atrium lobby, he was approached by a glamorous black woman in a slinky red evening gown. Hair in a French twist and dangling emerald earrings too big to be real, yet they were. Vintage Diana Ross, if Diana Ross had an Adam's apple.

"Hey, Jimmy."

"Whataya know, Poontang?"

"Jenny's back. I heard she'll be at Delmonico at six." News delivered in a voice that did not betray any secrets. Then she blew him an air kiss and glided off in the direction of the elevators.

Dot's wife had walked out on him months before. He didn't know whether to be thrilled that she was back or angry that she hadn't even bothered to call him, and before he could decide, a frisky blond spring breaker asked for an autograph. Handed him a Sharpie and pulled up her tank top.

Such was life for the man whose devilish smile was on the marquee and plastered on signage throughout The Fabulous. On billboards and taxi-tops all over town. Media hyped the hype with glossy photo spreads showcasing him in his work clothes: top hat, tails and orange polka-dot boxer shorts. All promoting the biggest show to open on the Las Vegas Strip in a very long time. Only a dozen weeks into its run, but already the Jimmy Dot Circus was such a big-titted hit that tickets were sold out through the middle of next year.

Dot was a grifter who had shepherded the neo-vaudeville spectacle from the humble beginnings of a late-night pop-up show in an abandoned carpet warehouse. Then, as with all performers no matter what the wattage of their star power, the wisecracking ringmaster along with his cast of social delinquents including a safe cracking swami, smart-ass midget Elvis and assorted sideshow freaks sought more attention. Looking to nudge the circus into the public consciousness and show the world that Las Vegas entertainment was not limited to past-the-expiration-date singers and by-the-numbers production schlock that spewed from the sphincter of most casino showrooms on the Strip. And attention is what they got, in spades, as evidenced by a front-page story in *USA Today*:

ROD STEWARD ASSAULTED ON STAGE IN LAS VEGAS

Five people were arrested in Las Vegas Thursday night for storming the stage at the Colosseum at Caesars Palace as a mini-Elvis struck singer Rod Stewart in the face with a pie. Blinded by banana cream, the stunned Stewart stumbled about the stage as another of the assailants blew a fireball while a gravel-voiced man in orange polka dot boxer shorts grabbed the

microphone and finished crooning "You Wear It Well"
as the capacity crowd of over 4100 cheered wildly
as they thought the attack was part of the show. Las
Vegas Metropolitan Police spokesman Lieutenant
Harry Kagel issued a statement saying that charges of
aggravated assault and criminal trespass were pend-
ing against the five who gave their names as Jimmy
Dot, Dr. Zazzo, Poontang Johnson, Jenn O. Cide and
Sparkle Short. Kagel added that further investigation
led police to believe that disruption of the show was a
publicity stunt designed to promote an underground
cabaret of curiosities known as the Jimmy Dot Circus.

They weren't in jail long enough for the baloney sandwiches, sprung by Blake Fuller, president of The Fabulous, who was in the audience and thought the stunt was the funniest thing he had ever seen. Which led to a multimillion dollar offer that would move the Jimmy Dot Circus from obscurity to a headlining gig on the main stage of the most amazing casino on earth. Enough money to set them all up for life. But Jimmy Dot did not think twice before saying no, as to him a dollar earned using his wits bought a lot more than a million made punching a time clock. A fundamental principle that had guided him since scamming classmates with fixed cockroach races in the sixth grade.

His wife Jenny admired his code of ethics. But what about Poontang, Sparkle and the rest of them? They wanted money and fame, and Dot knew they deserved it. But did he owe it to them at the expense of his own self-respect? A question he never got to answer as Blake Fuller had a black ace up his sleeve.

Faced with exposure of his most intimate secret, Dot was given no time to think it over. No time to consult an attorney. And before the ink dried on the contract, the ringmaster's mail was being delivered to a suite on the 74th floor of The Fabulous, where he would live under virtual house arrest for the next five years. Alone, because Jenny thought he had sold out and left him in a huff. So instead of greeting each new morning as a blank canvas of larcenous possibility, he was contractually obligated to hang out on the property a certain number of hours every day and pose for photos with obnoxious tourists who thought they had the right to butt into his business in the sports book, the barber shop and even when he took a leak. The victim of ironclad fine print packed with non-performance penalties so draconian he couldn't even quit. Sapping his mojo by placing him under a public spotlight so invasive it burned away almost all chance to ply his trade and take pride in just being himself.

"Hey, Everest. Whataya say? Whataya know?" Dot called to his friend in the red turtleneck and paisley vest as he climbed onto the shoeshine chair.

"Jenny's back and she'll be at Delmonico at six," replied the rich baritone of towering Everest Lincoln as he put down the newspaper he was holding.

"Jesus Fucking Christ! Am I the only one in town who didn't know she was back?"

Every day Everest read the *Wall Street Journal, New York Times* and half a dozen newspapers in between. Keeping up on current events allowed him to speak intelligently to his shine customers on just about any subject, though most conversations were sparked by the two Super Bowl rings he wore. Playing football in an era when a back-up tight end made less than the porter who cleaned the ashtrays at The Fabulous. An economic disparity that cost him eight years in the can for a botched liquor store heist, a sentence that could have been cut in half but he refused to rat out his accomplice. Eight lost years made the decision to go straight an easy one, and he got into the shine business.

After a long day on his feet Everest's dogs were barking. He took a load off his size fifteens, climbing onto the shine chair beside Dot's. Rubbed the jagged scar above his left eye that he told people came from a game against the Green Bay Packers, when it was actually a souvenir from a fight over a cigarette in Cell Block C.

"Big reunion and you're wearing that shirt?"

"Why not? It's my Wednesday shirt."

Jimmy Dot was equal parts excited and nervous, as he had not spoken to his wife since she walked out on him. Never given a chance to explain how Fuller had blackmailed him into signing the contract with The Fabulous. Agonizing months in which he had not known where she was. Lonely months in which he had learned the hard way that he could not live without her. And now, in less than two hours they would be face to face. Not knowing how she would react to seeing him, his guts knotted like a teenager scared to move in for his first kiss.

"Check it out."

Everest nodded toward the atrium where Blake Fuller, in his mid-thirties with styled dark hair and a sharp pinstriped suit, was sucking up to an arriving guest in that overtly kiss-ass way reserved for only the most elite VIPs. This VIP keeping the president of The Fabulous at arms length like you would an overly chatty bellhop.

"That's Randy Leeds," said the shine man.

"You say the name like it should be spelled in capital letters."

"He thinks so. Billionaire CEO of EcoGreen Pharmaceuticals."

Randy Leeds was over six feet tall and not quite forty. Great tan and swept back sandy hair. Acting every bit like he owned the world in a navy blazer and sharply creased cream-colored slacks accessorized by a magnificent woman half a step behind him. He swaggered toward them too quickly for Dot to get a clear read on the billionaire's body language, but the blond trophy wife in the classic Chanel suit was a quick study.

Abbie Leeds. Tall and striking with a huge diamond on her left ring finger, she had reached the age where women evolve from pretty to beautiful. About thirty, Dot guessed, watching her collect admiring glances from all directions as Fuller steered his VIP guests toward the concealed entrance to the private penthouse elevator. Her back straight and each step perfectly measured. Her smile flawlessly delivered. She carried herself with an unnatural Stepford precision, making it obvious to Dot that she was just an actress playing a part. And that despite all the money and privilege, the narrow focus of her eyes betrayed that she was terrified of a bad review.

"Careful, Jim." Everest saw the larceny in Dot's eyes as they followed the billionaire and his wife. "A fly fisherman ought not cast his hook for a shark."

"This mark puts his pants on one leg at a time, the same as everybody else," said Dot as he noticed Poontang exiting an elevator, minus the emerald earrings.

"How do you think Leeds grabbed the top spot at EcoGreen? He was third in line till a boating accident and a suspicious heart attack gave him the keys to the kingdom."

Dot laughed as he pictured Abbie Leeds serving Mai Tais while her badass husband gave a tour of the graveyard of vanquished enemies by their pool.

"Two dead executives ought to be enough to tell you that there's nothing this guy won't do to get what he wants. And absolutely nothing he won't do to keep it. You'd best wise up quick to the fact that Randy Leeds is cagey and dangerous and, whatever scam you're cooking up, the risk doesn't justify the reward." Everest had not lectured Dot like this since taking him under his wing when the funnyman first hit town as a cocky teenager. "Nobody's doubting your talent, Jim. You could sell virginity to a hooker and convince the pope that Easter is in July, but sure as ten dimes make a dollar, there's no way on earth you can con Randy Leeds."

"Wanna bet?"

"How much is enough, Jim? The Fabulous is already paying you more money than you could ever spend."

Dot gave the billionaire a closer look, knowing that with wealth and power came an enormous arrogance that usually exposed vulnerability if you pried deeply enough. But as he focused on Randy Leeds it became quickly evident that there was no need to look past the obvious. Everything about this guy was one big tell. The way he kept Fuller subservient in his own casino. The robotic wife programmed to walk half a step behind. He was a control freak who needed to lord authority over absolutely everyone, giving Dot an idea how to play him. And consequences be damned, as what he wanted from Randy Leeds was worth a lot more than money and the risk did justify the reward.

The man wearing Wednesday orange scratched a stick match on the leg of his chair and drew flame to a fresh cigar, holding it close to embrace the smoke, as it was always the first hit of tobacco that gave him the most pleasure. Hoisted his beat up army boots onto the footrests.

"Okay, my good man." Jimmy Dot's voice rang with a confidence not heard in months. "Put a first date shine on these shit kickers."

THE FABULOUS. WHITE BAR.
WEDNESDAY 4:29 PM

"**R**andy Leeds will have murdered these people the same as if he shot them each in the head." Revson put out his cigarette and fumbled with the pack for another. "All in the name of greed and nobody seems to care. I've been snubbed by the press and ignored by public health officials. I tried to place a full page ad in the *New York Times*, but they refused it."

"What did you expect?" asked Owen Howard, his gaze distracted by a well-favored cupcake wearing white contact lenses seated near them. "You're accusing the respected CEO of a Fortune 500 company of plotting mass murder."

"I post the truth all over Facebook and Twitter. I comment day and night on medical and pharmaceutical websites. Every word either ignored or ridiculed because without corroboration it's just another conspiracy theory. And I can't even get bloggers to listen because they only post their own conspiracy theories." The technetronic beat chafed Revson's ears as he drained his gin and tonic. He had not eaten all day but the alcohol didn't make him drunk, just more determined. "How do you stop a man who has his own private goon squad?"

"Goon squad?"

Revson displayed the deep cuts on his arm. Rolled up the right leg of his new white pants to expose the darkening bruise on his swollen knee.

"They'll stop at nothing to keep the truth from coming out."

Revson's phone beeped. A text from his granddaughter made him smile. Calmed him enough to ease a cigarette from the pack. The bartender served him another drink and reached a lighter across the bar. Everything about the bartender's face was familiar, though he could not imagine where he might have seen him before. He inhaled deeply, the smoke relaxing him for a moment.

Bill Revson had been well liked in his community. Coached Little League and mowed the neighbor lady's lawn. He was a guy people waved to when they drove by. Had a wife and two grown children, now estranged over the shame and humiliation his wild allegations had brought upon them in a town that might as well have been called EcoGreen, PA.

Even though the media had blocked the scientist from getting his case heard in the court of mainstream public opinion, tongues wagged in the stores and barber shops and taverns of EcoGreen, PA. Merchants knowing that their businesses would dry up and blow away if the pharmaceutical engine that powered the small town's economy sputtered or stalled. Making Bill Revson despised as a traitor whose unfounded accusations threatened thousands of jobs. A pariah with no home and no friends. His only family a freckle-faced nine-year-old who would probably be grounded for a month if her mother found out she was texting her Pop Pop.

"Do you have a wife, Mr. Howard? A favorite aunt? A kid down the street who feeds your dog when you go out of town?"

The journalist fanned away a wisp of smoke and again pushed the ashtray to Revson's other side.

"Pancreatic cancer is a horrible torture. Excruciating abdominal pain that spreads through to your back until eventually all other organs shut down and you have to gasp for every breath, making you wish you were dead. And it isn't long until that wish is granted. If we don't do something to stop this insanity before Monday, ZeeFil will be on the market and people you care about will suffer unimaginable pain and then they will die."

"Come on, Revson. Do you actually expect me to believe that the FDA would approve a drug that isn't safe?"

"When the FDA determines a drug to be safe, that doesn't mean there are no side effects. It means they have determined that the benefits of the drug outweigh the known risks."

"So you're saying that the FDA has determined that the benefits of stopping a runny nose outweigh the horrors of pancreatic cancer?"

"I'm saying that Randy Leeds bribed someone to put ZeeFil on the fast track." Revson crushed out his cigarette and lit another. "Because accelerated FDA approval is usually only given to drugs for life-threatening illnesses like HIV. Meaning that instead of years, the ZeeFil approval process took just a little over ten months. They sent a review team to evaluate our research, supervised the pre-testing on lab animals and conducted three phases of abbreviated human clinical trials, but there wasn't nearly enough time to do a thorough evaluation.

I know where they misinterpreted the data and I can show them if they will just agree to retest it."

Howard gathered his change. Counted it twice as it seemed to be $20 short. Oh well. He tipped the bartender ten and got up to leave, but Revson blocked his path.

"Why would I buy these ridiculous white pants just so I could get into this cockamamie bar and spill my guts if everything I'm telling you isn't true?"

"You never answered when I asked how you knew I was here?"

"I got a call a little while ago from someone who said she was a friend. She told me where you were and that you could help. That's all she said before she hung up."

"Assume for a minute that I believe your crazy psychedelic logic. If EcoGreen knows that the drug causes cancer, why would they risk all the potential lawsuits they would have to settle?"

"Payouts to victims are a budgeted expense. A drop in the bucket compared to the huge profits ZeeFil will generate. Plus sales of all their cancer-fighting drugs would go through the roof. It's illegal, immoral and insane."

"Interesting word, insane."

"Come on, Mr. Howard. You've made a career out of exposing corporate cover-ups. Fighting for what's right and standing up for those who can't stand up for themselves. Now you have a chance to prevent the deaths of innocent men, women and children. And for the life of me I don't understand why you won't help."

"Because your story is bullshit." The journalist snatched the cigarette from Revson's mouth and smashed it out, then slid the white ashtray far down the white bar. "Do you really think you're smarter than the Food and Drug Administration? Are you that delusional to believe that EcoGreen would sell a pill that kills everyone who takes it? I don't know what your beef is with Randy Leeds, but give up this idiotic crusade because you'll never win."

The pain in his knee throbbed unbearably as Revson sat back down on the barstool. No longer able to cope with the excruciating guilt of not detecting the side effect before the drug left the research lab and for not being able to stop it once it did. Eyelids heavy from lack of sleep and blown off by the media one final time, he printed words boldly on a cocktail napkin.

ONLY ONE OPTION LEFT.

"The coward's way out?"

"Don't be ridiculous," snapped Revson. "There's only one more thing I can think of to do, and I have to make it count."

THE FABULOUS. PENTHOUSE 777.
WEDNESDAY 5:38 PM

Twilight painted a bewitching panorama seventy-seven stories above the most exciting city on earth. Mountains east and west, dissected by a fabled thoroughfare primed to explode into full-blown neon illumination. And there was no better view of this jaw-dropping spectacle of color and light than from the toilet in the master bathroom of the penthouse that crowned the most extraordinary address in Las Vegas.

The magnificent villas occupying the two floors below were reserved for high rolling gamblers who bet millions of dollars a night at the craps and baccarat tables. But Penthouse 777 was beyond the reach of even those casino whales. A sprawling neo-modern sky mansion with soaring ceilings, formal dining room and a three thousand-bottle wine cellar. Four fireplaces, antiquarian library and an open air screening room with theatre seating. Two swimming pools, fully equipped gymnasium and wraparound terrace with a lawn of velvety Kentucky bluegrass a thousand feet in the sky. A penthouse so exclusive that it was not available to the public for any amount of money. Offered gratis only to Hollywood A-listers and the social elite.

Leo DiCaprio worked the camera as his supermodel girl-friend coaxed a facial from a white tiger. Bill Clinton shot a hooker in the head during a game of William Tell gone bad. Prince Harry snorted cocaine off the stiff cock of his brother, then wondered if that made him gay or just royal.

Such sordid tales of debauchery had become legend through gossip, much of it initiated off the record by the hotel's publicity touts. The reality, however, was that Penthouse 777 was not a tricked-out playhouse for wild orgies and bad behavior, but a residence of restrained elegance for the socially refined who used coasters and kept their feet off the furniture. Twenty-thousand square feet of style and sophistication befitting the lady on the toilet who, though completely alone, completed her task with the same poise and grace as if she were seated across a formal dinner table from the Grand Duke of Luxembourg.

It was not often that Abbie Leeds found herself alone, on account of an aggressive agenda scheduled by her better half to make certain that she had no friends of her own and zero opportunity to stray from the propriety of her station. Maybe that's why she was always in character, so deeply immersed that she had almost completely lost touch with Abbie Anderson of La Crosse, Wisconsin. The youngest daughter of a shopkeeper and a secretary who had moved to Los Angeles to pursue her dream of becoming a movie star, only to find stardom far from the silver screen as an accessory to extreme wealth and power. Programmed by a domineering husband to act with an affected poise and grace, even in her most private moments.

Her hair still wet from the shower, she stood in front of the mirror and brushed long blond tresses away from her face and prepared for the beauty regimen arranged in order on the vanity before her. A tangerine silk kimono hung loosely from her shoulders as she prepared to apply face cream, body lotion, antiperspirant. Foundation, eye shadow, mascara. Blush, lip stain, Chanel No. 5. But not just yet.

Taking advantage of the quiet time, Abbie went into the bedroom and lit a lavender scented candle. Fanned through pages to find her place in the biography she was reading about movie star turned princess Grace Kelly. She found the page, then abruptly closed the book and set it on the nightstand. Tied the sash of her kimono and picked up the telephone.

"Great tits should be shown off, not covered up."

Still holding the telephone, she turned to face an intruder, who made himself comfortable on a yellow slingback chair opposite the bed. In his mid-twenties probably. Very tan and fit like a surfer, with daring eyes and almost-black hair that grew naturally wild. He wore freshly laundered jeans, new sneakers and an untucked blue dress shirt. The confidence he displayed as he made himself at home in her bedroom was frightening.

"My h-husband will be back any minute." Abbie stuttered ever so slightly when she was nervous, the result of a childhood impediment she had not totally overcome.

"No, he won't," replied the intruder calmly, his gaze locked on her luminous green eyes. "He's playing squash with Blake Fuller and won't be back for at least an hour."

Burglar? Rapist? Kidnapper? Dizzying scenarios kaleido-
scoped through Abbie's brain, knowing that if he was going
to kill her he had plenty of time to do it before help could
arrive. So she put down the phone and sat on the bed, mentally preparing her defense for whatever would come next.
Then tensed as the intruder sat beside her. Took her hand and
admired her diamond ring.

"May I see it?"

She yanked her hand back.

"Please take it off."

"No!" Abbie was trembling, as she was even more frightened
of a husband who mandated the diamond never leave her finger. "Take something else. Anything else. Anything but this
ring. You could never sell it anyway because it's a very well
known historical piece. Please, I have other jewelry. Money
in my purse."

The intruder again took her hand, this time easing the ring
from her finger. He gave it an examining look then faced her
matter-of-factly.

"The Valliere diamond. Nazis liberated this sparkler from a
Parisian aristocrat during the occupation in World War Two.
Hitler gave it to his chick Eva Braun, and when the lovebirds
pussied out with a double suicide at the end of the war, a
Russian soldier stole it off her cold dead finger. Every word
of that story a load of hooey that years later some grifter
was able to put over as gospel to the schmucks at Sotheby's.
Then, three years ago, Randy Leeds, CEO of EcoGreen
Pharmaceuticals and your husband, had his publicist make a

big whoop in the press about him buying it to accessorize his new trophy wife, you."

"What's your point?"

"It's nothing more than a big ass diamond ring."

"Not to Randy." Abbie was scared shitless as she had witnessed her husband destroy peoples' lives over things as inconsequential as a parking space. "If he comes back and I'm not wearing this ring, he will ... please give it back. You don't know what he's capable of."

He set the ring on the nightstand.

Abbie exhaled a long sigh of relief.

The intruder raked his fingers through her still-damp hair. Inhaled her intoxicating fresh from the shower scent and kissed her neck.

She couldn't decide if this guy was a Romeo or a rapist, but either way the thought of sex with him made her sick. Just as the thought of sex with anyone made her sick. Her appetite for pleasure long ago destroyed by husband Randy, who defiled her with his increasingly depraved desires and zero attention paid to her own. Abbie could not even remember what it felt like to be romantically intimate, as the sexual acts he made her commit were so vile and disgusting that afterward it took several showers for her to feel even remotely human again. It made her wonder what sexual depravities Prince Rainier demanded of Grace Kelly.

The intruder's lips pressed softly against hers. She tried to push him away but was no match for his strength, and there was nothing within reach she could use to crack his skull. But it was probably best not to fight it, Abbie figured. Isn't that what the women's magazines said? Why provoke further rage that could result in a trip to the emergency room or even worse? You were going to lose the battle to superior strength anyway, so let him take what he wants and he'll leave. It certainly couldn't be any more monstrous than the disgusting things her husband did to her.

So Abbie played it smart and fought the urge to fight back. Let it happen, she told herself. Get it over with. Please get it over with. Close your eyes tight like you do with Randy and think about water skiing. Fashion or movies. But she couldn't, as the rage that had been building within her for so long had finally reached its boiling point. Enough was enough and she would no longer allow herself to be violated. Would no longer allow herself to be the victim of sexual depravities so disgusting that words of which could not be spoken. It was now or never. She had to strike back.

The telephone was now within reach and she could smash him in the face and run for help. No. Randy would not allow the scandal. Randy would say it was her fault. Randy would dish out punishment the way only Randy could. But Abbie could no longer take it. Would no longer be a victim. Had to find a way to turn the tables on her attacker. And with a reckless abandon that could jeopardize everything she had, took control of the situation the only way available to her. She kissed him back.

Seizing the power she became the aggressor, kissing him again and again until heat escalated to passion. Dominating the intruder. Forcing him into sexual submission where he did everything she demanded.

No longer a courtesan forced to commit the unmentionable, for the first time in three years Abbie was empowered by the feeling of free will. Able to think for herself and visualize life's possibilities. To expand her imagination to see music and hear color. She gestured toward the window, marveling at the neon now blaring full force.

"This is my first time in Las Vegas," she told him, her voice confident and steady. Buzzed by the rush of control. Revitalized by an inner strength that made her feel oddly at ease making conversation with this intruder as if they were on a date. "The only reason we're here now is that Randy is consumed with the crazy rumor that Preston Bond is alive and somewhere inside The Fabulous. That's why he's holding the annual shareholders meeting here on Saturday instead of at the corporate headquarters in Pennsylvania."

He laughed. A lot.

"It's not funny to Randy. He's had detectives snooping around this hotel for months but they haven't come up with anything more than rumors. He's positive that us being here is going to somehow change that."

"How so?"

"In Randy's world, enough money can buy absolutely anything."

"Including bringing a movie star back from the dead?"

"He's a narcissist addicted to getting his name in the paper for hanging out with celebrities, something anybody with a good publicist can do. He paid the Rolling Stones ten million dollars to play at his birthday party, something any billionaire can do. But Randy is obsessed with making himself a bigger star than any of them by doing the one thing nobody else can, having his picture taken with Preston Bond."

The intruder drew Abbie close, his tongue tickling her ear but she pushed him away. This was now her party. The scent of lavender in the air, she tantalized his desire with a strip-tease until tangerine-colored silk fell to the carpet, exposing a body as perfect as an Alberto Vargas drawing come to life. A body she now gave willingly as the gentle caress of a stranger had ignited a fire inside her she thought had forever been extinguished.

The next hour was beyond spectacular.

Abbie lay naked on the bed where passion had kicked handcrafted French linen to the floor. Then with an eye on the clock she slipped into her kimono and walked through the magnificent suite of rooms, arm-in-arm with her Romeo. Owning what was undoubtedly the most amazing true story ever to have occurred within the walls of fabled Penthouse 777. A story she could never tell.

"Who would have believed that an hour ago you were a stranger," smiled Abbie.

"Las Vegas is a sudden town."

Goodbye kisses at the door. An embrace neither wanted to break, until they both knew they must.

Abbie watched her mystery lover walk to the elevator, and then closed the door. Made her way back to the bedroom and turned white as a sheet.

"MY RING!"

The hallway to the men's room provided Jimmy Dot with a bird's eye view of his gorgeous six-foot six-inch wife with the flowing mane of blue-black hair, and the asshole sommelier who had always been hot for her. A little too at ease with each other, the way Dot saw it, as they stood at the head of a long table of conventioneers enjoying an extravagant wine dinner inside the glass-walled private dining room.

Jenny had been born in Athens, the only child of a dipso Greek sailor and Sri Lankan mother, and moved with the family to Las Vegas when she was two years old. The crossed blood lines blessing Jenny with exotic beauty, that right now more than anything, Jimmy Dot wanted to take in his arms and whisk away to happier times. This exotic beauty he adored more than a sonnet of thousand dollar words could describe, whose bewitching smile ignited each new dawn. This woman who shared his love of the Three Stooges, three cushion bank shots and the three original varieties of Cheetos.

Oblivious to the clattering of plates and intoxicating aroma of grilled meat wafting from the kitchen, all Dot could think about was how Jenny would react to seeing him after all this time. Was she still angry, thinking he had sold out? Had she come back to reconcile with him? How did the asshole fit into the picture? No way for him to be sure. No way for him to be sure of anything. Except that above all else his wife hated to be embarrassed, so he needed to be very careful how he made his move.

The eyeball pattern of Jenny's flowing sapphire velvet dress projected a mystical aura as she stood dutifully beside the sommelier in the tight-fitting black suit, listening to him announce the pairing for the first course. Blossomy adjectives justifying the price of overblown grape juice ending with "and all of you being dentists, I figured you would like to start off with a chardonnay that has a little bite to it."

Everyone at the table laughed. So stoked to be in Las Vegas instead of Springfield or Syracuse or whatever God-forsaken excuse of a town they came from, that they were primed to laugh at anything.

The sommelier handed a glass to Jenny, whose flinty blue eyes added sultry contrast to her exotic complexion. She winked at the dentists and seductively touched it to her lips, drawing her audience in before taking a sip. Swished the wine around in her mouth, then swallowed and smiled. "An expressive vintage, brilliant with notes of baked apple and just a hint of oak."

Then she took a bite out of the wine glass.

Dentists gasped in horror as the very tall tattooed beauty with the very long hair slowly and carefully ground her teeth into the shards of shattered glass. Hearing the pieces crack every time she bit down, they could not believe what they were witnessing. Cringing as she swallowed then took another bite. Then another, until all that remained was the stem of the wine glass that she placed on the table, smiled and said, "Enjoy, gentlemen!"

The dining room erupted with cheers and applause.

Dot had always been the one to assist with the wine bit on stage, at parties and even at their own wedding reception, and knew there had been no danger as Jenny bit against the curve and chewed the glass thoroughly. But he saw this particular performance as nothing more than cheesy shtick unworthy of her talent. Making it more than painful to watch his wife cheat on him by doing it with this asshole sommelier.

Dot knew how important it was not to cause a scene and not to embarrass her, and figured the smart thing would be to compose himself at the bar until she was finished. Approach her with a smile that was not tainted with contempt for the asshole. One of the things he remembered his father teaching him was that you never got a second chance to make a first impression, but right now he did have a second chance and could not risk blowing it. A chance to tell Jenny that his life was nothing without her. Convince her he was not a sellout by explaining why he had been forced to take the gig at The Fabulous. Feel the warmth of her smile that would let him know everything would be all right. But he held his position by the men's room, as no matter how painful it was to watch his wife with another man, he was so desperately in love that he could not take his eyes off of her for even a second.

Jenn O. Cide was a fire-eater, contortionist and multi-talented sideshow freak who had performed the unbelievable for amazed audiences around the country. A career spawned by pipsqueaks taunting her in the fourth grade because she was taller than the teacher.

The first time this happened she ran home in tears, but no one was there to soothe a little girl's fractured psyche as her mother was working and her dad was off on a toot. But what if they had been there? A few reassuring words and a kiss on the forehead wouldn't have changed the facts, so ten-year-old Jenny made an adult decision. Instead of retreating, she embraced being different. Happened upon a documentary about sideshow freaks while flipping through channels and soon became fascinated with all things odd and bizarre. Read books about sword swallowers, contortionists and tap dancing Siamese twins. And when she was twelve learned to eat fire when an uncle took her on a trip to the Ringling Bros. and Barnum & Bailey Winter Quarters in Florida. An education that would prepare her for life far better than the most prestigious cap and gown.

Before meeting Jenny, Dot had been happy with his life of pool hustling and imaginative larceny. But his wife was a performer and to solidify their bond he became one too. Created the Jimmy Dot Circus and kept it under the radar just enough to fit nicely into the ringmaster's off-the-grid lifestyle.

Jenny's cheeks dimpled when she smiled and boxing twice a week kept her body toned. She emitted a healthy effervescence unfamiliar in Dot's world of schemers and wise guys, and taught him to appreciate things he had never before taken the time to notice. She introduced him to Thelonious Monk and film noir. He taught her that a field goal was worth three points and that two of them were not enough to cover a six-and-a-half point spread. And since the day they met had eaten most of their meals in bed enjoying the shared pleasure of black & white detective shows. She was a thirty-two-year-old woman unafraid to attack life head-on, but having been denied the lessons of a conventional childhood made her on occasion as vulnerable as a fourth grader who couldn't fit in. Vulnerabilities Jimmy Dot had always been there to soothe, as he loved his beautiful wife in every way imaginable.

But what about his vulnerabilities as he was forced to stand on the outside looking in? Lurking like a peeper in a bathroom doorway a million miles from the happy reunion he had shined his boots for. His jealousy scorching to a boil as he watched his wife shill for the asshole sommelier who undeservedly shared the oohs and aahs that got her off. Gone for months without a word, then comes back and doesn't even tell him. Off to God knows where with God knows who doing God knows what. Had she been with this scum sucking mook the whole time?

Dot burst through the door of the private dining room, disrupting the smarmy sommelier's next line of wine bullshit to the rube dentists. Stood face to face with his wife.

"You walked out on me because you thought I sold out. What the hell do you call this?"

"You're embarrassing me, Jimmy."

"Let's go."

"Get out!"

"I said let's go."

"Get the fuck out!"

In a fit of crazed frustration Dot jumped onto the table, his army boots destroying carefully laid place settings as smashed plates and stemware flew into the laps of the stunned dentists. He eyed a bottle filled with brilliant notes of baked apple and oak. Kicked it like a football with all his strength, driving the heavy glass missile into the midsection of the arrogant sommelier.

"Get your own girl!"

Jenny was red with anger and the pissed off sommelier was on the floor with the wind knocked out of him. But the dentists loved it. Cheering as they recognized the celebrity in the orange Hawaiian shirt whose mug was on billboards and taxi tops all over town, and thought this dust-up was part of the evening's entertainment. When the reality was that Jimmy Dot was just a regular guy with a broken heart.

He exited to a standing ovation. Kicking himself harder than he had kicked the bottle, as he knew that his jealous temper had just ruined any chance of ever getting his wife back.

MAX E'S DELICATESSEN.
DOWNTOWN LAS VEGAS.
WEDNESDAY 6:40 PM

Lox and cream cheese on a poppy seed bagel sat untouched as the well-dressed older man in his usual corner booth was busy on the phone adding numbers in his head as he spoke.

"Potato chips, pack of Camels and a pint of strawberry ice cream. Total comes to $520. There in a half hour to forty-five minutes."

Jackie Fink ended the call, then made another where he repeated the order along with an address. Transaction concluded, he fussed a bit with his transplanted black hair, and then tore into the sandwich. Never one to waste much time chewing, he washed down the bite with a swig of icy ginger ale. Enjoying his meal without a care in this no-frills delicatessen, decades removed from the always-broke Gus Boyloygan who used to dine and dash more nights a week than he didn't. The Gus Boyloygan who rebranded himself as Jackie a couple generations after they were all called Jackie. A bust-out comic who ditched Cleveland in search of fame and fortune only to be rewarded with night after night of hecklers. Or worse yet, crickets. But these days he was living the dream.

Anything you wanted, any time of the day or night. Magazines, pretzels, toothpaste. Pizza, cocaine, a clean pair of socks. All you had to do was call Jackie Fink – provided you were lucky enough to have his number -- and one of his friendly female drivers would wrangle the order and deliver it to your door. Drivers who were so friendly one might call them prostitutes. In this case, the strawberry ice cream was a curvy redhead who would deliver the chips and smokes, then collect Fink's $500 delivery charge while negotiating her own fee for services performed.

Fink was medium in stature with heavy brows over deep-set dark eyes and a bit of a hook to his nose. He liked it at Max E's, a no-nonsense 24/7 salami depot tucked between a bail bondsman and a pawn shop on the no-mans-land taint of Las Vegas Boulevard between the Strip and downtown. Where the bankroll in his pocket allowed him to feel superior to all the wise guys and weirdoes who dropped by to recharge their batteries. Cops and crooks. Gamblers commiserating bad beats. Cab drivers and streetwalkers who gossiped the latest grapevine scuttlebutt.

Fink flicked a rogue poppy seed off the lapel of his light blue Armani suit. Dressing to the nines his way of overcompensating for an endless parade of one nighters on the comedy circuit that provided him the means for little more than one cheap suit with a reversible vest. Shoes were now custom made and he paid more for shirts and ties in a month than he used to pay for rent in a year, which would have made him look like an easy mark if all the swindlers in the joint didn't already know that he was so tight he could squeeze a nickel out of a penny. All flash. A creature of habit who ate the same thing in the same booth most every day of the year.

As Fink made short work of his sandwich, through the window he noticed Jimmy Dot getting off a bus on the corner. Dot didn't drive. Took cabs when he was in a hurry, but enjoyed the bus as it gave him time to be alone with his thoughts while taking in a pedestrian view of the Strip. Fink eyeballed him enter and breeze past the counter through the ambrosia of pastrami and pickles that overpowered a cacophony of other aromas in the busy storefront delicatessen. The color drained from his friend's face as he sat across from him.

"Jesus, Jim. You're pale as a fart." A pallor accentuated by the harsh glare of low hanging fluorescent bulbs.

The waitress brought Dot's usual bottle of Orange Crush. No glass. Then caught his sour vibe and knew to beat it.

"It's over, Jackie."

Dot's eyes were hollow. His words delivered with difficulty. Falling deeper and deeper into a bottomless pit, because at least when Jenny was gone he owned the hope that she would come back. Now all he had was a festering emptiness and a soul strangling job he couldn't even quit.

"Hey, Jimmy," called a man in slacks and a blazer who approached the table. Seemingly too well dressed to be down own his luck, but at Max E's things were not always as they appeared. "Think you could let me have a couple bucks till payday?"

"Get lost. Can't you see we're talking?" snapped Fink, then shook his head as Dot handed two hundred dollar bills to the man, who vanished as quickly as he had appeared. "What payday? That muzzler hasn't had a job since never."

"He has to eat too," said Dot, his voice weak as he stared blankly at nothing in particular. "I blew it, Jackie. I really blew it, and this time she's not coming back."

"So you're just gonna sit there like a pussy feeling sorry for yourself?"

Not the pep talk Dot had come there looking for.

Losing Jenny was a life-shattering kick in the nuts that made him think about his father. The son of Polish immigrants, Jacek Dotoski worked his ass off day and night in his small grocery in the West Park neighborhood of Cleveland. Same as his father before him, proud that the effort provided his family hot meals and a roof over their heads. But the downside of being in business for himself was that he wasn't around much, except on Sundays, when the family would go bowling or to the movies or to a ballgame. Then dinner out so that his mother, Elizabeth, could enjoy her day off as well. But his mother was a modern woman who needed more in her life than Star Trek reruns and one night a week out of the kitchen, and eventually took a lover. When his father found out, he put a bullet in his brain.

Dot was just a pup, too young to help and too old to cry. But he remembered vividly that rainy summer afternoon when Jackie Fink, his father's best friend, came to the house to deliver the news. How his mother had curled up in a ball on the sofa and cried. How his younger sister understood little of what was happening, except that there would be no more Sundays at the movies or the ballgame. But ten-year-old Jimmy had wise eyes. Had seen the signs, realizing that it probably could have been prevented if the old man hadn't been a slave to the grind six days a week. A rat in a maze, sniffing the false promise of cheese instead of being at home with his family. The circumstances of his father's death haunted Dot every day of his life.

Fink helped the family as much as he could until he took his comedy act on the road. And Dot never forgot that kindness; often wiring money to Western Union in the next town on the circuit during the years Fink was struggling.

"She fucked you over months ago when she took the powder." Fink licked a bit of cream cheese off his finger as he aggravated his friend's fresh wound. "Be glad it's over and that she's never coming back."

"You've been twisting the knife ever since I walked in here."

"Don't get pissy with me, boychick. I'm not the bitch who shoved five years of marriage up your ass."

Dot grabbed Fink's tie, knocking over the bottles of ginger ale and Orange Crush as he yanked him halfway across the table.

"Wise up, kid." Fink choked out the words, refusing to back off as soda spilled off the chipped Formica tabletop and soaked through the light wool fabric of his trousers. "Your wife couldn't have made her opinion of you more clear if she'd shit in your pocket."

Dot twisted the tie. "What kind of friend kicks a man when he's down?"

Fink's face turned color, unable to speak as his air supply was cut off.

"What kind of friend are you?"

Dot's fist twisted the tie even tighter. Fink unable to breathe, his head red as a boil that needed to be lanced.

"Come on! What kind of friend are you?"

Dot was enraged. Out of control. Then was somehow struck with a moment of clarity where he finally snapped out of it and let go, Fink collapsing backward in the booth.

"Sorry, Jackie."

Fink coughed, gulping to get his wind back.

"Jenny's got my head so fucked up I can't think straight," said Dot as the waitress cleaned the table and gave Fink a stack of napkins to wipe his soda-soaked trousers. "That's a reason, Jackie, not an excuse. Please forgive me. I'm really sorry."

"Look, Jim," Fink told him, finally able to speak clearly. "You have to quit blaming yourself and look at the big picture."

Dot sat back and let the reality of his life to come into focus. He was a grifter slowed down by a wife and overexposed by the media. A fish out of water at The Fabulous. More at home with the scufflers and dime store philosophers at Max E's.

"You gotta put this whole mess behind you and start thinking about yourself." Fink's tone had softened. "Why don't I send you over a nice scoop of French vanilla. On the house."

"No thanks."

"Did you hear me say it's my treat?"

Dot sat quietly, again staring blankly into a void.

"Not some alley tramp, Jim," explained Fink as he poked his thumb in the direction of two street-weary working girls sipping egg creams at the counter. "This new blonde I got is smokin' hot. Fresh off the plane from Paris."

Even though Dot's wife had dumped him he couldn't bring himself to cheat on her, because deep inside he held onto the same futile glimmer of hope as every man who had been kicked to the curb.

"Get back on the horse, Jim. Get yourself a cellphone. Learn how to use the Internet and see all the amazing things the world has to offer."

"What's the point?"

"The point is living. How about that scoop of vanilla and a scoop of chocolate? Or maybe strawberry? I got a busty red-head should be available in about an hour."

Dot sat quietly. Embarrassed by the scene he had caused at Delmonico. Ashamed of how he had manhandled Jackie. Appreciating that only a true friend would risk a beating by dispensing the tough love it took to smack him back to reality. Fuck Jenny. He had dedicated the last five years of his life to making her happy, only to have her cut him loose when the next guy came along. She didn't deserve him. He was a simple man with simple tastes who would go back to shooting pool and fleecing suckers like before he met her. But first, James Tiberius Dot needed to reclaim his mojo so he could skin a billionaire.

Dot considered the age-old gambler's adage: If you want to change your luck, fuck a fat girl. But he liked Fink's idea better.

"You got any green tea?"

"Any flavor of female you want, my friend."

"Send over the vanilla and a scoop of green tea after the show. And tell the girls to bring a bag of Cheetos and some Twinkies."

THE FABULOUS. JIMMY DOT THEATRE.
WEDNESDAY 9:27 PM

"**L**et's hear it for a great bunch of broads!" yelled the ringmaster as he made a grand gesture toward three old ladies in orange unitards and orange beehive wigs sleeping in wheelchairs stage right. "The Jimmy Dot Dancers!"

The crowd roared its approval as the dancers came alive and spun tight circles around a six hundred pound bearded lady in a teeny bikini, who stuffed her face with chili dogs while Sparkle wrapped her flab with a string of firecrackers.

"And a big hand for Swanky LaBeef and his orchestra!" yelled Dot as a spotlight hit a sweaty fat-faced man in a ruffled orange tuxedo shirt holding a cassette tape player. "Play us out, Swank!"

The place went berserk as Swanky pressed the play button that ignited *Viva Las Vegas,* as Sparkle lit the fuse that blew the fat lady to smithereens. Balloons and streamers cascaded from the rafters as the dancers rolled crisply choreographed figure eights. Sparkle chased Poontang with a giant flaming dildo and Jimmy Dot threw pies as he led his cast of oddball characters on a victory lap through the revved up intergalactic-themed theatre. Out the door in the direction of the gift shop to greet each and every ticket holder as the crowd filed out. The receiving line was both exhausting and time consuming, but Dot felt that anybody who forked over the major mazooma The Fabulous gouged to see the show deserved everything he could give them.

"This was the most fun I've ever had in my life!" gushed a sweet lady with rosy cheeks, not wanting to let go as the ringmaster in top hat, tails and orange polka dot boxers shook her hand.

Poontang glam-posed with adoring fans in a tight-fitting orange sequined gown.

A minister's wife asked Sparkle for an autograph but instead received a sketch of her pussy.

Dr. Zazzo, dressed in a white suit, white shirt, white tie and white turban, told fortunes and flirted with the girls.

The dancers snored in their wheelchairs. Contortionists contorted and a tap dancing monkey juggled bananas. The entire cast taking the bow except for Swanky, who was too shy to face the public up close. Who valued his privacy so much that when the show hit it big and the others moved into expensive digs, Swanky opted to stay hermited away in the seclusion of his one-room apartment above a downtown laundromat.

As the last of the audience finally filtered out, the ringmaster cornered Zazzo as the cast made its way back into the theatre toward their dressing rooms.

"You get it?"

"Piece of cake," smiled Zazzo as he fished a finger into the pocket of his whiter than white shirt and pulled out Abbie Leeds' diamond ring, then handed it to Dot. "How much do you think Poontang will give us for this sparkler?"

"She couldn't unload a famous stone like this. No fence could."

Zazzo was twenty-six and cocky. A homegrown cat burglar and ladies man conceived out of commercial passion, whose worldview had been shaped by the inside-out education the child of a working girl receives growing up in the moral twilight of the neon shadows. A man who had never once set foot outside of Las Vegas, figuring there was no point as everything he could possibly want from life was flown in fresh daily.

"Then what's the play?"

"First give me the dope on Abbie Leeds." Dot lit a cigar, enjoying the flavor of the dark Robusto. "What's she all about? Did she spill anything useful?"

"It seems the only reason Leeds moved his party to The Fabulous this year is that he's obsessed with finding Preston Bond. He's had detectives prowling the casino for months, but they got bupkis."

"You sure?"

"Less than bupkis."

Dot was confident that if he could get Leeds out of his comfort zone even briefly, he could make him dance like a goosed-up marionette. Then hit the daily double by using the bully billionaire to manipulate that suck-up Fuller into tearing up his contract, once and for all putting The Fabulous in his rear view mirror.

"Nice work, Zazzo."

"Can't wait to go back up there for an encore."

"Keep away from Abbie Leeds."

"Come on, Jimmy. That crazy cooze fucked like an animal."

"Do your fucking somewhere else." Dot examined the Valliere diamond. "By tomorrow morning I'll have her husband on the hook and I don't want that magic dick of yours to screw up my play."

"No problem, dude. Plenty of fresh tomatoes in this hotel."

"Then go impress some of that new talent." Jimmy Dot looked his over-sexed swami square in the eye. "Just don't go within ten floors of Penthouse 777."

UNLV CAMPUS.
WEDNESDAY 10:31 PM

"**J**ailhouse Rock."

"Heartbreak Hotel."

The answers always flowed quickly until they got past the obvious. Then it slowed to a battle of wits, as the first one to be stumped in this game of trivia owed the other a pizza.

"Spinout."

"Girl Happy."

The competing reek of tacos and falafel fouled the night air as the two men leaned against the fender of their rented black Town Car parked in the lot of a small shopping plaza across the street from the campus. A copy center, a bar, fast food and a handful of other store fronts buzzing with activity even though school was out for spring break.

The taller of the two men sported a scruff of chin spinach and a ginger buzz cut. Wore a snug ass-length brown jacket. His partner was dark and slick with black leather over a V-neck tee and Guido necklace. The pair could have been cast as either cops or crooks on any 1970s TV show, and though age put them a bit out of range for coeds, some hot stuff coming out of the bar gave them an inviting eye. Not that they noticed, concentrating on a competition that had little to do with pizza and everything to do with bragging rights until the next time they would pit their knowledge of music or sports or movies against one another. On the plane that morning it had been Super Bowl MVPs and next week it might be Rolling Stones albums. Tonight it was Elvis Presley movies.

"Clambake."

"Kid Creole."

"*King* Creole."

"Bullshit. It's *Kid* Creole."

"You're thinking of *Kid Gala*...."

The word snapped off in the crisp night air as they spotted their target. Quickly making tracks across the parking lot toward the copy center, where they intercepted Bill Revson before he could get into a waiting cab. Slammed him against cracked stucco on the side of the building away from foot traffic. The bookish scientist's wire-rimmed glasses knocked to the ground as they wrestled away the box he was holding and ripped it open. Five hundred copies of a flier that proclaimed: ZEEFIL CAUSES CANCER, with the particulars in smaller print below.

"Did you really think we would allow you anywhere near the shareholders with these?"

Bullies gloated with the power of being in control as they mocked the defenseless middle-aged man in the ink-stained shirt and white pants that still had the price tag on the pocket. But Revson stood boldly in the face of professional muscle that had already beaten him to a pulp the day before back in Pennsylvania.

"I have every intention of telling shareholders the truth on Saturday."

A punch to the gut dropped Revson to the pavement. The wind knocked out of him but still defiant, he got up only to be kicked back down. Got up again and felt the cold steel of a switchblade, the sharp point of the knife drawing more than a trickle of blood as it scraped across his throat.

"Unless you stop harassing Mr. Leeds and his company, you won't be anywhere on Saturday."

French Vanilla was as delicious as advertised. Silken hair that fell past her shoulders, long wrap-around legs and an eagerness to provide pleasure. Green Tea was a black-haired reverse image. Tits at attention, the naked girls kissed and playfully fondled each other, straddling Jimmy Dot who laid spread eagle in the middle of the oversized bed.

The neon radiance of the Strip filled the windows of the spacious suite as Vanilla slid her hand inside his orange polka dot boxer shorts while Green Tea fed him a Twinkie. Dot's mind quickly lost in a vortex of ecstasy as Vanilla tickled his cock with her tonsils while Green Tea nibbled beneath his balls. A lot of men thought about baseball to keep from coming too quickly, but Dot didn't care where the pleasure led him, ready to explode for the first time in a long time as he knew these girls would stay around for encores all night if he wanted them to. Lost himself in the moment. Almost there as Vanilla bobbed her head in a rhythm that had the funnyman on the express train to....

A blazing fireball scorched the air just above the bed. Both Green Tea and Vanilla screamed as they tumbled to the floor, frightened out of their minds as Jimmy Dot looked annoyedly toward the bedroom door at his wife Jenny.

They glared at each other. Wife angry that her generous overture of reconciliation was met with strange pussy and snack food. Husband blowing his cork that she had the balls to be mad after leaving him high and dry all these months.

"Why create that scene at the restaurant when it's obvious you don't miss me at all?" Jenny was beyond indignant. Towered above the bed as she spit words in her husband's face. "How long have you been cheating on me, Jimmy?"

"Not as long as you've been fucking that asshole sommelier."

"At least I never fucked him in our bed."

He couldn't believe she had the audacity to claim a bed she had never once slept in.

"You're a sellout, Jimmy. You threw away our marriage for money."

"You know that's not true."

"You never told me any different."

"Because you never gave me the chance to explain before running off to who knows where with that asshole."

"He's not an asshole!"

"Fucking my wife makes him an asshole."

"I hate you, Jimmy."

"Why? Because I know you're fucking the asshole?"

"Now it's you who's not giving me a chance to explain."

"So explain."

"You're a prick, Jimmy."

"Because I'm old fashioned enough to think a wife should only fuck her husband?"

"But it's okay for you to fuck hookers in our bed?"

"It's not our bed. You never set foot in this room until two minutes ago."

"Because you're a sellout."

"ENOUGH!" yelled Dot.

The room fell so quiet they could hear each other breathe. Each feeling the sting of betrayal, their eyes locked with animosity. Daring the other to blink but neither did. Until finally Jenny's expression eased, looking at Dot through the eyes of a wife who adored her husband no matter what their current differences.

Green Tea tried to sneak out.

"Hey! Chop Suey," yelled Jenny. "Get back in bed and tear open that bag of Cheetos."

Vanilla clutched her clothes, not knowing quite what to do.

"You too, Blondie. Get that hot ass over here. We're having a party."

BLAKE FULLER'S HOME. SUBURBAN SUMMERLIN.
THURSDAY 6:06 AM

Wearing skin tight electric-green bike shorts and matching shirt, Blake Fuller was all business as he stood at the kitchen counter of his desert-landscaped ranch house putting baby spinach and organic raspberries into a blender to fuel his morning ride.

"The key to a good smoothie is more green and less fruit," he called to a visitor in the living room. "That's where people make their mistake. Maybe it's not as tasty this way, but it will keep you a step ahead of the competition."

"When you said breakfast, I figured you meant bacon and eggs."

"Clogs the arteries. This smoothie will keep you right as rain."

"Got some coffee? I didn't come all the way out here to eat weeds like some fucking hippie."

"Excuse me?"

"Sorry, Mr. Fuller." The reply was quick and contrite. "I just get jittery without my morning jolt. And it's awful damn early."

Fuller always got up early so that all day he would be an hour ahead of everyone else. He dumped heaping tablespoons of protein powder and natural whey into the blender, added bottled water and liquefied his concoction. Filled a tall glass and took a satisfying swallow. Then drained the rest of his smoothie and joined the other man in the modern living room, which looked downright provincial compared to the supersonic design of his workplace.

"Casino surveillance cameras caught one of the circus performers, the one you call Dr. Zazzo, bluffing his way past security and getting onto the private elevator to Penthouse 777 yesterday evening. What was he doing there?"

"Search me."

"Mrs. Leeds was alone in the suite because her husband was playing squash with me. Why did Jimmy Dot send him up there?"

"What makes you think Zazzo didn't go on his own? He's got mad skills with the ladies."

"Don't be ridiculous."

With only one degree of separation, it was obvious to the casino boss that Jimmy Dot had sent Zazzo to see Abbie Leeds. But why? And why corner the wife and not the man with the money? And why hadn't Dot gone himself? Fuller was very close to cashing in on the score of a lifetime and could not allow his criminal ringmaster to monkey wrench the payoff by trying to pull a fast one on the high-profile billionaire.

"What has Dot been saying about Randy Leeds?"

"Nothing except what I already told you."

"No talk about trying to rip him off?"

"Not a word."

"And nothing about why he sent that bullshit swami up to see the billionaire's wife?"

"Nope."

Fuller nudged a glossy art magazine ever so slightly so it conformed to the corner edges of the glass coffee table.

"Well, it's obvious that Dot is up to something. Are you positive you haven't heard anything? No loose talk backstage about Leeds? About me?"

"Not a peep. And with what you're holdin' over Dot's head, I don't see where he'd have the balls to try anything. Besides, don't I clue you to every move he makes before he makes it?"

"And you're going to keep on doing it. Because I'm sure I don't have to remind you that I'm holding something over your head as well."

THE FABULOUS. JIMMY DOT'S SUITE.
THURSDAY 9:53 AM

Jenny's fingertips playfully weaved through the thicket of dark hair on her husband's barrel chest, and then danced provocatively lower toward the spot that would send him into orbit. But Jimmy Dot flipped the record, because as much as he loved how she got him off, he loved getting her off even more. Worked his tongue like a virtuoso until she shook with an orgasm so electrifying no adjective existed to properly describe it, then held her possessively in his arms. Neither of them wanting to break the embrace. Grateful to have rescued a love that had almost slipped away.

While the suite did not exude the over-the-top opulence of Penthouse 777, sleek lines and state-of-the-art amenities made it spectacular in its own right. Including touches of whimsy like dancing Martian girl lamps and an animation cel of a wide-eyed Judy Jetson hanging above the toilet that gave it more character than most of the sterile high-end flops on the Strip. But aside from seven orange Hawaiian shirts hanging in the closet and a cigar humidor on the dresser, Dot kept no personal effects anywhere inside the spacious suite. Refusing to get comfortable in a place he would never allow to become his home.

As for Jenny, as much as she despised The Fabulous for coming between them, she loved the room service. Breakfast in bed making a fantastic morning even better as she delighted in lobster benedict while Dot shoveled home poached eggs with savory short rib hash. And floating on the cloud of a new beginning, she wasn't trying to ruin the mood by asking her husband why he didn't just break his contract with the hotel.

"There's so many pages of fine print that I'm a slave to this place," Dot told her, then stuffed his gob with warm apple Danish that allowed him a moment to choose words carefully so to not rankle their still unresolved issue.

"You're an employee, Jimmy. Get yourself fired."

"It's not that simple."

"Sure it is."

Jenny reached her hand toward the nightstand and pressed a button that dissolved the tint on the floor-to-ceiling windows, splashing morning sunlight into the bedroom. Then another that would kick the day awake with music. Miles Davis, Beatles, Sinatra duets. She scrolled further down the menu until she found the Ramones. Jenny thought the world would be a better place if everyone ignited their morning with the punk energy of the Ramones.

"Pick some high roller's pocket. Skip a show. Shit in a punch bowl."

"Anything that would normally be cause for termination doesn't get me fired. It adds years to the contract." Dot bounced out of bed and went over to the room service cart. "It's legal quicksand, Jenn. The more I fight it, the deeper I sink."

"You've watched enough episodes of Perry Mason to know there's no way a bullshit contract like that can be legally enforced."

He averted his eyes and poured a cup of coffee.

"Please tell me you didn't sign the contract without showing it to a lawyer first."

"It wasn't that simple."

"Dammit, Jimmy!" She sat erect and pulled her knees to her chin as she looked at him with pointed suspicion. "What does Blake Fuller have on you?"

"Nothing."

"Bullshit. What leverage does that prick have where you would agree to sign a ridiculous contract like that?"

"I did it for Sparkle, Poontang, Zazzo and Swanky. We're a family. And as the head of that family, like it or not, sometimes I have to make decisions that are best for everyone." Dot dropped his bare ass onto a chair by the window. "And that includes my star fire-eater."

"Don't try to make this my fault."

"Don't try to make me feel worse than I already do."

"Then don't play on my sympathy." She blew away a strand of hair that was tickling her nose. "You screwed up, sure. But the Jimmy Dot I married would never sit still and take this bullshit. We'll get a lawyer."

"No."

"No?" She brushed some Cheetos crumbs off the sheets, and then slid out of bed. Six-and-a-half naked feet of angry womanhood crossed the room and confronted her husband. "What is it you're not telling me, Jimmy?"

Dot knew that the truth would extricate him from this cross-examination. But the truth would also hurt his wife deeply, so he kept his mouth shut and took the grilling. Continuing to hope that he could resolve the situation himself so that she would never have to feel the pain of it.

"If you're not going to be completely honest, Jimmy, I'm leaving. This time for good."

"Back to that asshole sommelier? I'll kick his fucking teeth in."

"Is violence your answer to everything?"

"It is when the asshole is fucking my wife!"

The words sucker punched her and she sunk to the floor. Hurt. Insulted and betrayed. Head down and still as sculpture for what seemed like minutes until finally she spoke calmly.

"I know your anger comes from what your mother did to your father, but you have to let it go," she said, finally looking at him. "Finding out who the man was she cheated with and getting some answers might give you closure, but too much time has passed and it's never going to happen. You have to accept that and move on. Take pride in the fact that you're a better person than either of your parents, and that you have a wife who adores you more than the moon and stars."

Jenny took a sip of his coffee, and then set the cup on the carpet beside the chair. Clasped her husband's hands securely in hers.

"Since the day we met I've never been able to look another man in the eye. I've never cheated on you and I never will.

And I won't work any more wine events because I know how much it bothers you. I'm yours, Jimmy Dot. Today, tomorrow and forever."

"Then we'll find a way to get out of the contract, I promise you."

"I thought it was unbreakable."

"We'll do the impossible. Whatever it takes," he vowed to his wife, and then cracked the devilish smile she had so long ago fallen in love with. "Because I would never expect you to be stuck living in a dump like this."

Her face lit up and she threw her arms around her man.

"I knew you had a plan." She looked at him to be sure. "You do, right?"

Dot told her about his bet with Revson. About Fuller, Leeds and the Valliere diamond.

Jenny stood and looked out the window. A 74th floor view of the city which, like most cities in the stark light of day, was a graceless stepsister to the gorgeous doll that appeared at night. Her gaze zipped past the long stretch of casino hotels that had taken root in the sand and grit, and focused on a small building a couple blocks off the boulevard near downtown. It was so close, yet seemed so far away.

"So in the next few days we're going to break an unbreakable contract and pull a fast one on an arrogant billionaire?"

"That's exactly what we're going to do."

"And then we go home?"

Dot followed her gaze out the window toward the small building near downtown, and then promised, "Back in our own apartment in time to read the Sunday comics."

THE FABULOUS. PENTHOUSE 777.
THURSDAY 11:02 AM

As much as Randy Leeds enjoyed flaunting his wealth and all the trappings that went with it, it seemed very much out of character that he had declined services of the butler and other domestics who regularly staffed the penthouse suite. But behind closed doors he preferred privacy to ritual servitude, which on this particular morning proved to be especially precognitive as he was in the middle of a violent argument with his wife when the doorbell chimed.

Leeds ignored it, as he was in no mood to receive callers. Then as the chiming persisted, he stormed into the foyer and pulled open one of the red oversized double doors.

"Well?" Leeds snapped at the man he did not recognize. "What is it?"

"I'm Jimmy Dot, your downstairs neighbor." He reached into his shirt pocket. "I think this belongs to you."

The Valliere diamond.

Leeds snatched the ring from Dot's hand and examined the stone.

"Your wife left it downstairs at the jeweler to be cleaned. I was on the way up to my room and they asked if I'd drop it off."

Abbie Leeds breathed an audible sigh of relief, only to be confronted by an even greater fear. This man had the ring. Did he also possess the story of how she came to lose it? Of course he did, or he wouldn't be feeding her husband that malarkey about getting it cleaned.

"I must say, Mr. Dot. This is a rather unorthodox way of delivering a priceless diamond."

"Vegas is a rather unorthodox town."

"Forgive my manners, but I'm afraid I haven't thanked you." Starched button-down shirt, pressed slacks and calfskin loafers tried to make sense of Thursday's orange Hawaiian and army boots. Fascinated that a man of Jimmy Dot's dubious ilk could be trusted to courier a priceless gem in his shirt pocket. "Won't you please come in?"

Leeds' voice rang with a measure of authority as he introduced his wife, then led their guest past a long floor-to-ceiling aquarium into the great room and sat opposite a white stone fireplace, a hint of ponderosa pine permeating from the ashes of the night before.

"Can I offer you some refreshment?"

"Black coffee, thanks."

"And a Perrier with lemon," he told Abbie, and then turned back to Dot. "You say you live in the hotel. That must be interesting."

"Do you mean interesting in the living in a fish bowl sort of way? Or in the, at this very moment in room 5612 a high profile family values congressman is shacking up with a woman not his wife sort of way?"

"Is it Tessner from South Carolina?"

"What makes you think that, Mr. Leeds?"

"Call me Randy."

"Look Randy. I'm not comfortable ratting the guy out."

"Nothing like that, Jimmy. Just some juicy gossip between friends." To be filed away until the time came for Leeds to use the information to his advantage. "Besides, I know Tessner is in town for the Christian Leadership Summit and rumor has it that he promotes family values by banging his wife's sister."

"Is his wife's sister a Russian prostitute?"

Dot kept Leeds amused with tales of hotel intrigue as Abbie served the beverages, then sat dutifully beside her husband. She looked pretty and proper in a canary yellow cashmere sweater accented with a single strand of perfectly matched pearls. Dot tried to imagine her as a crazy cooze who would fuck a burglar like an animal. He couldn't. Though he had no trouble keeping Leeds enrapt with the story of how someone he knew had sold an Arab prince the Pacific Ocean three times.

"Even after three trips to the cleaners, this sucker was still one of the richest men in the world."

"But not the richest." Leeds spoke of wealth with the same enthusiasm that most men talked sports. "My father was a linoleum salesman in Catoosa, Oklahoma. He told me that I could grow up to be president and I told him it wasn't enough. Even then I knew I was going all the way."

"Number one is everything and number two is Nowheresville?"

"To paraphrase my professors at Stanford Business School."

Dot sipped his coffee, enjoying the aroma more than the taste and wished he had asked for a beer. Analyzing his host as his host had been analyzing him. Though Dot had the advantage of a primer from Everest.

In the sea of billionaires Leeds was at the moment a minnow. But with ZeeFil set to hit the market his EcoGreen stock would skyrocket, inflating his net worth several times over. Add bonuses, options and side deals, and a new accounting could easily boost him into the top ten or even the top five on the Forbes list. And with a bankroll that size to work with, plus a little luck, he might indeed go all the way. Especially since Randy Leeds had a history of making his own luck, beginning when he had his sister infect Timmy Douglas with the measles so he could take over his paper route.

"So is this your first time at The Fabulous?"

"It is," Leeds told him. "The hotel has such a sensational reputation, I thought it might be a treat for the shareholders, so I scheduled my company's annual meeting here."

"You're gonna love it, Randy. Swim-up movie theatre and a basketball court where you can play against NBA all-stars. A virtual reality art studio where you can have your portrait painted by Pablo Picasso. Not to mention farm-to-table restaurants where celebrity chefs actually work in the kitchen."

"You're omitting the hotel's most popular attraction."

"That's very kind of you to say."

"Of course, your show" replied Leeds, suddenly realizing he had seen Dot's bulldog face a hundred times on billboards and all over the hotel since arriving in Las Vegas the day before. "I'm told it's a huge hit. But I was referring to Preston Bond."

"Our resident ghost."

"But Bond isn't dead, is he Jimmy?"

"How could I possibly know that?"

"Because you live in this hotel, and from our conversation there seems to be very little that goes on here of which you are unaware."

"Believe what you want."

"What do you believe?" pressed Leeds.

"That you seem very interested in Preston Bond."

"Everyone is interested in Preston Bond, Jimmy."

"But not everyone has had detectives turning The Fabulous upside down for months looking for him. Only to come up empty."

"Not empty, Jimmy. They're positive that Bond is alive and somewhere in this hotel. And I'm positive that nothing goes on in this hotel of which you don't have first-hand knowledge. What's it going to cost for you to take me to him?"

"I can't do that."

"Can't or won't?"

Dot let the question hang.

"But you do know how rich I am."

"I also know that Bond doesn't want to be found."

"Before we were married, my wife was an actress." Leeds looked at Abbie. Exceptionally lovely and twice as obedient. He slipped the Valliere diamond on her finger, and then asked a question to which he already knew the answer. "Weren't you in one of Preston Bond's movies?"

"It was only a s-small part." Abbie was unable to control her stammer.

"No need to be nervous, my love."

Yeah, right. Lying about the ring. Sex with the burglar who had stolen it. Fright trumped nerves as her fate was in the hands of a stranger whose motives were as yet unclear.

"There are no small parts, only small actors," Dot reassured her, citing a line from memory. "But movie stars, that's another species all together. They like to push the boundaries of absolutely everything, including some legendary debauchery right here in this penthouse."

Abbie shifted uncomfortably in her seat as Dot looked around the fabled surroundings.

"You know, rumor has it that there's a video of Cameron Diaz being double-penetrated by a python in front of this very fireplace. Funny people, celebrities. They think money and fame allow them to violate laws of man and nature without consequence. They already have everything, yet they want more." Dot looked at Leeds. "You've got a beautiful wife and more dollars than you could spend in a dozen lifetimes. So, what's left? What's the one thing you don't have and can't buy?"

This time Leeds let the question hang.

"The answer is fame, Randy. Which is why you booked your company shindig here at The Fabulous, hoping to trot Bond out in front of your shareholders. Because you know that the person who unmasks Bond will be almost as famous as the man himself."

"Let's cut to the chase, Jimmy." When Leeds wanted to make a deal, that deal got made. "Deny it all you want, but we both know he's in the hotel and that you could take me to him right now. Name your price."

"I learned recently that there are things in this world far more valuable than money or fame."

"People who make statements like that seldom have either. Fame is addictive, Jimmy. Even more than money."

"It's not in my nature to seek a greater spotlight."

"Then what is it going to cost me to get face to face with Bond? You don't seem to give a shit about wealth or fame. What's left, Jimmy? You want to screw my wife?"

"I don't want anything, Randy. I just stopped by to drop off the ring."

Dot stood and shook hands with Abbie.

"Thank you for the coffee, but I'm afraid I have to leave. My wife and I have a date to shoot pool."

Goodbyes were said and promises made to get together soon. Then as Dot was shown the door he asked, "Do you like to shoot pool, Randy?"

THE FABULOUS. BLAKE FULLER'S OFFICE.
THURSDAY 12:19 PM

The executive assistant in the outer office was an attractive brunette pushing thirty. All business in a tailored navy blue jacket and skirt, though under that skirt were no panties to impede access to her most delectable asset. Or so portrayed the drawing Sparkle handed her as he leaned his pint-sized frame against the desk.

"Look familiar?"

"Time for you to go."

"Shy, huh?" The midget inched closer, and then leered. "I can cure you of that."

She picked up the phone but before she could dial, Sparkle knew to beat his Elvis-clad ass out of there as fast as his sawed-off legs would carry him.

Original artwork added a bit of warmth to the clipped neatness of the ultra-modern inner office, where Blake Fuller reacted angrily when informed by recently retired Las Vegas Metro Police Lieutenant Lew Bernard that an hour earlier Jimmy Dot had entered the private elevator to Penthouse 777.

Known on the street as Hard Bernard, he liked to boast that it was because he was hard on the bad guys, a claim no one would dispute, as he was a gorilla of man whose head looked like it had been chiseled crudely out of concrete. But even though he had built his reputation by viciously beating confessions out of criminals the old fashioned way, those who knew him would tell you that the genesis of the moniker had nothing to do with meting out justice to bad guys and everything to do with a more personal violence.

After twenty-two years on the police force Bernard now worked at The Fabulous, taking care of certain matters off the record. A retired Las Vegas cop gets to keep his badge, a prop that came in handy executing his duties as a fixer who covered up celebrity overdoses and made sure dead hookers were discovered far away from hotel property. And even though his finger was on the pulse of everything that went on behind the scenes at The Fabulous, the naturally unpleasant former vice cop did not understand why Fuller insisted he keep an eye on Jimmy Dot.

"Why do you care if Dot's up in the penthouse?"

"That's none of your business," snapped Fuller, his eye on a painting that may or may not have been a fraction of an inch off kilter.

Hard Bernard scratched stubborn whiskers that itched after a few days of not shaving, then unbuttoned his checked sports jacket and relaxed on the long silver sofa. "You think he's trying to sell Leeds Las Vegas Boulevard? Or somehow cash in on the fact that this billionaire is obsessed with finding Preston Bond."

"Why would Leeds care anything about Preston Bond?"

"Who knows why rich people do what they do, but he's had ghost busters snooping around the hotel for months." Bernard noticed Fuller's facial muscles tighten; alerting a detective's instinct that he had hit a nerve. He dry swallowed a blue pill and some Chinese herbs, then smirked. "You didn't know?"

FAA investigators reported that no one had survived the plane crash two years earlier in the remote mountains of Wyoming. But because the movie star's body was never found the rumor mill exploded with reports that he was seen here, there and everywhere. So, Blake Fuller figured at the time, why not have him seen at The Fabulous?

It was genius exploitation of a rumor the public was eager to believe, as he set up the long-established local gossip columnist to stumble upon planted evidence that Bond was in the hotel. Validated by this hint of journalistic legitimacy, within minutes the scoop blew up Twitter and within half an hour the story was on all the news wires. By morning, media outlets around the globe poured gas on the fire with their own rumors of Preston Bond at The Fabulous. Blake Fuller's well-orchestrated denials gave those rumors merit. And the more emphatic his denial, the more the public bought fiction as fact. It was that easy.

Room rates skyrocketed when the rumor leaked out that Bond had surgically altered his appearance and worked at hotel. Graveyard business tripled because it was said that Bond, wearing a different disguise every night, often hung out in the casino until the wee hours. And no one ever saw him arrive or leave because Bond lived in a secret penthouse deleted from all blueprints and construction records. Fuller manipulated these rumors like a master puppeteer, perpetuating the link between The Fabulous and the man more famous in death than he was in life. And the world believed every word of it. The board of directors believed in recognizing a job well done, rewarding Blake Fuller with an unprecedented promotion from the public relations department to president of The Fabulous.

He was given a seven-figure salary with stock options. Plus a twenty million dollar performance bonus due to kick in soon if certain revenue projections were met, which they undoubtedly would be as long as he could keep the ghost of Preston Bond haunting the casino. The bonus was also contingent upon signing the Jimmy Dot Circus to a contract extension and, most importantly at the moment, not generating any negative headlines, like if the hotel's star attraction should fleece a high profile billionaire guest.

"Now, unless you feel it necessary to waste any more of my time," grumbled Hard Bernard as he got up from the sofa, stretched his husky frame and checked to make sure he had his phone and that no coins had fallen between the cushions, "I've got better things to do."

Fuller watched the fixer pack his craw with more Chinese herbs and walk out of the office, then straightened the painting on the wall. An abstract by Warner Jezzler, one of a new generation of artists whose work could be had for a song but might someday be worth millions. Fuller prided himself on staying ahead of the curve and on his eye for value. Not a dime's worth of difference between a struggling artist and an obscure circus sideshow if you had vision. But right now he worried that his vision of cashing the twenty million dollar bonus check was being jeopardized by the scheming street hustler he had bailed out of jail and made into a star.

Could Dot really be trying to exploit Randy Leeds' obsession with Preston Bond? It wasn't possible. Or was it? The question gnawed at Fuller as he paced back and forth in front of floor-to-ceiling one-way glass that overlooked the action of the revolving multi-tiered casino. Maybe Dot was simply planning to rob the billionaire, extort him or liberate his credit cards. Whatever the play, Fuller knew that if he couldn't keep his star attraction away from Randy Leeds he would not only lose his bonus millions but more than likely be fired as well. Blackballed in an industry where he would be lucky to get a job writing newsletters at a Motel 6.

Fuller picked up the telephone on his desk and flung it hard, ripping a hole dead center in the Jezzler.

TOP HAT BALLROOM. SKID ROW
LAS VEGAS.
THURSDAY 1:01 PM

The lingering haze of cigarette smoke accompanied by the musty stank of sweat and stale beer did not evoke reminiscence of the bar at the Newport Yacht Club, though the point could be argued that the denizens of the Top Hat were every bit as intriguing as the elite of blue blood society. Back-sore laborers still ripe with the ooze of a hard day's work knocked back aged-in-the-glass whiskey with dent-faced stool jockeys who hadn't punched a time clock since before forever. Recycled pussy you wouldn't fuck with your worst enemy's dick worked harder hustling drinks than they would have at any nine-to-fiver. It didn't take much talent to be broke in Las Vegas, and the Top Hat was a clubhouse where people on the downside of advantage could tell stories of what used to be and what might have been, embellished a little more with every page that fell from the calendar.

"Buy a round for the house," Dot told Davey Klubs, the no-nonsense ex-marine with a bushy moustache who held sway over this motley crew of day drunks, as he placed some money on the bar. Then slipped the bartender an extra hundred as they shook hands. "And get yourself some good cigars."

A couple hours earlier, Randy Leeds would have believed it a lot more likely that he would spend his afternoon playing tiddlywinks on the dark side of the moon than shooting pool in a Skid Row dive. He missed an easy shot then cursed his warped cue stick.

"Perhaps this instrument might serve you better," offered a slender old gentleman in a gray suit as he handed Leeds another cue, slightly less crooked than the first. A man past eighty with erect posture and thin white hair oiled perfectly into place. Whose natty suit and tie captured the style of the day, if it was a day when Reagan was president.

"Randy, I'd like you to meet a good friend of mine. Dr. Frank Ballinger." Dot blew a tight smoke ring as he introduced his friend. "Frank, this is Randy Leeds. A very important man in the pharmaceutical business."

"The fellow making deals in the bathroom is also an important man in the pharmaceutical business." Ballinger nudged Leeds with his elbow. "Know him?"

Frank Ballinger was known as The Doctor in honor of a long career separating people from their money with surgical precision. A confidence man so skilled that he once sold some schnook the city of Cincinnati. Ballinger was the best in the business until he found himself in a losing battle with Johnnie Walker. Then Hiram Walker. Then any rot gut with enough kick to steady his hands. Battles that these days were subsidized by Jimmy Dot, who believed that this man had earned the right to live out retirement in whatever manner he wished. A man who years ago had nurtured the potential of a boy who had hit the road after his mother died from the shame of causing his father's suicide. Who taught fifteen-year-old Jimmy Dot style and technique and gave him the confidence to succeed in the confidence racket. Taught him that unless the sucker was begging for it there was no percentage in taking more than enough. To push himself until he could accomplish the impossible, then move on to an even greater challenge. Taught him the social graces and that doing a crossword puzzle every day would keep his mind sharp while building his vocabulary. Jimmy Dot owed this aging gentleman in the out-of-style gray suit a huge debt. And if whiskey was the currency required to satisfy that debt, then so be it.

Jenny and Abbie sat at a high top table, drinking beer and watching their husbands shoot a game of eight ball. Abbie liked the Top Hat as the timeworn blue-collar atmosphere and over-flowing ashtrays took her back to a bar in La Crosse where she and her friends drank when they were underage. She also liked Jenny, enjoying the simple pleasure of girl talk for the first time in a long time. And even though Jenny's job was to keep the wife happy while Dot sprung his trap on the husband, she liked Abbie as well.

Dot bought the wives another round of beers plus a double shot of the good stuff for Ballinger who was caught off guard by a sneeze, pulling out his handkerchief just in time.

"A good sneeze is like an orgasm." The old gentleman winked at the ladies. "Or as close as I get these days."

Dot struck a stick match on the sole of his boot, rotating the end his dying cigar to the flame so it would burn evenly. A good pool hustler not only possessed the ability to make shots whenever he needed to, he knew when and how to miss. Jimmy Dot banked the five ball in the side pocket then missed the seven.

"Why did you steal the Valliere diamond just to return it?" asked Leeds as he lined up his shot. "You knew it would be easy enough for me to check and find out the ring had never been taken to be cleaned. Why did you go through the whole charade? You made it very clear that I don't have anything you want."

"I've got money in my pocket and the love of a good woman." Dot winked at his wife. "What else is there?"

"Fame, as you so pointedly told me back at The Fabulous."

"I also told you that I prefer to stay in the background."

"Says the man with the most recognizable face in this town." Twelve in the side. Thirteen in the corner. "You're a ball of contradictions, Jimmy Dot. You dress like a slob yet you have the manners of a gentleman. You earn millions, yet I believe you really are content with just the money in your pocket."

"Not everyone aspires to be the world's richest man."

"I overcame huge odds to get where I am today, Jimmy. Not like a small time schemer we know who accidentally became a star and likes to stack the odds against himself so that the payoff will be more satisfying when he wins. Which is exactly what you did yesterday when you bet Bill Revson $10,000 against a hot dog that you could get me to admit in public that ZeeFil causes cancer."

"Does ZeeFil cause cancer?"

"No, Jimmy. It doesn't." Ten ball in the corner followed by the fourteen. Eleven in the side. "And for the life of me I don't understand why you would make a bet that you can't possibly win. You would have been better off lighting cigars with that money."

Dot knew Leeds' backstory because Everest read half a dozen newspapers every day and Leeds probably learned a few odd facts about him by placing a quick call to Blake Fuller. But Fuller did not know about the bet, meaning that someone he trusted was selling him out. But who? And why?

"I'm enjoying our little game of cat and mouse, Jimmy." Leeds looked at his wife sharing a laugh with Jenny as Ballinger delighted them with card tricks. "And as you can see, Abbie is having a good time with your wife and that rummy doctor."

"Let's cut the cards for a hundred," Jenny challenged Ballinger.

"It wouldn't be fair of me to take advantage of an amateur, dear girl."

"Two hundred then."

"Never let it be said that Dr. Frank Ballinger refused the invitation of a lady."

Jenny shuffled, and then Ballinger cut the cards and showed her the nine of spades. Jenny's cut produced the king of diamonds, which she buried in the deck without showing.

"You're right, Frank." Jenny handed over $200. "An amateur should never play cards with a pro."

Leeds enjoyed observing disadvantaged people, as it reminded him how far he had risen since denouncing his birthright as the prince of linoleum in Catoosa, Oklahoma. Watching the lower classes from a safe distance, like his luxury box at Yankee Stadium or through the darkened windows of a limousine. Not amid the suffocating odor of hopelessness and shattered dreams in a place God must have created when he was hungover. Yet that was the price he was willing to pay to find out what Jimmy Dot had up his sleeve.

"He's here. Isn't he, Jimmy?"

"Who?"

"Preston Bond. Why else would you bring me to this shithole bar?"

"To shoot pool and have a few beers."

"Nobody with any tangible connection to the outside world would ever set foot inside this dump." Leeds saw a windowless rotgut asylum of the Devil's rejects. Grime-filled cracks in the floor and mirrors so blemished with decades of nicotine they absorbed rather than reflected. "What better place for a famous man to hide from society."

"True enough," agreed Dot. "What A-list celebrity wouldn't want to live here? Cot in the stock room, peanuts in the machine and all the beer you can drink. Only drawback I can see is that he'd have to share a bathroom."

"Save the wisecracks, funnyman. It's obvious that you returned the diamond to gain my confidence, and that you're trying to jockey me into position to trade Preston Bond in exchange for a ZeeFil confession."

Busted. Dot shifted gears.

"There's more than one way to win a bet, Randy."

"You're even crazier than that putz Revson," laughed Leeds as he sank the nine ball in the side pocket. Fifteen in the corner.

"He's not so crazy. A friend of mine told me that yesterday afternoon Revson was having drinks at the White Bar with an investigative journalist who seemed very interested in what he had to say."

Leeds scratched his next shot.

"This journalist have a name?"

"I wouldn't worry about it, Randy. After all, you said it yourself. Revson is just a putz."

"Cards on the table, Jimmy. What are you after? No matter how big a rush you get stacking the odds against yourself, we both know you're not going to these great lengths just to win a one dollar hot dog."

Dot's cigar danced in his mouth as he sank the four ball in the side pocket. One in the corner. Six in the opposite corner.

"I have no idea whether your sniffle pill is any good or not, Randy. All I care about is winning my bet with Bill Revson. Which I guarantee you I will do."

Dot dropped a two-seven combination in the side. Then sank the two.

"I don't care how clever you think you are, Jimmy. You don't stand a Chinaman's chance of tricking me into making any statement against my will."

"It won't be against your will, Randy. And just as sure as I will sink this three ball in the corner pocket, before the weekend is over you will announce to the world that your new miracle drug causes cancer."

"But ZeeFil doesn't cause cancer."

"Doesn't matter. You'll say it does."

Dot smiled as he sank the three ball in the corner.

"Your confidence is dazzling, Jimmy, but you're out of your league. Way out of your league. Give that pest Revson his ten grand and maybe he'll go home and stop trying to harass me." Arrogance dripped off every word. "I want Preston Bond, but I don't need him. You should have quit when you had the diamond, because our little game is over."

"Keep thinking that."

"There are many men I once liked who learned the hard way that it's not healthy to try to put one over on Randy Leeds." He leaned on the edge of the pool table until he was face to face with the shorter man. His eyes cold. His threat very real. "So whatever your end game is, Jimmy, I cannot suggest strongly enough that you forget about it before you and your wife get hurt. Go back to bar bets and conning tourists out of their lunch money before I stop liking you. Do we understand each other?"

"I heard you." Dot tapped the eight ball into the corner pocket to win the game. "But you're still going to tell the world that your sniffle pill causes cancer."

THE FABULOUS. CASINO POOL.
THURSDAY 1:56 PM

Girl from Mars working the pole at a Florida strip club. Mother of six caught in a tryst with the family dog. Miracle cold cure causes cancer.

Typical social media postings. Preposterous stories rarely given a second thought by a world inundated with such a bottomless cesspool of online misinformation that people kept scrolling until they found a tasty headline accompanied by a celebrity photograph. But none of Bill Revson's posts included images of nightclubbing movie stars or pop diva side boob. Just the truth. And he had found out the hard way that nobody cared about the truth if it wasn't sexy.

#ZeeFil. #Cancer. #DeathDrug. Bill Revson's online assault was relentless, but resulting comments were chapter and verse the same responses he had gotten from the press for weeks while trying to alert them to the lethal side effect of EcoGreen's miracle cold cure. The FDA had declared it safe, leaving the one man who could prove that it wasn't to be looked upon as nothing more than a disgruntled former employee. Lunatic, crackpot, kook.

Revson had finally slept, if only for a few hours. A hot shower and clean sport shirt, buttoned all the way up to cover the switchblade scar across his neck, had given him fresh energy, but to accomplish what? Continue his futile online blitzkrieg of Facebook, Twitter, pharmaceutical blogs, consumer protection agencies and medical associations? Without corroboration nobody would give him the time of day. He had already checked out the event center where the EcoGreen shareholders meeting would be held, and was confident of a couple ways he could sneak past hotel security. But Randy Leeds' goon squad would be there on high alert for him, so what was the point? He racked his brain for the next move in his one-man humanitarian fight where he was all but out of ammunition. But Bill Revson believed that when you fought for what was right, you were never out of ammunition.

He had not had a bite of food for two days as stress had sapped his appetite for anything more nutritious than tobacco. Had bent his wire-framed glasses back into shape the best he could, but they rested slightly askew on the bridge of his nose as he leaned on the railing that circled the center of the casino. Eyeballing the action a level below as hotel guests swam with mermaids in the white sand pool beneath a hundred foot waterfall. As tropical cocktails were served by waitresses in silver bikinis ringed with illuminated galaxies of orbiting stars. As tourists played slot machines, keno and a strike-it-rich interactive game exclusive to The Fabulous called Rocket Billionaire.

Revson shook his head as he noticed a slot player give a cocktail waitress five dollars for a free drink. Shifted his attention to the happy vacationers enjoying food and drink by the pool, just like when he and Carrie Leaper used to people watch at the mall when they were teenagers. It had taken skinny and shy Billy Revson all of sophomore year to muster up the courage to ask Carrie for a date. And they went steady up until he earned his scholarship to Dartmouth that paved the way for life in EcoGreen, PA.

Revson wondered a lot lately what life might have been like if he had followed Carrie to Colorado State. Married her and landed in another town. Worked for a company that was not trying to give the world cancer. Where friends had his back and bosses respected a job well done. Where a nine-year-old would not be grounded for texting her Pop Pop.

He and Carrie used to lean over the railing on the upper level at the mall and pick strangers out at random, giving them an identity and backstory. The jock in the letterman jacket from Rival High was on probation for vandalizing a Burger King, and had to go to summer school to pass the eleventh grade. The red-haired lady with the oversize purse was an undercover policewoman looking for shoplifters, while at the same time shoplifting herself. The two girls in Catholic school uniforms, window-shopping dresses they couldn't afford, did not know that they were both dating the same boy. But they sure as heck would on Saturday night when all three showed up at the spring dance.

People watching was fun. Everything was fun and uncomplicated back then. Revson wondered if Carrie ever thought about him and about those times together at the mall. He imagined what she might be doing right now. Having lunch with ladies from her book club before spending the rest of the afternoon shopping. Home in time to have a pot roast on the table when her husband returned from work. Planning a fun weekend with her children. A month from this weekend curing her sniffles with a ZeeFil. A year from this weekend listening to a doctor say her cancer was spreading so rapidly that she would not see Christmas.

Revson's eye caught a stunning poolside waitress who more than filled out her futuristic bikini, but all he could see was her pale shriveled body in a hospital bed hooked up to a ventilator. He saw pretty twin sisters with long dark hair, both bald from chemo. He saw the lifeguard being lowered into his grave.

Revson knew that you could lead people to the truth, but it took a hell of a salesman to make them believe it. And the past months had proven he was no Dale Carnegie. Not even Willy Loman, and he could no longer bear the unimaginable guilt of being the cause of all the suffering and death the future held for these innocent people. A rage swelled inside him as the clock was ticking and he had absolutely no idea what to do.

He heard a commotion behind him and turned to see people straining to get a look at Killer Kong, who walked through the casino with that over-cologned midget Elvis on his shoulder. A vicious heavyweight boxer who had once killed in the ring and wore a necklace of teeth smashed from the mouths of fallen opponents. Who had been knocked out by the champ a year ago in a slugfest down the street at the MGM Grand in what the boxing media called the greatest fight of all time. Now Kong was at The Fabulous training to avenge that loss, vowing that this time the champ would not leave the ring alive. He was a mountain of solid muscle, but when Bill Revson caught a glimpse of the boxer, all he saw was a cloak of loose skin draped over cancer-riddled bones and a midget who had crumbled into dandruff.

A few deep breaths calmed the shakes as Revson composed himself, but his injured knee was killing him and he needed to sit. He lit a cigarette and turned to walk away, only to find himself face to face with an oversized promotional photo of Jimmy Dot. The wiseass smile mocking him. Demanding his hot dog.

Confronted by the question he had been obsessing about since the day before, he again asked himself, what kind of idiot bets $10,000 cash to win a one dollar hot dog? Was getting it for free that much of a thrill? Was it really free if he was wagering money to win it? Revson often overlooked the central question to analyze the reasoning behind it. Had been that way ever since wondering why Peter Dumich ate his beans but not his burger at the Boy Scout jamboree. It was just how the scientist was wired as he again tried to figure out why someone would make such a ridiculous bet. Only to veer a bit off course, pondering why people fell all over themselves to get something for nothing even when they knew there was a catch.

Free popcorn and balloons for the kids was the hook to get mom and dad to the dealership to buy a new minivan. A free cruise got people to buy time-shares. So why not give something free to a group of EcoGreen shareholders in exchange for a few minutes of listening to the facts about ZeeFil?

Revson was onto something. He couldn't afford to hand out cruises, but there had to be something he could offer that would get the peoples' attention. Though even if he knew what it was, with the goon squad watching his every move he would have no way of giving it to them. Putting him right back to square one with all questions and no answers.

He noticed another slot player give a cocktail waitress money for a free drink, making him think about how he was guilted into tipping the shuttle driver for his free ride from the airport. Blackjack dealers, towel attendants and maids all had their hands out. Owen Howard had tipped the white-clad bartender ten bucks for a couple of over-priced Budweisers and there was even a tip jar by the cash register in the gift shop where he bought his cigarettes. Las Vegas may have been a town built on gambling, but it was fueled by gratuities. And Revson had seen enough movies to know that the one place you got actual value for your tip was the bell desk. Bellmen knew everything that went on in a hotel and would get you absolutely anything for a price. Giving Revson an idea.

If he had it figured correctly, it would take just one bell-man to accomplish what a thousand pleas for help to news outlets and social media could not. His mind raced to flesh out the idea. An idea so brilliant in its simplicity that the scientist could not possibly fail to make his voice heard at the shareholders meeting on Saturday. But he didn't want his enthusiasm to get the better of him. It was a can't miss idea on the surface, but he needed to carefully analyze the play. Quantify the variables into a formula to determine the probability of success. The number of positives minus the negatives divided by the intangibles equaled … equaled … Fuck mathematics! It was the first time in his life that Bill Revson had not viewed numbers as an exact science. Also the first time he had uttered the work fuck, even to himself. And it was the first time in weeks that he knew exactly what to do.

Buoyed with a fresh confidence, Bill Revson enjoyed the chilly deliciousness of a thick vanilla milkshake as he relaxed at a poolside table waiting for his cheeseburger. No longer guilty about being the cause of all the suffering and death ZeeFil would cause, because he now had the power to stop the cancer-causing drug before it reached the public.

The scientist admired the beauty of the stunning waitress in the futuristic bikini. Smiled as he looked at the twin sisters with the long dark hair and the lifeguard who flirted with them. All of their futures bright and full of promise. Revson texted his granddaughter.

"I'll be home soon, Sweet Pea. Love Pop Pop."

THE FABULOUS. BILL REVSON'S ROOM.
THURSDAY 3:47 PM

I n his time at The Fabulous, the clean cut young bellman in a snazzy space cadet uniform had had his palm greased with crazy amounts of cash to fulfill even crazier requests, but this was by far the biggest tip he had ever gotten. Five grand, and it didn't involve hookers or drugs or anything even remotely illegal. And another five grand when his task was complete. He thought of his brother the chiropractor. What a schmuck.

"So are you absolutely clear as to what I need you to do?" Bill Revson asked him for the third time, stepping away from the window. He was scared of heights, and the floor-to-ceiling pane of glass unnerved him.

"Get a couple thousand of these fliers printed." The bellman held up a copy of the flier the goon squad had taken away from Revson the night before. "Find out where the annual reports are stored that EcoGreen will give out to all their shareholders at the event center on Saturday, then slide one of these fliers inside each report."

"And if you can't gain access to the annual reports?"

"I pass on some of this lettuce to somebody who can, and he slips the fliers into the reports. Either way, everybody at that shareholder meeting will have a piece of paper in their hand that says ZeeFil causes cancer."

AMBASSADOR APARTMENTS.
DOWNTOWN LAS VEGAS.
THURSDAY 3:59 PM

An early spring breeze swayed the towering palm trees fronting the Ambassador Apartments; sixteen units designed with asymmetrical mid-century modern lines nestled in a resurgent neighborhood near downtown. In its heyday, the Ambassador played host to more than its share of legendary Vegas characters indulging in legendary Vegas debauchery. But these days the action at the well-maintained address was mostly low key, as tenants generally kept to themselves or made the scene elsewhere. Then there was the landlady in apartment number one, who had been there for all of it.

Gladys surfed the cable channels, searching for a certain yogurt commercial she liked in which a wisecracking baby judged a beauty contest. Twice through the loop with no success, she settled for singing juice boxes, then leaned back in her plush velour recliner to enjoy the thirty second serenade.

The landlady loved commercials. The way people with short attention spans preferred magazines to books. She was pushing eighty and looked every minute of it with a platinum Eva

Gabor wig, pince-nez glasses and red Capri slacks bulging at the waist. But back in the day, Gladys had been a knockout. A showgirl who dated high rollers in exchange for expensive gifts and hundred dollar chips with which to gamble, until eventually she found love. But when that love died in Vietnamese jungle, she withdrew to the rent-free solitude of managing the Ambassador.

For almost fifty years she existed on television and short visits with passing neighbors, eventually glomming onto religion as a way to give her life meaning. But in a town perpetually reinventing itself, the landlady ultimately did the same by chucking her plastic Jesuses into the trash when real purpose came calling. Gladys was again a showgirl. Back on stage as one of the Jimmy Dot Dancers.

"Anybody here order a pizza?" called a voice through the screen door.

Gladys hummed along as the juice boxes finished their jingle.

"Pepperoni and black olive. Your favorite."

"Jenny!"

Gladys scrambled out of the recliner, as quick as old lady possible, and gave Jenny a long hug as she came inside and set the hot pizza on the coffee table.

Jenny looked around at artificial tulips, mismatched furniture and photographic memories of a gorgeous young showgirl. Inhaled the familiar potpourri of Shalimar and Ben Gay, and knew she was home.

Gladys had bonded with Jenny almost immediately after she and Dot set up housekeeping in apartment twelve right after they were married. Taught the new bride how to properly poach an egg and make a pineapple upside down cake, while Jenny bought the old lady a smartphone and taught her how to use all the hippest new apps. And Gladys adored Jimmy, as they often drank wine deep into the night, playing gin rummy and trying to top each other's most outrageous stories. Dot usually won at cards but was no match for memories like the one about the old lady's affair with Sinatra, that she later admitted in a boozy moment was just a quick blowjob backstage at the Sands.

Jimmy and Jenny were true friends Gladys could count on no matter what. Best friends who had become family and made an old lady's golden years a little brighter. A lot brighter. Jimmy and Jenny were always together, always smiling and so much in love you could feel the heat a block away. But for months she had seen only Jimmy, minus the smile, as every day he came by to check apartment twelve to see if his wife had come home.

Gladys set out plates, napkins and Jenny's favorite, raspberry iced tea. Then crunched the plastic cover as she sat beside her on the couch ready for some answers.

"Enough stalling, girl. Let's have it. Where have you been these past months? I've been worried sick."

"Remember Blammo, the old sideshow freak I told you about who taught me how to eat fire when I was a kid?"

"Sure," Gladys replied through a mouthful of pepperoni and olives.

"He was in really bad shape after his fourth heart attack, and I went down to the Barnum & Bailey Winter Quarters in Florida to help take care of him. He died last week, so I figured it was time to come back and face the music."

"You could have called."

"Sorry, Glad. I know I should have let you know where I was, but I didn't want you to tell Jimmy."

"You think he sold out, but I know Jimmy as well I know my cholesterol level. Greed isn't what gets him out of bed in the morning, and you should have known he didn't go to The Fabulous for the money."

"What was I supposed to think?"

"Did you give him a chance to explain?"

""Without honesty a marriage is nothing."

"Same with trust. Jimmy is an honorable man and you should have believed in him. If you would have just listened to what he had to say, you could have saved everybody a lot of heartache. He's been awfully miserable without you. Came by every single day with a fresh bag of Cheetos tied to a heart shaped balloon, hoping you'd be here. Can barely open your apartment door there's so much of that stuff in there." Gladys was a sucker for a happy ending. Especially this happy ending. "Have you seen him yet?"

Jenny's eyes brightened and Gladys not only had her answer, but also realized that pizza tasted a lot better when you had a friend to share it with.

"You're right about everything, Glad, and I believe in Jimmy one hundred percent till death do us part. I know now that he didn't do it for the money. He hates the money, because everywhere he goes now people have their hand out. People he counted as friends turned out to be nothing more than a bunch of moochers." Jenny picked the olives off a slice and licked the grease from her fingers. "How do you avoid the spongers trying to get their mitts on the cash you have left after buying the Ambassador?"

"I got myself this high definition big screen TV and a comfy new recliner, then sent the rest of the money to that man on the commercials with all those starving seventy-three-cents-a-day kids with the flies on their faces," explained the old lady about an unexpected multimillion dollar windfall that had landed in her lap a couple years before. "Nothing left in the bank except cobwebs."

"Every gutter snipe who can steal a newspaper knows how much The Fabulous is paying Jimmy. He was happier hustling pool for the grocery money." Jenny took a bite with just pepperoni and chased it with a satisfying swallow of iced tea. She felt so good to be home and regretted that she had ever left. "Do you know the hotel makes him hang out in the casino four hours every day like a trained seal and pose for pictures with any square who asks him, even in the men's room? I don't even care anymore why he signed that contract. Only how he's going to get us out of it."

"He has a plan?"

Jenny's eyes again brightened.

"He promised me we'd be back home in our apartment in time to read the Sunday comics."

"Jimmy want me to accidentally burn down the theatre? Everybody knows old people can't be trusted with matches."

The action in Dot's late night stories never included props as notorious as Elvis' cock, but Gladys loved when he explained to her the anatomy of even the simplest scam. Loved it even more when he clued her in ahead of time, so she could feel like she was part of it. And even more on those occasions when he let her shill for him, and actually be part of it. She was so excited about how he was going to get the best of The Fabulous, that when her eye caught the baby judging the beauty contest she didn't give the little wisecracker a second thought.

"You know, Glad, when Jimmy breaks the contract the show will close. You'll be out of a job."

"I was on top when it meant something to be on top." The old lady looked fondly at framed photos of herself on stage at the Dunes and Desert Inn. After hours with Dean Martin, Red Skelton and Danny Thomas. "So screw The Fabulous. What can I do to help?"

"On Sunday you can bake a pineapple upside down cake."

"A welcome home party?"

"We'll bring Chinese and some wine." Jenny smiled suggestively. "Maybe even invite Frank Ballinger,"

Gladys blushed and straightened her wig.

"This is really happening? My kids are really coming home?"

"When Jimmy Dot promises he can do the impossible, he does the impossible. So put on your sweater and let's go to the grocery store and pick up what we need for Sunday, because I have every confidence that my husband knows exactly what he's doing."

THE FABULOUS. BLAKE FULLER'S OFFICE.
THURSDAY 4:34 PM

Jimmy Dot had absolutely no idea what he was doing. With Leeds now suspicious of his every move he would have to dig deep into his bag of tricks to bait another hook, with no guarantee of being able to use the billionaire to manipulate Blake Fuller. Meaning that if he was going to make good on his promise to Jenny, Dot would have to take aim directly at the casino boss. But how?

"Go right in, Mr. Dot," said the executive assistant in the tailored jacket and skirt. "Mr. Fuller is expecting you."

What did Fuller fear losing more than anything? He had no family, not even a dog Dot could put the snatch on. All his boss seemed to care about were his crappy paintings that may or may not become valuable some day. He was pretentious, narcissistic and addicted to the power that came with his job. And all this information added up to exactly nothing, meaning that maybe Jenny was right when she suggested that he shit in a punch bowl and take his chances.

"Hello, Jimmy," welcomed Fuller with a smile, seated behind his broad slate-topped desk enjoying a greenish-colored smoothie. "Have a seat. Can I offer you something to drink?"

Dot remained standing.

"You can tell me what is so damn important that you had to drag me away from an afternoon with my wife."

"How is Jenny? It must be nice to see her after all these months."

He was a mean-spirited prick and a health nut. Wore bespoke suits that fed his arrogance. Nothing Dot hadn't known before as he sized up his boss looking for an angle, any angle, he could use to try to break his contract. Even the thought of the word boss made him gag. Fuller was his first and would be his last.

"You haven't answered my question."

"Yes, of course." Fuller fiddled with some pencils on his desk, taking his time until they were arranged just so. Then handed Dot a document. "I'd like you to sign this. It's an addendum to your original contract, extending your obligation to The Fabulous for another five years."

"What the hell makes you think I would sign that?"

"The same reason you signed the original. To prevent your wife from being deported."

"That cheap shakedown won't work twice. My Jenny is as American as Uncle Sam's whiskers."

"Your Jenny came to this country from Greece when she was two years old. Neither she or her parents, before they died, were ever naturalized or granted green card status, making her as much an illegal alien as any wetback who swam across the Rio Grande."

"She married a citizen and that automatically makes her a citizen."

"It's not automatic these days."

"A good lawyer can beat that."

"I hear you've been to three of the best and they all told you that she doesn't stand a chance. Especially with a grand theft conviction on her record."

"She was only eighteen. The kid driving said it was his father's car and Jenny had no way of knowing it was stolen."

"She pleaded guilty."

"In exchange for a suspended sentence and a guarantee that the whole matter would be expunged from her record."

"No conviction is ever completely expunged." Fuller enjoyed having the upper hand. Held out his fountain pen. "Sign it, Jimmy."

"Fuck you, Fuller. I'll go see Mal Williams. He's not only a fan of the circus, he's a lawyer. And the most powerful member of the United States Senate. He'll get Jenny a green card and you'll be left with nothing but an empty theatre."

"The senator can't help you," announced a voice behind him. "Immigration is a hot button issue and he has an election coming up."

Dot turned to see a fit-looking man wearing a dark polo shirt with a stitched government logo get up from the sofa, walk across the office and lean his rear end on the edge of Fuller's desk.

"This is Harry Gunther," Fuller told Dot. "He's a special agent with the Las Vegas field office of the U.S. Citizenship and Immigration Service, which is part of the Department of Homeland Security. He has a warrant for the immediate arrest of Jennal Alexis Dotoski, formerly known as Jennal Alexis Todonides."

"This is bullshit!"

"Sign this addendum to your contract and Agent Gunther will tear up the warrant, and forget he ever heard of your wife's immigration status."

"Go piss in your hat."

"Just sign it, Jimmy. Then you and your wife can live happily ever after."

"Fuck you!"

If he signed it he would lose Jenny. If he didn't sign it he would lose Jenny. But Dot knew he had nothing to lose by smashing Blake Fuller's face through the one-way glass behind his desk.

"Right now your wife is grocery shopping with an elderly woman named Gladys Anderson," Agent Gunther informed Dot, then took his phone from the pocket of his pleated chinos and held it like a weapon. "And my men are in position to arrest her the moment I give the word. She will be placed in a detention cell until her expedited hearing in the morning. And before you get a chance to say goodbye, your wife will be on a one-way flight to Athens, deported and never again allowed to set foot on U.S. soil."

"No fucking way. I've talked to enough lawyers to know you can't deny her the right to due process."

"We're Homeland Security. We can do whatever we want."

Dot was livid as he felt his world beginning to crash around him. Saw how much Fuller was enjoying this.

"How much is this blow dried asshole paying you to ruin our lives?"

"Dotoski is Polish, isn't it?"

"My parents were both born in Cleveland, Ohio, USA. I'd invite you to check on that, but I'm sure a creep like you already has."

"I know everything about you, Dotoski. And everything about your parents and their parents."

Blake Fuller held up a file folder labeled DOTOSKI.

Dot wanted to throw Fuller through the window and the immigration agent right after him.

"Gunther. German, isn't it?"

"That's right, Dotoski."

"Maybe after I shove that warrant up your ass I'll sue you for starting World War Two."

Dot and Gunther now stood face to face, each daring the other to make a move. And as much as Fuller delighted in yanking his ringmaster's chain, enough was enough, as Dot's signature on the dotted line would virtually ensure his twenty million dollar bonus.

"Let it go, Gunther." Then Fuller turned to Dot, "Just sign the damn paper, Jimmy, and all of this will be forgotten. It's early yet. You and Jenny have plenty of time to enjoy a nice dinner before your show."

"Which means this fucking Nazi has plenty of time to toss a few Mexican families in the jug before going home to beat his wife."

Fuller unscrewed the cap of his fountain pen and placed it on the desk beside the addendum.

Dot picked up the document and glanced at it. "I'll sign it later."

"Sign it right now, or your wife is gone forever."

"Fuck you, Fuller. I'm going to read this one first."

Dot folded the addendum and put it in his back pocket, and then accidentally on purpose crashed his shoulder hard into Agent Gunther as he walked out of the office.

THE FABULOUS. SPORTS BOOK.
THURSDAY 5:11 PM

"**M**otherfucker!"

Jimmy Dot snarled the words loudly as he stormed through the casino, prepared to unleash the full force of his anger on the first asshole tourist to demand that he pose for a selfish or selfie or whatever the fuck these brainless idiots called them. Looking for any excuse to dispense a dose of the old ultra-violence so scathing that even Dot's celebrity could not keep him from being tossed back into the same downtown lockup where this whole nightmare began. But fortunately his growling bulldog expression kept the photo seekers at bay until he reached the sports book where he plopped himself down in the center of a row of empty red leather armchairs.

"Usual Jimmy?"

He nodded to the waitress in the frisky space age get up then unwrapped a fresh Robusto, trimmed the end then struck a match.

"Let me do that." The intergalactic cutie took the match from between his fingers and held it to the business end of the dark cigar, taking care to administer the fire evenly so that he would enjoy a smoother smoke. "Be right back with your beer."

The beer did nothing to take the edge off, as Dot was boiling with so much hatred toward Blake Fuller that a handful of Valium would not have tempered his urge to destroy the man who was trying to destroy him. Whose blackmail had driven his soulmate away for months and now threatened to exile her forever. Extortion 101, as the casino boss knew that if you wanted to make someone act against his will, threaten the person he holds most dear. Revenge logic dictated that Dot simply turn the tables. But he knew that Fuller was such a narcissistic prick that the only person he cared anything at all about was himself, meaning that Dot would have to find another way to extract his pound of flesh.

Cheers erupted sporadically from sports bettors as they sat glued to the giant high-definition video images of baseball, basketball and hockey games that bombarded the state-of-the-art bookmaking theatre from all directions. But Dot was oblivious to the raucous action around him, as hatred had given him focus to figure out what would hurt Fuller the most. Where he was most vulnerable. He leaned his head back and closed his eyes, hoping that psychological adrenaline would drive him in the direction of an answer.

"Come to pay off?"

Dot grimaced. Thought process derailed.

"Don't pretend you can't hear me," pressed Revson, as Dot's eyes remained closed, trying to tune out the familiar voice that trespassed on his privacy.

The timid scientist seemed all of a sudden cocky, making Dot figure he had probably gotten laid. A thought quickly dismissed, as he knew that a stiff like Revson would never come across with the cash it took to make it with the high-end gash that prowled The Fabulous.

"I want the $10,000 you owe me."

Arrogant too. What had come over this guy since yesterday?

Dot finally opened his eyes. "If you win the bet, you'll get your money Saturday night like we agreed."

"It bothered the heck out of me that I couldn't figure out why you would bet that you could get Randy Leeds to admit in public that his miracle drug causes cancer. You had to know it was a bet you couldn't possibly win, and it didn't make any sense to me until just now."

"You finally figure out that winning means nothing without the chance of losing?" Dot aimed his sniffer toward the aroma wafting from the hot dog cart. "And that the more the odds are stacked against you, the sweeter the victory."

"No, Jimmy Dot. I finally saw what should have been obvious all along." Revson lit a cigarette and took a deep drag, smoke streaming from both nostrils as he continued. "You're one of those guys who likes to lose. It's as simple as that. You're nothing but a loser."

Revson ordered a gin and tonic from the outer space cutie.

"Just give me my money." More of a demand than a request, as Revson tapped his cigarette above the ashtray on the drinks table wedged between their chairs.

"You need it that bad?" Dot looked at the disgraced lab geek whose only social skill, it seemed, was being bothersome. Who probably couldn't summon up enough moxie to be the life of the party on bingo night. "I don't see you as a man who could have any vices to feed except maybe a little Cinemax after your wife falls asleep. So what's the rush?"

The $10,000 cash advance he had just taken on his MasterCard to toke the bellman. A transaction that fueled this newfound confidence, though it had done nothing to put the brakes on the scientist's curiosity to know the reason for absolutely everything. He finally had Dot figured out, but what about the bum in soiled sweatpants and a ripped Metallica T-shirt leaning against the betting counter? The guy looked like he hadn't eaten in a week or bathed in a month, yet there he was in this high-end sports book pretending he belonged. Revson thanked the waitress as she served his drink, reasoning that the casino dressed her as if she was from the ninth ring of Saturn because that's where you would find Las Vegas if you looked closely enough at a map.

Revson had to wait two days until ZeeFil's cancer-causing side effect would be exposed at the EcoGreen shareholders meeting, so he figured it wouldn't kill him to wait to collect his money from Jimmy Dot. In the meantime, he was in Las Vegas at the most spectacular hotel anyone had ever set foot inside. His quest to stop the most dangerous mass murderer in American history had suddenly become a vacation, which Revson prepared to enjoy as the throbbing of his knee reminded him that he had more than earned every minute of it.

"Maybe I'll check out your show tonight."

"Sorry, Poindexter. It's sold out." Dot admired a perfect smoke ring, then drained his beer. Got up and glared menacingly at Revson. "I sat here and took your shit because right now I have bigger fish to fry. But if you ever again call me a loser, I guarantee you will regret it."

As he watched Dot walk out of the sports book, Revson sat back and drank his drink in short sips, feeling relaxed for the first time in months. Began watching a basketball game but his eyes would not allow it, drawn instead to the bum at the counter who was now engaged in a serious discussion with a ticket writer and two supervisors. Then came the Twilight Zone moment as the bum slipped a rubber band off of a baseball-sized roll of hundreds, snapping off several thousand dollars and pushing the cash across the counter. What kind of inside-out town was this where a bum had that kind of money? He had finally figured out why a rich clown bet ten grand to win a hot dog, but where was the logic in a bum risking money that could feed him for a year? And his sweatpants had no pockets, so where did the money come from?

"They say if you hang out in Las Vegas long enough, eventually you will see everything."

He turned to find Owen Howard making himself comfortable in the seat Jimmy Dot had just vacated. No white outfit this time. He wore a yellow button down shirt and blue jeans.

"I've been looking all over for you, Revson."

"Why? You believe me now?"

"Maybe." The journalist noticed something very different about Revson. No longer begging to be taken seriously, he seemed almost cocky. "Did you convince some other writer to run with the story?"

"I took care of it myself."

"As far as I know, ZeeFil is still scheduled to go on sale Monday."

"Not a chance."

"So you no longer need me to write about it?"

"Are you saying that you would?"

"I came to Las Vegas to file a career making story about finding Preston Bond, but I'm getting nowhere fast. And I certainly don't want to leave Las Vegas as the joke of my profession because I passed on a story that could be, like you told me yesterday, even bigger than Bond. So if you can show me some proof, anything at all that even somewhat substantiates your claim that ZeeFil causes cancer, I will write a story that credits you as the hero who saved the world, while getting my byline on every media outlet from Boston to Beijing and Miami to Mars."

Three short hours ago the beleaguered scientist was at the end of his rope. Riddled with excruciating guilt as he stared down a ticking clock with absolutely no idea what to do. Now between the bellhop and the journalist he could attack ZeeFil on two fronts, meaning that as he sat amid a couple hundred screaming sports bettors, one way or another he was about to become the biggest winner of them all.

"I don't have any actual proof. No lab reports or company records, or I would have already shown them to you and every other journalist I spoke with. But I do have a personal journal with all my notes that will show the FDA exactly what to look for."

"We don't need a smoking gun. A company the size of EcoGreen doesn't buy a box of pencils without leaving a paper trail a mile long. Your journal and my story will be more than enough to get a temporary injunction until all their relevant documents can be subpoenaed. In the meantime, ZeeFil won't go anywhere near the public. So what do you say, Mr. Revson. Will you show me your journal?"

"It's in my room." Revson finished his gin and tonic, sucking the final hint of juniper from the ice cubes. Thrilled that someone had finally believed him. Excited that the ordeal that had cost him his family, his career and his reputation was rapidly drawing to a very just and very safe conclusion. He was no longer cocky or arrogant. He was calm. Guilt free. At peace, as he was about to be vindicated. "Let's go."

Howard checked his watch. "I have a massage appointment in a few minutes. How about we meet in your room around 7:00."

"I'm in 2631. I'll go up now and get the journal from where I have it stashed."

"Are you kidding?" laughed Howard. "You're the luckiest man in Vegas right now. Go play cards for an hour."

THE FABULOUS. SHOESHINE STAND.
THURSDAY 5:47 PM

A pair of scantily clad girls, too young to have discovered the more effective subtlety of women, launched star fucker smiles in Jimmy Dot's direction as he walked through the casino toward the shoeshine stand. He smiled back, as his contract demanded, then climbed onto the chair beside Jackie Fink, whose Italian loafers were being buffed to a mirror shine.

"Hey, fellas. Whataya say? Whataya know?"

"Same words, different tune," Fink told him as he inspected Everest's work.

Other than shopping for ties and sampling his own merchandise, there was never much on Fink's agenda. So as long as his phone was in his pocket to conduct business, most days he would bounce from here to there flashing a roll and showing off expensive threads. He made a big production out of paying for the shine, and then went off to do just that.

Everest, who wore a lime-green turtleneck under his paisley vest, handed Dot a couple of folded newspapers then hoisted his considerable frame onto the vacant chair. "Wondered when you'd be by for these."

"No crosswords today." Dot set the papers down. "Not in the mood."

"Don't let Leeds drag you down. Him getting wise to your play at the Top Hat was probably for the best."

"Back off, Everest. I've already been called a loser once today."

"You know I didn't mean it like that, Jim. It's just that there are a lot of guys who learned the hard way not to mess with that dude. I'm just glad you didn't end up being one of them."

"The day I'm scared off by a punk like Randy Leeds is the day I pack my polka dot Speedo and sell Popsicles at the beach."

"Then you haven't given up trying to con him?"

"Hell no. Before I'm through with that one way asshole he's gonna wish he'd never left Cow Pie, Oklahoma."

"There are only two things in this life necessary to make a man completely happy. Money and the love of a good woman." More than a hint of envy in the shine man's voice as he looked his friend in the eye. "You're one of the lucky few who has both, so why in the world would you risk it all just to satisfy your ego?"

"I told you to back off."

"And more importantly, how are you even going to make a move when Leeds knows it's coming?"

How did Everest know that Leeds had called his bluff at the Top Hat? Why was he so interested in his next move? Dot quickly retracted these thoughts, feeling guilty about even thinking that the man who had been one of his closest friends for over twenty years might possibly be the one who was selling him out.

"And what about Fuller?" wondered Everest.

"What about Fuller?"

"Something happen in his office to put this bug up your ass?"

"What makes you think there's something new between me and Fuller?" asked Dot, suddenly a little less guilty for being suspicious. Maybe Everest was tired of the endless cycle of bending his back to clean shit off peoples' shoes, only to end up right back where he started. Maybe he finally felt entitled to some of the gash and flash that paraded past him six days a week. Sometimes seven.

"I know every move you've made since you had pimples and a full head of hair," the shine man told him. "Same as I know everything else that goes on in this casino."

It was true that certain things did not add up, but Dot refused to doubt this man who had stepped in and saved his cocky teenage ass from a beating when he made the rookie mistake of lifting the wallet of a quick tempered wise guy. This man who taught that kid street smarts then, when he was ready, graduated him to learn the finer points of his craft from Frank Ballinger. The man who spent extra years behind bars rather than rat out someone he barely knew would never betray one of his closest friends. Making Dot certain that not only had Everest not sold him out, but that it was he who had betrayed the shine man by even thinking it.

THE FABULOUS. STARSHIP LOUNGE.
THURSDAY 6:16 PM

Blake Fuller sat across from a VIP in a long narrow fuselage with seats alongside windows that gave the illusion you were hurtling at warp speed through the galaxy. Like a classic railway club car teleported into the twenty-fifth century, where smoking hot space chicks delivered enthusiastic cocktails amid a soundtrack that seemed to resonate from instruments not yet invented. The casino boss stroking the high roller's ego a bit before turning him loose to assault the craps tables.

Most high rollers were demanding. The whales especially, who made unbelievably outrageous demands that had to be met with a smile or their action would be lost to any of a dozen other casinos within walking distance. Even the smaller fish copped major attitude. Send a private jet, discount my losses and get my girlfriend off my back by treating her to a shopping spree. But this duded-up cowboy, who had sold his ranch but was smart enough to retain the mineral rights, demanded nothing. Came to The Fabulous a couple times a year to lose a million or two as fast as he could so that he could get on with the important part of his evening. Meaning that all it cost the casino to empty his pockets was a steak, a few drinks and a night in one of the magnificent villas complete with two high end working girls to keep him happy until a hotel limo delivered him to Delta Airlines in the morning. Didn't they have women in Montana? Not like these they didn't.

Babysitting VIPs was usually left to the casino hosts, but Fuller liked the cowboy, as he was a change of pace from the rest of the invited gamblers. And though he would never usually insult a VIP by taking a call, as his phone vibrated he excused himself and walked over to the flight deck bar to take this one.

"What's Dot's new plan?"

Fuller listened, not happy with what he was hearing.

"He was in the shoeshine chair half an hour ago. Didn't you get any information out of him?"

Fuller's expression hardened as he listened.

"I don't want excuses. The fact that he didn't sign the contract yet means that swindler has something up his sleeve. And if you know what's good for you, you'll find out what it is. And fast."

THE FABULOUS. BLACKJACK PIT.
THURSDAY 6:34 PM

Revson had fourteen and the dealer's up card was a five. The other players at the table cringed as, against both probability and common sense, he signaled for another card. A six, beating the dealer's eventual nineteen.

He had little idea how to play the game of blackjack other than the object was to get close to twenty-one without going over twenty-one, but luck, as it so often did in life, trumped skill and he was winning. Not a lot of money because he was playing small and not pressing his bets, but Revson had run a $50 buy-in up to almost $300 and was brimming with the confidence that came from being the luckiest man in Las Vegas.

He had seen a movie once, based on a true story about some students from MIT who learned how to gain advantage at the blackjack tables by counting cards. These were some of the finest young mathematical minds in the world that ditched sky-is-the-limit futures to play blackjack. Card counters had been around casinos forever and their statistical advantage translated into big bucks as long as they flew below the radar. And the MIT kids raked it in as well, until they got cocky and blew the whole shebang. Revson wondered what would have happened if he and his lab partners had chucked Dartmouth to go to Las Vegas and play cards.

Revson had thought a lot lately about all the what-if moments in his life, but now it was time to bury the past and look toward the horizon. He was blackballed in the scientific community, but once ZeeFil was exposed as a health risk and his credibility restored, would any respected laboratory hire him? Or would they just look at him as the guy who screwed it all up in the first place? And maybe that was fair; scientists were supposed to stop epidemics, not start them.

He had been branded a kook and a crackpot and a lunatic. Was disowned, ostracized and beaten to a pulp. But he stood up to the challenge. Risked everything to make it right so that not one person would suffer or die because of his mistake. One balding middle-aged man against an evil empire of power and greed and, against all odds, he prevailed. He would be hailed a hero and maybe he would write a book about it. And maybe the book would be made into a movie. Revson loved going to the movies, and he couldn't imagine a bigger thrill than munching popcorn while watching a major Hollywood star play him on the big screen.

Revson held an ace and a six and the dealer had a queen showing. She was a somewhat attractive thirty-something whose uniform was intergalactic but not revealing. Nice enough to the players where he almost thought she cared, but robotic enough to know she didn't. He followed his instinct and stood pat with the soft seventeen as his attention was distracted toward a passing couple holding hands.

They were about his age, and from the look in their eyes he could tell that they had been in love for a very long time. It made him think about how a wife was supposed to believe in her man even when no one else did, and stick by him no matter how rough things got. His better half, however, had dropped him like a drooling leper rather than endure a few dirty looks at the dry cleaner and the grocery store.

Again a winner as the dealer busted, Revson finished one cigarette and lit another. A smoker-friendly environment was just about the only thing that made sense to him in this town he still viewed as three exits past surreal.

His son and daughter had not spoken to him in months. More concerned with negative Facebook comments than hearing what the man who had nurtured them through chicken pox and puberty had to say. No benefit of the doubt for the man who went without many simple pleasures to make sure they would not be saddled with a lifetime of student loan debt. But with his reputation about to be restored, he was certain they would fight their mother to be first in line to bask in the reflected glory of the conquering hero upon his return. But would Revson allow them their fifteen minutes? Not on your life. He wouldn't go back to EcoGreen, PA at all if it weren't for his freckle-faced granddaughter. Nine years old and she understood unconditional love more than any of them.

Revson had no idea where the coming years would take him, but he looked forward for the first time in his life to seizing control of his own destiny. Maybe he would teach or do volunteer work. Maybe his next research project would be a road trip to find the perfect fried chicken. He fully understood that he was not the hero Howard's story would make him out to be, just the luckiest man alive.

Ace of clubs topped the ten of spades. Blackjack.

Bill Revson had not been this optimistic since the day he summoned the courage to ask Carrie Leaper to the spring dance. He couldn't wait to wake up tomorrow and greet the first day of the rest of his life.

THE FABULOUS. BILL REVSON'S ROOM.
THURSDAY 6:58 PM

Easy money and free drinks. Maybe Las Vegas wasn't such an absurd place after all, Revson thought as he stepped aside, allowing two nearly-naked women to exit the elevator. Tall, strikingly gorgeous women who wore nothing except clinging see-through fabric with images of the queen of hearts and ace of diamonds. As the elevator whisked him up to twenty-six, his only thought of the encounter was that the two cards equaled blackjack, as after little more than a day at The Fabulous he was finally beginning to appreciate the anomaly that is Las Vegas and take it all in stride. All was right with the world as, even with his injured knee, there was a spring in his step as he breezed down the hallway and opened the door to his room.

"Is this all of it?"

Owen Howard sat in a high-back chair fronting the window, holding up a notebook he had found tucked between the mattress and box spring. He wore a navy blazer over his yellow shirt and jeans. And tight black leather gloves.

"Did you kill the real Owen Howard?" asked the scientist, his analytical mind not having to strain itself much to see that he had again fallen victim to Randy Leeds' goon squad.

"You got me wrong, Revson. I'm not a violent man. The real Owen Howard is in Bumfuck, Iowa, snooping into farm subsidy graft or some such bullshit." The imposter stood and walked toward him. His voice evenly measured. "And I'm not going to hurt you. I just need to be one hundred percent sure that this journal is the only documentation you have."

Revson's fliers would be distributed at the shareholders meeting, but with so much at stake he pushed for insurance. "How can you in good conscience let innocent people suffer and die when you have the ability to help me stop it?"

The imposter kicked Revson in the balls. The toe of his boot crushing the scientist's nut sack, and dropping him to the floor.

"Is this journal the only documentation you have?"

"Yes," whimpered Revson faintly through pain too excruciating to imagine.

"I don't believe you." He opened the mini bar and cracked a cold Budweiser. "We're going to keep talking until I'm convinced you're telling me the truth."

"It's everything, I swear to you." Revson gathered enough strength to sit on the edge of the bed. Still woozy. Still in great pain, the bookish middle-aged man looked up at his overpowering assailant. "I knew something wasn't right when your face didn't quite match Howard's online photos."

"Didn't matter. You were so frantic to get a journalist to listen to your story that you wanted to believe I was Howard."

He took a swig of beer, and then laughed. "With a haircut, dye job and colored contacts, you would have believed Mickey Mouse was Owen Howard."

"You may not be a journalist but you have my notes, and as part of the EcoGreen cover-up you also have inside knowledge. With that corroboration we can stop this horror before it starts. Please Mr. ... What is your name?"

"I'm Tommy C."

Revson had seen enough gangster movies to know that if the bad guy suddenly spilled the truth, the other guy's future was probably short. He had nothing with which to bribe him. Could only hope to reach his conscience.

"Look Tommy ..."

"Tommy C. Even my mother calls me Tommy C."

"Do you love your mother?"

"What kind of dumb fuck question is that? Of course I love my mother."

"Try to imagine the horrific pain she will suffer before finally dying, just because she took a pill to cure a runny nose. Think of all the other innocent men, women and children who will die if ZeeFil isn't stopped. Please, Tommy C. You have the power to help me prevent it!"

Tommy C swung both fists hard, boxing Revson's ears. A screaming pain shot through his head, then the goon pulled him up by the hair.

"Are there any copies?"

"No."

Tommy C punched him in the face, shattering his glasses. Blood trickling from the bridge of his nose.

"Are there any copies?

"Whatever Leeds is paying you to kill me is just a drop in the bucket compared to what you can make if you blow the whistle. You'd be a national hero."

"You just don't know when to quit, do you?" Tommy C carefully placed a gold cuff link on the floor near the bed, then grabbed a Baby Ruth from the mini bar and put it in his jacket pocket. "And you can forget about stuffing your fliers in the annual reports, because I gave your bellman some serious cash to double cross you. Time to give up. It's over."

"You're not doing this for the money, are you?" Revson spit up blood then wiped his mouth with his sleeve. "You enjoy hurting people."

"It's better than sex." A lascivious grin as he finished his beer and tossed the empty bottle into the trash. "A lot better than sex."

"Then you must be pretty damned excited, because you're about to fuck half the country."

"Starting with you, my friend."

Tommy C picked up the chair he had been sitting on and swung it hard, smashing the window. Grabbed Revson by the shirt and yanked him to his feet. Ripped the Dartmouth class ring off his finger and stuck the souvenir in his pocket.

"I know you're scared and I know you've got some regrets." He slapped the defeated scientist's broken glasses back onto his blood-smeared face and shoved him toward the window. "My only regret is that you couldn't get a room on a higher floor, but you can make it up to me by not closing your eyes on the way down. I don't want you to miss one second of this ride."

Bill Revson was scared out of his wits as his greatest fear was about to be realized, falling to his death from a great height. Forced to stare down fast approaching mortality. Each second hurtling him closer and closer to the unimaginable pain of finality. All of life's what-ifs kaleidoscoping through his brain as he fell. Twenty-six stories was approximately 290 feet, multiplied by the rate of acceleration and ... No. Not this time. For once let curiosity be damned. His life was over and the only thing he cared about was the only thing still within his control. Choosing his final thought. Not ZeeFil, as he would not give EcoGreen the power. Not his failure as a scientist and the human suffering it would cause. Would hugging the mental image of his smiling freckle-faced granddaughter cancel out the pain of smashing into the ground? Would death and pain be simultaneous so that he felt nothing? Would ...

Revson's eyes bugged-out with fright as Tommy C seized him by the collar and thrust him head first through the broken window, almost giddy as he watched the flailing body became smaller and smaller as it fell. Wishing he could see the action in slow motion as Revson bounced off the edge of the porte cochere, then smashed face down on the pavement in front of a group of drunken bachelorettes wearing plastic tiaras exiting a party bus.

Tommy C stood at the window for a few moments admiring his work, then pulled his phone from his pocket and made a call.

"It's done."

THE FABULOUS. POONTANG JOHNSON'S DRESSING ROOM.
THURSDAY 7:33 PM

"**W**here do you get the bat shit idea that I'm not a romantic?" demanded Zazzo as he carefully placed the three of clubs on top of a rising house of cards. "I've romanced more women in this hotel than anybody."

"That's sport fucking." Poontang added a hundred to the stack of bills beside the cards as she looked across the red lacquer table at the man in his white-on-white stage costume. "The most romantic thing you've ever done is promise not to come in a girl's hair."

"I give these tomatoes the attentiveness they don't get from their men at home, plus a Vegas affair that they can brag about to their girlfriends."

"What woman wouldn't want to brag about the fake swami who fucked her in the ass, then stole her diamond earrings?" Poontang rocked a towering Afro wig and stunning low-cut orange Valentino gown. Added a card. Less than ten left in the deck. "You ever been on a real date, Zazzo? Nice restaurant. Goodnight kiss at the door."

"Why are you bustin' my balls?" he shot back, beginning to resent the aspersions to his character as he tossed a hundred onto the pile. "Don't take it out on me because your new man doesn't bring you flowers and candy."

"My new man is a gentleman."

"Does this gentleman know that your pussy is really a ten inch cock?" cracked Sparkle as he scarfed meatballs and crudité from the pre-show spread.

The top-billed cast members each had their own dressing room, though Sparkle's was more of a full service pornography depot and Zazzo's a tricked-out fuck pad. Swanky's and Dot's digs served as little more than pit stops to change their clothes and take a leak, which is why they all hung out at Poontang's before every show. The décor was Chinese modern with cushioned furnishings and framed photographs of Jean Harlow, Marlene Dietrich and a dozen other glamorous stars from Hollywood's golden era.

"Why the sour puss, Jimmy?" Swanky asked Dot, noticing that something was obviously bothering the ringmaster, who walked in looking dapper in top hat and tails, minus the pants. "Everything okay with Jenny?"

"Jenny and I are great, Swank."

"One of the epic romances of all time," Poontang schooled Zazzo. "You could learn a lot by watching those two."

The sour expression on Dot's face came from guilt. While his brain percolated with an idea that would hopefully put the screws to Blake Fuller and allow him to keep his promise to Jenny, his guts gnawed at the problem of how to tell the cast that Saturday's show would be their last.

He could soften the blow to the dancers, the freaks and the rest of the supporting cast by digging deep into his pocket. But for Sparkle, Swanky, Poontang and Zazzo, it was less about money and more about the fact that the show had become a major part of who they were, making Dot feel like a first class asshole for putting his happiness ahead of theirs by kicking them to the curb. He tried several ways to justify it, but his conscience wouldn't allow it. He hoped they would understand, and he would understand if they didn't. Figuring the best way to tell them would be to just come right out with it.

"Listen up, guys. I have something important to ..."

"Hey, Jim!" interrupted Jackie Fink as he as he rolled in under a head of steam. "That egghead you made the crazy hot dog bet with just took a dive out of his twenty-sixth floor window."

"Revson wouldn't kill himself. No way."

"I ran into a cop I know who said the guy left a suicide note."

"It's not possible." Dot pictured the man who only a couple hours earlier was upbeat and cocky. Who had gotten under his skin by calling him a loser. "If he flew out a window, somebody pushed him."

Dot said it in a way that got everyone's attention.

"Who would want to murder a harmless old dude like him?" wondered Poontang.

"I know who killed him. And I also know why."

"Then tell us and we'll split the reward," Sparkle chimed in through a mouthful of salami. Then looked at Fink. "I'll give you my end of the money for a scoop of every flavor ice cream you got on the menu."

"Forget it, Sparkle. Cops don't offer a reward when the stiff leaves a note."

"Cops don't know shit. Jimmy says it's murder, so it's murder."

"Just pay for your pussy like everybody else."

Poontang held her breath as she ever so delicately added another card. It held steady for a second, and then the house of cards collapsed.

"Winner!" crowed Zazzo as he grabbed the stack of hundreds and stuffed them into the pocket of his white suit jacket, then laughed. "Maybe I'll blow this wad on a romantic dinner and hope I get a goodnight kiss."

Dot knew this murder confirmed that everything Revson told him had been the truth. ZeeFil did cause cancer, and people would die if the drug went on sale to the public. And it would go on sale to the public because with Revson dead, nobody was even trying to stop it. Truths that anointed Jimmy Dot as the only person left to step up and do what was right. A job for which he was ill prepared. A job for which he had no time, as he was trying to get his own life together. But what kind of life would that be, knowing that his inaction had caused innocent people to die? It was up to him, and only him, to prevent an unthinkable evil. Proof positive that there was no god, as no omniscient deity would entrust a clown in orange polka dot underwear with such a crucial task.

Bill Revson's mistake was that he kept bashing his head against the wall by doing the same thing again and again hoping for a different result. And, like it or not, it was now up to Dot to find a better way to convince someone who could put a stop to this insanity and do it fast. But how? What could he do? Call the newspapers and the Feds? Revson couldn't get them to take him seriously, and he was the chemist who came up with the key component of the formula, so why would they listen to the wisecracking ringmaster of a Las Vegas circus? Could he call EcoGreen's competitors? Call Oprah? And say what? He had no proof, just an unthinkable truth. Dot could hear himself trying to convince people with the same word for word spiel Revson had laid on them, and getting the same one-word responses. Lunatic. Crackpot. Kook.

The stage manager knocked on the door. "Two minutes."

THE FABULOUS. FUGAZI LOUNGE.
THURSDAY 11:57 PM

Taylor Swift acknowledged a spirited ovation as she and Tommy C finished their duet, then he waved to the crowd and descended the scaled-down concert stage and made his way past a dozen rows of theatre seats to the bar in the rear of the crowded lounge and ordered a beer.

"I'll get that," called out Jimmy Dot as he handed the bartender a twenty and waved off the change.

"Thanks," said Tommy C, whose expression lit even brighter as he recognized the funnyman. "You're Jimmy Dot."

"And you're Owen Howard."

"You liked my song? I guess you did if you're buying me a beer," smiled Tommy C, seeing that he needed to masquerade as the journalist a bit longer, still jazzed with adrenaline. "I mean I killed, right?"

"It's a shit song and you're a shit singer. So bad that you're an insult to all the other shit singers waiting their turn to pay $99 for a video of themselves caterwauling on a Las Vegas stage with a hologram of their favorite pop star."

That's what Dot would have said had he not wanted something from the karaoke clinker. Instead, he faked a smile for the better part of two beers until the time was right for him to get to the point.

"I assume you heard about Bill Revson?"

"He finally get someone to believe that crazy ZeeFil story?"

"He's dead."

"You serious? How?"

"Header out of his twenty-sixth floor window."

"A lot of talk around the hotel tonight that there was a jumper," said Tommy C. "It was Revson?"

"He didn't jump. He was murdered."

"Police say who did it?"

"They're calling it a suicide."

"Bullshit!" yelled Tommy C, loud enough to be heard over Pitbull screeching on stage with some trilby-topped hipster.

"I agree. We both know that he never would have killed himself as long as ZeeFil was still a threat to the public. He was murdered by Randy Leeds in order to shut him up, meaning that everything Revson said about the drug being dangerous is true." Dot took a sip of beer. Struck a match on the bottom of his stool and fired life into a fresh Robusto as he attempted to urge on the man he believed to be a journalist. "Which gives you all the proof you need to write a story that will blow the lid off all of this."

"Is there any tangible proof? Did the cops find anything in the room with Leeds' prints on it?"

"All they're saying is they found a suicide note on a bar napkin stuffed in the pocket of a pair of white pants in his closet. It said *Only One Option Left*. That was enough to make them close the case."

"That's nothing more than circumstantial." Tommy C kicked himself for overlooking the note. "It's not even circumstantial."

"All the pieces are there," prodded Dot. "Make them fit any way you want as long as your story brings out the truth."

"I'd love to tie Leeds to this, but how do you expect me to convince anybody it wasn't suicide without proof?"

"What kind of investigative reporter are you? Do your job for chrissakes."

"How come you care so much about this?"

"How come you don't?"

The ringmaster had no way of knowing it, but Tommy C did care. Cared very much, except that his loyalty had already been bought and paid for by the other team. A fee he was prepared to earn no matter how many upper story windows he had to smash.

"All you have to do is tie Leeds to the murder and you can stop ZeeFil in its tracks."

"On what evidence, Jimmy? No offense, but don't you find it strange that in months of running his mouth to the press, the FDA, bloggers and social media, the only person Revson was able to convince of this conspiracy is you?"

"I find it strange that you're in a position to save lives, but don't seem to give a shit. I'm not as shortsighted as Revson. So you and the rest of the media can suck my hairy ass if you think I'm not going to do whatever it takes to keep ZeeFil away from the public."

"Good luck with that," laughed Tommy C as he unwrapped the Baby Ruth candy bar that had been in the pocket of his navy blazer.

THE FABULOUS. PENTHOUSE 777.
FRIDAY 1:10 AM

She reached for the $5000 casino chip, but Leeds pulled it back. Held it to her lips and made her lick it, then inserted it into her pussy as if he was plugging a slot machine.

The prostitute liked this game. Liked it crazy. Liked it kinky. A welcome change of pace from most Las Vegas Johns who usually just wanted a quick come and go so they could get back downstairs to the casino for another shot at converting cold dice. But this situation was anything but usual as she writhed naked on Spanish marble in front of the blazing white stone fireplace. The penthouse offered twenty-thousand square feet of comfortable elegance, yet Randy Leeds wanted this action on the very spot where Cameron Diaz had been videotaped banging out a bestiality daily double.

Leeds told his wife to suck his cock as he inserted another $5000 casino chip into their guest. The prostitute loved the game and begged for more, then more still until it began to hurt. But she didn't care, concentrating on trying to keep track of how much as he kept jamming the money inside her, the walls of her box stinging from the hard edges of the compressed clay gambling tokens crammed in at awkward angles.

Every one that fit belonged to her, that was their deal, and it reminded her of the old joke of why Jewish women wore gold diaphragms because they wanted their husbands to come into money. The walls of her pussy pounded like a sharp headache, but the money just kept coming. Then it stopped. She was full.

Randy Leeds pushed his wife away. Ordered her to bury her face between the prostitute's legs and remove the casino chips with her teeth.

Abbie did as she was told, filling a chip rack as their guest wondered if the money being excavated from her pussy was enough to buy a new Mercedes.

Leeds hovered over the action, stroking himself faster and faster until his spooge splattered both women. Commanded his wife to lick up the mess, then finish filling the rack and to be quick about it. Playtime was over.

"Dig deep. Make sure you get all of them."

Abbie did as she was told, disgusted and humiliated as she completed her task.

The prostitute got dressed, and as she reached for the rack of chips, Leeds snatched it away from her.

"You can go."

"Not until you give me the money you promised. Every last chip."

"You're right. I'm sorry," Leeds acquiesced, carrying the rack of chips as he escorted her to the foyer and pulled open one of the red double doors. Then gave her a hard kick in the stomach that knocked her into the hallway and ass backwards onto the carpet.

"You owe me that money!" she screamed up at him.

"Owe you? You didn't even fuck me." He threw one casino chip at her. "More than you deserve, you greedy whore. Now get the hell out of here before I call security."

He slammed the door and faced his humiliated wife.

"And what's your problem?"

Abbie backed away.

"You think I'm an asshole for making you do that?"

"I didn't say that, Randy." Abbie was scared as she had seen this side of him all too often. "I didn't say anything."

Leeds smashed his fist into her face, the force of the punch slamming her backward into the wall.

"That's for thinking it."

THE FABULOUS. JIMMY DOT'S SUITE.
FRIDAY 6:47 AM

Jenny remembered asking Jimmy after they first met what pleasure he could possibly get from watching a TV show more than once. Do you buy a record and listen to it only once? That was his answer and soon she shared her husband's enjoyment of black and white television. Of reliving a well-acted scene, the soundtrack behind the patter and nuances missed in previous viewings.

Jazz cat *Johnny Staccato* crushed crime between gigs. *Mr. Lucky* played fast and loose with the law on his floating casino, while stylish private eye *Peter Gunn* single-handedly took down the bad guys 114 times without wrinkling his suit. Jenny clicked on these titles, adding them to the classic DVD box sets of *M Squad* and *Racket Squad* already in her shopping cart. Overnight delivery so that when they got home to their apartment, other than answering the door for the pizza man, she and her husband would not have to get out of bed for a month.

Jenny entered her payment information and completed the order, logged out then placed her phone and credit card on the desk. The sun had begun to recharge the city for another go around, and she looked expectantly past the long stretch of casino hotels to that small apartment building a couple blocks off the boulevard near downtown that no longer seemed so far away. Only two more days.

Dot sawed logs while Jenny picked up clothing that the lust of a few hours earlier had strewn about the bedroom. Hung her velvet dress in the closet and tossed yesterday's orange Hawaiian into the laundry bag, then as she folded Dot's trousers his wallet fell to the carpet along with a folded piece of paper.

She put the wallet on the desk and took a look at the paper. Re-read it as to make no mistake what it said. Put on her robe and pulled the sash tight, then laid on the bed beside her husband until eventually he was roused by morning wood. Made a move, but Jenny pulled away.

"Why did you do it, Jimmy?"

Dot rubbed the sleep from his eyes and looked at his angry wife.

"What did you possibly hope to gain by stringing me along?"

"What are you talking about?"

"You know motherfucking well what I'm talking about!"

"Dammit, Jenny. If we're going to fight, at least tell me what it's about."

"You promised me that we'd be home by Sunday and never have to set foot inside this soul sucking hotel again."

"And we will be."

"You're a liar, Jimmy. Not only do you have no intention of quitting the show, you're signing on for an extra five years."

"You got it all wrong," he explained, realizing that she must have found the addendum to the contract. "Fuller is trying to strong arm me into an extension, but I didn't sign it. You saw the paper, Jenn. You know I didn't sign it."

"Not yet." She was quickly simmering to a boil. "I asked you yesterday what Fuller had on you to get you to sign the original contract, and you said he had nothing. Now you're telling me he has enough to strong arm you into signing an extension. What the fuck is going on, Jimmy? I want the truth."

Dot slid out from under the covers and walked naked into the other room. Cracked open a beer from the cooler behind the bar and came back to face his angry wife. Paced back and forth in front of the window looking for the right words, and then realized she would soon find out anyway. So he just came out with it.

"Immigration has issued a warrant for your arrest. Fuller has it fixed so that you'll be deported back to Athens unless I sign that extension."

"They can't deport me, I'm an American citizen."

"Not according to the government and the three lawyers I went to for help."

"Fuck you, Jimmy!" She exploded into a full-blown rage. "What kind of bullshit are you trying to pull?"

"Were you ever naturalized? Do you have a green card?"

"Why the fuck would I?"

"Neither did your parents. Meaning that after the original travel visas expired, for the rest of their lives they lived here illegally. Same as you."

"If you want to sign the extension, sign it. But don't invent some bullshit story making it my fault."

"Immigration agents were going to arrest you yesterday when you were at the market with Gladys unless I agreed. I told Fuller I'd sign it later, buying me some time to figure a way out of this."

"One lie to cover another, then another and another. You're not even a good con man." Jenny's rage turned hollow, deep-sixing her into the bottomless emptiness of betrayal. "I take it back, Jimmy. You're a great con man. You had me fooled right from the start when you conned me into marrying you. Why? I don't have a clue. There are thousands of hookers in this town, so it certainly wasn't for the sex."

"You don't pay hookers for sex."

"That's right. You pay them so they'll leave when you're finished having sex. But you didn't want me to leave. Why, Jimmy?"

"How can you ask me a thing like that?"

"I'm asking. Why, Jimmy?"

"Because you're my everything, my soulmate. You have my love and my loyalty one hundred percent, and I've never wanted to be away from you even for an hour. Why do you think I became a performer and started the circus?" Dot was getting tired of having to defend himself to a wife he felt should have his back no matter what. "But you're loyal only when it suits you. Instead of stepping up and helping figure a way around Fuller when he blackmailed me into signing that original contract, you left me high and dry. And now that I'm behind the eight ball again, all you can think about is yourself.

A marriage stops being a partnership when one of the people involved is a selfish chicken-shit coward."

"Coward? You have the nerve to call me a coward because I went to Florida to help a dying friend, rather than stick around to hear more of your lies?"

"What lies? You called me a sellout then ran off for months before I had the chance to say one word to you. And this time, when I do have a chance to explain, you don't believe a damn thing I say."

"Blackmailed into signing a contract against your will? A crooked immigration agent forcing you to sign another one?" A condescending laugh. "I thought a con man's lies we supposed to at least sound believable."

"On the square, Jenny. Fuller is going to have you deported unless I sign that new contract."

"That's another great thing about hookers. They'll believe anything you tell them as long as the meter's running." She got off the bed and hung up her robe. Threw on a sweater and jeans. "A marriage stops being a marriage without honesty and respect, and you've proven again and again with every lie that you don't respect me, and you certainly don't love me. Well, I don't love you either, so you can read the Sunday comics right here by yourself because this time I'm leaving you for good."

That was the moment Dot found out for the first time in his life that words can cut deeper than the sharpest blade. Wounded. Speechless. Watching helplessly as his forever and always picked up her phone and credit card then opened the door to leave.

"I never loved you!" yelled Jenny as she stormed out, slamming the door behind her.

"**I** assume you understand there is value in making an ally of a man with great wealth," stated Randy Leeds, wearing a blue sweater pulled over a blue polo shirt, as he crouched to line up his shot on the putting green seventy-seven stories in the sky above the Las Vegas Strip. Then stood and with an even stroke tapped his golf ball into the hole. "Of course you do. That's why you've been sucking up to me ever since I arrived. That's why you warned me about Jimmy Dot trying to trick me into admitting something about ZeeFil that most assuredly is not true."

"And I will continue to have your back while you are a guest at my hotel," replied Blake Fuller, dressed in a light gray suit, morning dew on the grass spotting the calfskin uppers of his new two-tone Italian Oxfords.

"You mean the hotel where you work," scoffed the billionaire. "And certainly not for much longer, once Preston Bond shows his face and takes the air out of your inflated graveyard numbers. You will not only be out of a job, but also the twenty million dollar bonus you're counting on."

Fuller's face registered surprise, as no one outside the executive offices knew about the bonus, but he recovered his composure quickly.

"Preston Bond is dead, Mr. Leeds. And I plan to keep my job as well as my bonus."

"I'm afraid bravado will not make either of those statements true. I will have my picture taken with Preston Bond at the EcoGreen shareholders meeting tomorrow afternoon. And to that end, I will be in your debt if you will provide me with something I can use as leverage against Jimmy Dot."

"I find it hard to believe, especially after I warned you about him, that you would allow that swindler to con you into thinking he knows anything at all about a dead movie star."

"Quite the contrary. He claims to know absolutely nothing about Preston Bond, though you and I both know that's not true."

"Believe what you want. But what makes you think I have anything that you could use as leverage against Jimmy Dot?"

"Oh, come now, Fuller. Jimmy Dot is a very unusual man in that he is not working at this hotel for the money or the celebrity. It's obvious that you're employing some form of coercion to get him to take the stage each night."

"And what if I am? Why in the world would I help you destroy my career unless you are willing to pay me the twenty million?"

"Not a penny."

"Then why would I help you? What's in it for me?"

"A favor," offered Leeds. "I assume you're smart enough to understand that a favor from someone soon to be the world's richest man can be worth a lot more to you than twenty million."

"The investigators you've had snooping around the hotel for months have come up with nothing. Yet somehow Dot has convinced you that Preston Bond is in the hotel and you want him to show you where. And you also want him to quit mouthing off about ZeeFil." Fuller was hungry, as the early morning summons to appear had caused him to miss his breakfast smoothie. He eyed the array of fresh fruit on the buffet table beside the infinity pool and helped himself to a plate of fresh papaya and mango. "So for twenty million, plus a favor of equal or greater value, I will provide you with ammunition that will make Jimmy Dot do absolutely anything you want him to."

"Since you do not seem to grasp the value of having a billionaire in your debt, perhaps you can comprehend the devastating consequence of having that billionaire as an enemy. So I will ask you one last time to provide me with something I can use as leverage against Jimmy Dot."

"Don't underestimate me because I work for a paycheck. Either I get the bonus from the hotel or I get it from you."

"I admire that you have all of a sudden found the backbone to stand up to me, but that confidence is misguided. I suggest that you again weigh the pros and cons of having me as an ally or an enemy."

"And I can't believe that you have the colossal gall to expect me to give you something that would jeopardize both my job and my future in exchange for a favor that you could withdraw at any time. You want my help, the price is twenty million. Payable right now."

"I don't need your help, Fuller."

"Of course you do, or you wouldn't have demanded that I come up here at the crack of dawn."

"Granted, your assistance would make things easier, but I have another way of getting everything I want from Jimmy Dot." Leeds put away his putter and smoothed the crease of his slacks. Checked his watch, a priceless one-of-a-kind timepiece that he never tired of showing off. "I have a tee time in thirty minutes. Finish your breakfast and get used to looking over your shoulder. You'll never know how or when it's coming. But make no mistake, that one day I will take great pleasure in destroying you."

THE FABULOUS. JIMMY DOT'S SUITE.
FRIDAY 9:39 AM

Jimmy Dot had hitchhiked onto the dead scientist's outrage, and vowed to stop an inevitable horror no matter what it took. But how? It was obvious that no short con or last minute manipulation was going to bring EcoGreen to its knees, filling him with so much self-doubt that he could think of no other recourse than to simply use the telephone. But two hours of this straightforward attempt to derail the ZeeFil express had gotten him nowhere fast.

He had hoped his personal physician might be able to tell him who he could speak to that might have enough juice to at least call attention to the matter. No dice. He spoke to the publishers of both local newspapers who told him that without proof it was no more than a slanderous accusation, and if printed they would most assuredly be sued. He called all three lawyers he had recently met with, and each told him with absolute certainty that not even a drunk judge would issue a temporary injunction to stop the drug from going on the market without at least enough credible evidence to in some way substantiate his claim.

Dot was spinning his wheels, but no one had called him a kook or a lunatic. At least not yet. As he sat at the desk looking at the list of names he had written on a piece of hotel stationary, he knew that none who had yet to be crossed off had the power to slam the brakes on ZeeFil. But he only needed one person with the connections to refer him to someone who could. Next up was Alec Baldwin, who had given him his cell number at the circus' opening night party. Like everyone else remaining on the list he was a long shot, but the actor had a big name and a big mouth and knew a lot of important people. As Dot began to dial the number there was a knock at the door.

Trying times sometimes knocked couples out of sync, but as long as their love was strong, they could talk and they could work things out. Dot's love was strong. And so was Jenny's, or why else would she have come back? But his wife would have to do a lot of apologizing to take the sting out of hurtful words that could not be unsaid. Should he greet her stone-faced or with a smile? Best not to press his luck, he figured, as she was back and that was all that mattered. But that smile dropped as he pulled open the door and faced a badge.

"Get lost. I'm busy."

As Dot pushed the door shut, Hard Bernard slammed it back in his face and muscled his way inside. Dry-swallowed a couple pills then did a quick search of the suite to make sure they were alone.

"James Dotoski, you are under arrest for the murder of William Revson."

"I don't have time for your psycho bullshit, Bernard. Besides, you haven't been a cop for over a year so you can't arrest me. You can't arrest anybody."

"But I can sure as hell hold you until the homicide boys get here."

"Fuck off, Bernard. The cops are calling it suicide."

"You and I know different."

It was common knowledge that Hard Bernard was a violent psychopath, and that the Benzedrine and Viagra he popped like Pez gave him a perpetual hard on. He screwed several women a day, motivated not by lust or conquest but by rage as he used his cock like a weapon to fuck these women violently, and if they dared to fight back he made them regret it. Hookers used to give it up in exchange for a get out of jail free card. Suspects traded wives and girlfriends for the promise of freedom, only to be double-crossed as he booked them anyway. Even naïve teenagers fresh off the bus from Nowheresville were not immune to the pain and humiliation inflicted by Hard Bernard. But sex was no more than a gym workout to keep his rage focused, while speed, Viagra and Chinese boner herbs fueled a viciousness that usually got him whatever he wanted.

The hulking ex-cop pulled out handcuffs. "Turn around."

"Fuck you, Bernard. I can prove I was never anywhere near Revson's room."

Hard Bernard picked up the desk chair. Flipped it upside down and, as easily as snapping a day old wishbone, his massive hand broke off one of the legs and held the jagged piece of wood to Dot's throat. "By the time I'm finished with you, you'll be begging to confess that you were."

"One day somebody's going to save a lot of innocent people a world of hurt by getting rid of your ass once and for all."

"You?"

"Could be."

"You better worry about your own ass first." Hard Bernard swung the chair leg and smashed a vase of fresh tulips. "Casino surveillance video shows you in the sports book arguing with the victim less than two hours before he flew out the window."

"He tried to collect on a bet he hadn't won yet."

"That's your story."

"You know damn well I didn't kill Revson, so why are you really here? What the fuck do you want from me?"

"Preston Bond."

"You think I've got him stuffed under the bed? It's the one place you didn't look."

"Just tell me where he is."

"Why does everyone all of a sudden think that I know where Preston Bond is?"

"I don't give a shit why. I just want Bond."

"So you can go three floors up and sell him to Randy Leeds? The guy who actually killed Bill Revson."

"You killed Bill Revson."

"Revson was going to blow the whistle, which would cost Leeds billions of dollars, ruin his reputation and probably send him to jail."

"You're the one going to jail if you don't give me what I want." Hard Bernard brandished his jagged weapon. Glanced at the shattered vase. "Right now, or the next one cracks your skull."

"Knock off the macho bullshit and listen, you junkie moron."

Hard Bernard's rage swelled as he stepped toward him, but Dot stood his ground.

"You are going to give me evidence of something I can use to blackmail Blake Fuller. Set him up if you have to. As long as it's something that will ruin him. Do that before the end of the day, and I'll introduce you to Preston Bond."

"Take me to him right now, and this officially stays a suicide."

"You already made a deal with Leeds, didn't you?"

"For more money than you could ever imagine."

"Big mistake promising Randy Leeds something you can't deliver."

Hard Bernard stepped menacingly toward Dot, who did not flinch. "I'll deliver."

"Are you aware of Leeds' reputation for destroying the people who cross him? Give me something to use against Fuller and you won't have to find that out the hard way."

"Last chance before I beat a murder confession out of you."

As Hard Bernard viciously swung the weapon, Dot sidestepped the blow and smashed both fists into the hulking ex-cop's chest, knocking the wind out of him and sending him crashing backward into the desk. Jumped on top of him, knees neutralizing the much larger man by pinning his shoulders to the carpet.

"How many women that you raped will come forward with their stories and sue the police department when you have a popular Vegas headliner arrested on some bullshit charge that couldn't possibly stick? How many men that you've beaten confessions out of do you think will go to the D.A. when they see me on the news with two black eyes? You may not be a cop anymore, but that's not going to stop them from throwing your sorry ass in prison where there are no bennies or boner pills. How long do you think you'll survive in a cellblock filled with criminals you put there? You want Bond, help me set up Fuller. That's the only way it's going to happen. You have until the end of the day." Dot released his hold, got to his feet and kicked Hard Bernard toward the door. "Now get the fuck out."

Dot walked across the room to the bar and poured a cup of coffee, allowed himself only a moment to recover his composure before pulling a sturdy chair to the desk and getting back to work. He picked up the phone and dialed the number that was next on his list.

"Hello Alec. It's Jimmy Dot."

THE FABULOUS. BLAKE FULLER'S OFFICE.
FRIDAY 10:04 AM

"**W**ho knows what that piss ant has up his sleeve, but I'm not going to wait to find out," snapped Blake Fuller into the telephone. "I want you to arrest Jenny Dotoski."

He paced back and forth on the silver carpet in front of his desk as he listened to Agent Gunther.

"Yes, right now. This morning."

He listened again then exploded.

"I don't give a fuck how many Mexicans you have scheduled for today. Do what I'm paying you to do! Find her, arrest her and put her ass on the next plane out of the country!"

Fuller slammed down the telephone. Took a moment to compose himself, and then straightened the painting he had just hung in place of the wounded Jezzler. A striking photorealism acrylic by Ryder Corralez he had picked up for a song at an East Hollywood gallery, that might someday be worth a million. And if not, he was positive one of his many other finds would be. An ego-inflated confidence validated by the latest issue of *Zoom Bop*, a modestly circulated but well respected art mag, in a recent piece about his growing collection. No dilettante. No dabbler. Confirmed in print that this Las Vegas casino boss had the eye. And right now that eye was on the future.

As soon as he collected his bonus he would be out the door. Goodbye to The Fabulous. To Las Vegas. To an arrogant billionaire's threats. His windfall would finance the career he had always dreamed about. He would become an art dealer. A respected player in the high stakes world where a good eye and shrewd dealing might one day make him an arrogant billionaire.

Satisfied that the Corralez hung properly, Fuller slipped into the jacket of his light gray suit, shot his cuffs and walked into the outer office.

"I'm going downstairs to look at carpet samples and check progress on the remodeling of the keno lounge," he told his executive assistant. "Come with me. I want your opinion."

She hesitated a moment until her boss passed on his way out the door.

"What are you waiting for? Let's go."

The pretty brunette straightened her skirt as she rose from her chair, exposing a three-foot Elvis on his knees beneath the desk. The midget waited until their voices faded down the hallway, then popped up and went into Fuller's office. A kid left alone in a candy store.

Sparkle dragged a chair over to the credenza by the window that overlooked the casino, climbed up and took the lid off the water compartment of a coffee maker. Whipped out his dick and unleashed a stream of frothy piss that would spice up Fuller's next jolt of caffeine. He pulled the chair back to its proper place, then stood at the desk and opened drawers one by one. Pencils. Note pads. Envelopes. Worthless office supplies. Phone charger. Sunglasses. BINGO! Fuller's personal checkbook.

The midget checked the balance in the ledger then tore five blank checks from the back of the pad and found a copy of a memo he could use to trace Fuller's signature, stashing the documents into the side pocket of his white jumpsuit. Then he opened the top drawer and saw a file folder marked DOTOSKI. What he found inside was pure dynamite. He took out his phone and photographed each page, careful to keep the papers in order, then returned the file to the drawer and closed it.

With a letter opener the midget loosened the screws supporting the desk chair, nudged the Corralez ever-so-slightly off kilter and walked happily out of the office with the taste of executive pussy still fresh on his tongue.

SHADOW CREEK GOLF COURSE.
NORTH LAS VEGAS.
FRIDAY 11:02 AM

More private than a country club, Shadow Creek was one of the most beautiful golf courses in America. Amid the rolling green hills, cascading waterfalls and towering pines, one might wager a year's salary that it was not within a hundred miles of the desert.

As the last member of a foursome hit his tee shot on thirteen, a golf cart came barreling toward them up the fairway and fishtailed to a stop.

"Hi-ya, fellas!" called Jimmy Dot.

An annoyed Randy Leeds told the others to go ahead and he would catch up.

"What is it, Jimmy?" It was a picture postcard day, cool and pleasant like most every early spring day in Las Vegas. But at the moment Leeds wasn't feeling it. "You steal my wife's ring again?"

"I want you to do the right thing and delay the release of ZeeFil so it can undergo further testing."

"Even if further analysis was warranted, which it most definitely is not, it would be virtually impossible to recall a product that has already shipped. Not to mention that the loss of public trust would cause EcoGreen stock to plummet."

"How greedy are you? Is everything about money? Don't you even care that you're going to give people cancer?"

"You're talking out of your ass, Jimmy." With a soft cloth Leeds wiped a few blades of grass off the head of his driver and put the club back into his golf bag. "The drug has been thoroughly tested, and not one person got cancer in the FDA trials."

"I don't know which is more heinous, Randy. You putting countless people at risk by bribing somebody at the FDA, or killing Bill Revson to shut him up."

"I didn't bribe any FDA supervisors. I didn't kill that idiot Revson. And I'm not putting a pill on the market that is going to give cancer to the people who take it."

"Revson was about to ruin you, and you killed him."

"Revson was a crackpot who couldn't get even one journalist to listen to him." Leeds laughed. "Can you imagine that? In this day and age, not being able to float a conspiracy theory?"

"Look Randy, I'm giving you one last chance to do the right thing."

"Drop it, Jimmy."

"Or what? You'll throw me out a window too?"

"Give me one reason why I shouldn't."

"Don't you see that by pulling the drug yourself you can save face, fix the problem and make your money later. Your publicist can spin it to look like you put the welfare of the public ahead of profits. You'd be a hero."

"I have to catch up to my foursome."

"Come to my show tonight."

"So you can drag me on stage and have that swami of yours hypnotize me into saying something against my will?"

"No, Randy. I'm hoping that after a few laughs you'll lighten up and see that hitting the pause button on ZeeFil is the right thing to do."

"You don't give a damn about the drug. You're just trying to win that stupid hot dog bet. But why? You can't collect from a guy they're still scraping off the driveway."

"Tell me the truth, Randy. Next time you catch a cold are you going to take a ZeeFil?"

"Falling toward the pavement at a hundred miles and hour must be a terrifying way to die."

"Not nearly as terrifying as the fall from grace that will leave you closer to being the poorest man in the world than the richest."

"Return that golf cart to whoever you stole it from and stop meddling in my affairs, or you are a dead man. Look me in the eye, Jimmy. A dead man."

HILDA'S COUNTRY CAFE.
SUBURBAN HENDERSON.
FRIDAY NOON

"Am I right, Jimmy?"

Malvin Williams was a tell-it-like-it-is cowboy who over the years had risen from a stable hand mucking out barns to his current position as majority leader of the United States Senate. And he would be the first to tell you that he was always right.

"It is the best apple pie I've ever tasted, Mal," replied Dot enthusiastically as he scraped the last crumbs of buttery crust off his plate and into his mouth. "That's a fact."

"Next time try it a la mode. Old gal hand cranks her own ice cream every morning." He waved to the sturdy woman with white hair who was busy behind the counter. "Hey, Miss Hilda. Bring our friend a bowl of vanilla, will ya please."

Dot had met the man in the western shirt and black Stetson only once before, but the senator made him feel at ease as if they were old friends.

"Back when Henderson was just a quiet little speck on the map, Miss Hilda would cool pies on the window sill so the aroma would attract passers by."

"Like with hobos in the old cartoons."

"Never did have a TV till I had kids of my own, and even then never paid it much attention. But I do know that anytime a fella down on his luck came to the back door, the old gal would make sure his belly was full before sending him on his way."

Dot always enjoyed stories about the good old days, even if they were someone else's good old days.

"And you'd never guess it from the urban sprawl, but my brother and I used to ride our horses here after school and she'd give us each a glass of milk and piece of pie. Cherry for him and apple for me. Been hooked on it ever since."

Hilda cringed as she set down Dot's bowl of vanilla. "Hate to think how old that makes me."

"But still pretty as a bunch of fresh picked daisies, Miss Hilda," smooth-talked the senator, making her blush at a dose of the cowboy blarney that had endeared him to the Nevada electorate five times.

As Hilda disappeared into the kitchen, Williams looked out the window at the traffic buzzing past on the busy thoroughfare. The KFC and Taco Bell that squeezed the café from both sides.

"A lot of folks call that progress. What's your take, Jimmy?"

"I think we both should have another piece of pie."

They dug in, savoring warm apple spiked with cinnamon, nutmeg and another flavor Dot's taste buds identified as possibly a hint of maple. And as they enjoyed round two, Dot told the tale of ZeeFil, cancer and murder to one of the most powerful people in America.

"I called the Cancer Society, the AMA, even TMZ. And they all said the same thing."

"That they wanted to see some proof? But I imagine there isn't any, or Miss Hilda and I would not be enjoying the pleasure of your company."

"Bill Revson didn't have any lab reports or official EcoGreen documents, but he told me he kept a journal containing all his notes. A journal the police didn't find in his room."

"Making all of this circumstantial."

"Just because it's circumstantial doesn't mean it's not true." Dot stressed the urgency. "There's too much at stake for you not to call the Food and Drug Administration and make them retest the drug. And it has to be today. Monday will be too late."

"I can't make the FDA do anything, Jimmy. They're an independent agency."

"Not entirely. Their commissioner had to be approved by the Senate."

Williams pushed back the brim of his hat and raised an eyebrow.

"That's right, Mal. I've learned a lot today about how things work."

"Then it should be obvious to you, now that he's been confirmed, that the commissioner can tell the Senate to pound salt and there's not a blasted thing we can do about it."

"But you being the top man, he'll take your call." Dot noticed a little kid sneeze a couple of tables away. Nodded for Williams to look as the mother handed the boy a Kleenex. "And he'll have no choice but to listen to what you have to say."

"Then he'll chew out my rear end for making a wild accusation without even a whiff of proof. Besides, even if a drug is fast tracked it undergoes months of clinical testing plus review boards and gosh only knows how much other scrutiny. I don't see how any drug could possibly make it through such an involved process without a cancer causing side effect being detected. There are too many checks and balances. Too many people involved."

"EcoGreen has a lot of money."

"Now you're just spitting in the wind."

"Check to see which one of the supervisors involved in the process has a new Corvette in his driveway."

"It's not possible, Jimmy. And not to beat a dead horse, but you've got no proof."

"Revson had the proof and Leeds murdered him for it."

"And then destroyed it?"

"Probably. He sure couldn't take the risk of anyone finding it."

"You ought to write for the movies," chuckled the senator.

"Movies have happy endings, Mal. Like the good guy becoming a national hero and being elected president."

"Hey, Miss Hilda," Williams called across the small café. "If I become president, can I eat here for free?"

"You'll pay your check just like everyone else, Malvin Williams."

"President, huh?" The senator finished his pie, then contentedly laced his fingers on the prosperous paunch that hung over a silver rodeo buckle. "I guess it can't hurt to make that call."

"You won't regret it, Mal. I promise you." Dot had gotten what he came for, but he kept pressing. "My wife is being threatened with deportation by a crooked immigration agent. Is there anything you can do to stop it?"

"Killer cold pill, billionaire murderer and now a crooked agent." Williams slapped his knee and laughed. "I'm not kidding, Jimmy. You really should write for Hollywood."

"I'm serious, Mal." Jenny may have ripped his heart from his chest, but James Tiberius Dot was not going to let the Feds bum rush his wife out of the country on a one-way ticket to a place where she didn't even speak the language. "She's been here since she was a squirt, but the lawyers say that even though she's married to a citizen, it doesn't make a dime's bit of difference."

"She from south of the border?"

"Greece."

"That's something in your favor. But even so, strings like that are hard to pull these days." The senator saw the worry in Dot's eyes. "I assume you and your missus have a good bit of money in the bank. Is it in a joint account?"

"What does that have to do with Jenny's immigration status?"

"I'll let you know." Williams placed some cash and the check under his coffee cup, and then looked Dot square in the eye as he got up from the table. "You're sure about ZeeFil?"

"As sure as Miss Hilda makes the best apple pie on God's green earth."

No sign. No phone. Off the main drag and not listed in any guidebook. Hop Louie's was a dimly lit hideaway where the food was good, the drinks were better and Christmas music played in a continuous loop whether it was January or July. Where ancient Chinese men with wispy white whiskers sat at the bar gambling on games of cards and dice not found in any casino.

Poontang, Zazzo and Everest sat at a round table finishing their lunch, as near the kitchen Sparkle tried to chat up the waitress. She was young, pretty, and the only English she knew was off the menu. Sparkle showed her a sketch of her pussy. No reaction. Complete with hand gestures he showed her again. No reaction.

"What the hell's wrong with that gash?" grumbled the midget as he came back to the table. "Girls either smile or tell me to fuck off. Nobody ever just says nothing."

"She's fresh off the boat. Maybe she didn't understand."

"They got pussy in China, Poontang. It's slanted, but it's still pussy."

"Chase tail on your own time," scolded Everest. "And tell us what's so blasted important that I had to shut down my shine stand in the middle of the day and drag my carcass to Chinatown."

"Yeah, dude. Speed it up," Zazzo chimed in. "I got a tomato waiting whose daddy owns ten thousand acres of money in Texas."

Sparkle pushed aside his plate of chow mein and told about finding the file marked DOTOSKI in Blake Fuller's desk drawer.

"Not a good idea to rummage through Fuller's office. Best to put back whatever you stole."

"I'm not stupid, Everest. I took pictures of the file." Sparkle eyed the big man curiously. "Besides, what's it to you?"

"Forget Fuller. It's not right to go through Jimmy's personal stuff," lectured Poontang as she wedged a menthol 100 into her diamond cigarette holder. "How would you like it if we went through your stuff?"

"Who wants a bunch of stroke mags with the pages stuck together?" cracked Zazzo as he snapped open his Zippo and gave her a light, and then looked seriously at Sparkle. "We don't want to invade Jimmy's privacy. Delete the pictures."

"Even if they give us the name of the asshole who caused Dot's old man to croak himself?"

The table got quiet as they were all familiar with the story, and how not knowing the name of the man his mother had cheated with had haunted Dot his entire life. Sparkle pulled up a photo of a police report on his phone. Handed it to Everest who read it carefully then showed the others.

"We can't tell him."

"He deserves to know the truth."

"Even if it hurts him?"

"We all owe Jimmy way too much not to tell him the truth."

"That's exactly why we can't tell him."

They argued the point until everyone's plate was clean, eventually agreeing that Dot had to be told so that he could have closure. They also agreed that closure wasn't enough.

"We need kill the mother fucker."

"And deny Jimmy his revenge?"

"Break his legs? Cut off his balls?"

"None of that," Zazzo told the table. "I've got a better idea."

And he did. Captivating their attention as he laid out the simple set up and the role each of them would play.

"Ooh, Zazzo. You have a nasty mind," cringed Poontang. "I vote yes."

"You guys?"

"I'm in."

"Hell yeah."

The waitress set the check in front of Sparkle. He took a look at it and screamed bloody murder.

"This is bullshit! This is fucking bullshit!"

"Give it to me, you cheap fuck," said Zazzo as he grabbed the check. Then started laughing, and showed everyone where next to the total the waitress had drawn a sketch of two stubby legs framing a tiny nub.

"Who the fuck do you think you're dealing with, you tight ass chop suey slinger?" yelled the midget as he climbed up on his chair and ripped open his white jumpsuit which dropped around his knees. Standing triumphantly in all his glory as if he had just won Olympic gold. "I'll cram this beast so far up your ass it'll come out your nose, and I'll still be horny again in an hour."

"Lordy, lordy," demurred Poontang as she fanned herself.

Around the restaurant chopsticks dropped and conversations skidded to a halt at the sight of the pint-size man with the king-size dick. Everest shook his head. The waitress stared. Zazzo was envious. The gamblers didn't even notice.

Sparkle jumped up and down on the chair like a wild man, yelling at every woman in the place.

"Who's first? I know you all want it!"

Camera phones flashed at every table.

"Come on. Get in line and I'll fuck every goddam one of you!"

"What the hell are you waiting for, ladies?" yelled Poontang. "Somebody service that monster before it destroys the neighborhood."

DEAD END BAR & GRILL. WEST OF THE STRIP.
FRIDAY 1:40 PM

Jenny offered Abbie a bite of her cheeseburger as they camped out on barstools in the timeworn booze haunt, where beer signs and video poker machines provided the only light. Just the right amount of light.

"I can't."

"Who's going to know?"

"Easy for you to say," said Abbie, complimenting how great Jenny looked in her light blue sweater and tight jeans tucked into black boots. "You're probably one of those women who can eat whatever she wants and never gain an ounce."

"So you gain a pound from eating a burger once in a while. What's your husband going to do, divorce you?"

"There are worse things than divorce."

"Oh, for chrissakes." Jenny pushed away Abbie's salad plate then told the bartender, "Throw these weeds in the garbage and bring another burger plus a double order of onion rings. And two more beers."

The Dead End had been around since the 1950s, and a first-timer might think it hadn't been cleaned since the 1950s, but every morning it got a disinfectant scouring everywhere that counted. It was a biker bar after dark: shots and beers, barbeque and loud rock 'n' roll. No MC colors allowed inside, but that didn't stop the occasional bottle from being cracked over somebody's skull for putting the moves on the wrong pair of tits. During the day, however, the place was quiet with regulars who stopped by for their usual number of beers before stumbling home in time to watch *Wheel of Fortune*.

"I feel like I'm getting away with something," smiled Abbie as she enjoyed a bite of the burger, then took another.

Jenny pointed to a schmutz of burger grease trickling down the chin of the very proper woman in the vivid Dior dress that had probably cost more than her first car.

"Oh my God," gasped Abbie, quickly wiping her chin with a paper napkin. "I'm so embarrassed."

"Lighten up, girl." Jenny sat straight on her barstool and let out a hearty belch. "Where is it written that only men can be slobs?"

Abbie wasn't allowed many friends and had extended the invitation to luncheon for some long overdue girl talk, but when Jenny called the audible of burgers and beer she had wanted to lighten up. And finally was relaxed enough that she did lighten up. Put her elbows on the bar like back in La Crosse. Tried to force a burp but couldn't.

"You need more ammo. A few of these onion rings ought to do it," encouraged Jenny who then signaled to the bartender for two shots of Irish whiskey.

"I shouldn't drink whiskey."

"You should and you will."

She did.

"Now let's get down to the business of what women do when they drink their lunch," said Jenny as she chased her Irish with a swig of beer. "Bitch about our husbands."

"What do you have to complain about? I saw the way Jimmy smiled at you at the Top Hat." A lot of envy in Abbie's voice. "And I saw the way you looked at him. Even now you've got him in your eyes."

"The moment I met Jimmy, I understood why people write love songs." Jenny ordered two more shots. "But he lied to me."

"A lie? One lie?"

"Does Randy lie to you?"

"When you have total control over someone, you don't have to lie."

"Why do you stay with him?"

"I love him."

"Try again."

"And he loves me."

"I can see how much he loves you," said Jenny as she looked at the makeup covering Abbie's black eye from the night before. "Why the hell do you put up with it?"

"I signed a prenup."

"So what? Take the short money and make a fresh start while your face is still in one piece."

"It's a bad prenup." Abbie knocked back her second shot, the booze loosening her tongue. "A really bad prenup, where if I divorce him I get next to nothing. And if I give him grounds to divorce me, all I get is a dollar."

"Is that even legal?"

"I went to a lawyer who says it is."

"No way it can be that one-sided. Isn't he accountable for anything?"

"The lawyer said if he goes to prison or something, I can petition the court on moral grounds to void the prenup, then sue for a fair divorce settlement. But that's not a sure thing. And even if it was, men as rich as Randy don't go to prison." The more they drank, the more Abbie opened up. "Maybe he'll do me a favor and drop dead on the golf course so I can get the life insurance money and marry the man I should have married in the first place."

She reminisced about her first love. How it started as a high school crush, then blossomed into the real thing that lasted until she made the biggest mistake of her life by moving to L.A. in search of stardom.

"Here's a picture of us at a softball game the day I turned twenty-one," smiled Abbie as she showed Jenny the image on her phone. Both wearing T-shirts and jeans. Abbie's brown hair tied in a ponytail, and if Jenny didn't know better she never would have believed it was the same girl. Then Abbie showed her a more recent photograph, where the one who got away had bulked up and cut his hair very short. A beaming smile and not bad looking, but probably handsome as hell through the eyes of a woman in love. "And this is him now. Lives in Chicago."

"Is he married?"

"Nope." Abbie swallowed some air and grimaced until she emitted a pop that was as close as she was going to get to a burp. It made her giggle. "And he still loves me. I reconnected with him recently and we talk all the time."

"Then divorce Randy and move to Chicago."

"I'd like nothing more, but don't you think I'm entitled to something for all the abuse?" Abbie's voice turned bitter as she pointed to her camouflaged black eye. "A lot more than something?"

"Why did he hit you?"

"Same reason he always hits me. Because he felt like it."

They ate and they drank, Abbie eventually becoming a happy drunk as Jenny steered the conversation away from the topic of men. Talking about this and that, eventually finding a common interest in books. Abbie touted biographies and the latest best sellers, while Jenny recommended pulp fiction that spawned classic film noir. They pumped money into the jukebox, cracked jokes with the day drunks then shot a game of pool that made Jenny think about her husband.

She looked at Abbie, serving a life sentence in a cruel and brutal marriage that kept her from the man she actually loved. Felt grateful that she was lucky enough to be with the man she loved, and how stupid she had been to walk out on Jimmy after letting her pride get in the way. Reasoning that just because his explanation about the contract made no sense did not mean he had lied. She had just assumed it, and he was right in calling her selfish for not listening to him. He was right in calling her a coward for taking it on the lam rather than having his back when he needed her the most. Felt lousy that she fired back in the heat of argument by saying she had never loved him. Would give anything to be able to un-ring that bell, as she could only imagine how devastated she would be if he had said those words to her.

Jenny felt truly sorry that Abbie's marital scrapbook included knuckle sandwiches and who the hell knows how many other horrors, while her own eyes brightened at the thought that Jimmy learned to cook her favorite foods and often brought home flowers just because. A man like that deserved the benefit of the doubt, and when they left she would haul ass back to The Fabulous and listen to every word he had to say. Do whatever it took to repair the damage her hurtful words had caused until she saw her husband smile. Not the devilish grin he flashed for the suckers, the private smile that was theirs alone. The one from the heart that meant everything was all right.

They drank up, paid up and Abbie texted her driver that they were ready to be picked up. As Jenny's eyes adjusted to the bright sunlight outside the bar, she at first didn't notice that the man who opened the door of the Town Car was not the driver who had dropped them off. This guy wore an ass-length brown leather jacket, and Jenny knew she was in trouble the instant he climbed into the back seat beside her. Tried to escape through the door on the other side but was forcibly pushed back inside the car by a second goon with slicked back hair and a Guido necklace who then got behind the wheel.

"I'm sorry, Jenny," called Abbie from the curb as she pointed to her black eye. "Randy made me do it."

Before Jenny had even an instant to wonder why, the Town Car quickly disappeared into the flow of eastbound afternoon traffic.

THE FABULOUS. CASINO.
FRIDAY 2:13 PM

He was still working other angles, but with the most powerful man in the United States Senate pushing the FDA to retest ZeeFil, Jimmy Dot felt confident as he made his way through the always busy casino on his way to set in motion the solution to an even more pressing problem.

He breezed past Naked Lunch, where topless waitresses served burgers and fries, then PizzaPalooza and Bacon&Beer. Dot especially enjoyed Bacon&Beer, but with a double order of apple pie resting happily in his belly he took a pass. Continuing on past Restaurant Row until he approached the under construction keno lounge, where he stopped dead in his tracks as he saw Everest huddled in conversation with Blake Fuller. He watched for a few moments until the two men shook hands and parted company. Then confronted Everest.

"You've known every move I've made since I had a full head of hair. And now, so does Fuller."

"You've got it all wrong." Everest's rich baritone cracked up an octave as he tried to defend himself against Dot's obvious conclusion. "Come on, Jim. You know I would never sell anybody out. Especially you."

Dot said nothing. Gagging on the bitter pill of being betrayed by a man with whom he had entrusted his innermost secrets his entire adult life.

"Please believe me, Jim. It's not what it looks like. Next week they're moving my shine stand and he was showing me the new location."

"Goodbye, friend."

"I'm not talking about Girl Scouts in their underwear. This creep Fuller has explicit videos of grown men having sex with both boys and girls around six or seven years old," explained Hard Bernard, as Killer Kong put on a show for his fans by promising to knock out ten sparring partners in ten rounds. Nine up and nine down as challenger number ten answered the bell for the final round. "He keeps it all on a laptop bought and registered with a phony name, and downloads the smut using public Wi-Fi. It's like a burner phone he can just throw away because there's nothing else on it and no way it can be traced back to him."

"And you know this, how?" asked Dot as he lit a cigar.

"I'm on the inside. I know more about Blake Fuller than he knows about himself."

"Then you've seen this laptop?"

"If a judge ever got a look at the browser history on that thing he'd lock that pervert up for a thousand years. Once Fuller knows you have it, he'll be begging to let you out of your contract."

The sold out crowd urging him on, Killer Kong delivered a flurry of punishing body shots, then a quick one-two to the head. A fighter who had earned his nickname as a vicious killer, he was the ultimate antihero. A cult figure whose popularity had swelled to such an extreme that he had become a mainstream superstar adored by millions of fans who kept current on social media of every move he made. Each and every one of them wishing they were at the pavilion as Kong staggered his opponent with a ferocious roundhouse right.

"Excuse me."

Dot felt a hand on his shoulder. Turned around to see a man seated with his two teenage sons.

"There's no smoking allowed in here."

"It's an open air pavilion."

"You're not allowed to smoke anywhere that children are present."

Dot was about to acquiesce and let his dark Robusto burn out, when he noticed that the man's two boys could each use a shave. He puffed life back into the cigar and blew a smoke ring.

"I said you can't smoke here."

"Then don't smoke." Dot again faced Hard Bernard, "How come you never used the laptop to blackmail Fuller yourself?"

"It was my ace in the hole. An insurance policy in case things ever went south around here." From their ringside seats, Hard Bernard looked on as an overmatched young heavyweight hoped to make a name for himself by landing one lucky punch. Wondering how he himself would do going toe-to-toe with a beast like Killer Kong. The bent ex-cop was so hopped up he liked his chances. Then looked at Dot. "Besides, Fuller doesn't have the kind of money that Randy Leeds does."

"Is Fuller feeding Leeds information about me?"

"He was, but they've been on the outs since this morning, when Fuller tried to shake some money loose," Hard Bernard told him. "Though for some reason he's still hell bent on keeping you away from Leeds so you don't screw up something else he has going. Something big, though I'm not sure yet what it is."

"When you find out, let me know."

"Depends on what it's worth to you."

Number ten was a game opponent, ducking and weaving, trying valiantly to counterpunch his way out of trouble. But Kong was just toying with him. Getting in his three minutes of fun before knocking the kid flat. The crowd on its feet, screaming for blood as an uppercut followed by a flurry of body blows staggered the overmatched challenger backward into the ropes.

Again the hand on Dot's shoulder.

"I'm afraid I must insist you put out that cigar, or I'll tell an usher."

"You do that, pal," said Hard Bernard as he turned and flashed his badge. "And while you're gone, I'll tell these kids who their real father is."

"As Kong continued to pummel his opponent, Dot asked where he could find the laptop."

"Inside a safe in the closet of the master bedroom of his house," Hard Bernard told him. "He removes the battery after every time he uses it. Thinks that makes it safe from detection."

"Does it?"

"He thinks so. But his fingerprints are all over it inside and out, so once the laptop is in your possession you'll have him by the balls." Hard Bernard dry-swallowed two bennies and a Viagra. "Now where's Preston Bond?"

"What's the combination of the safe?"

"Since when does a yegg like you need a combination?"

Only seconds left in the round as the crowd chanted *TEN ... TEN ... TEN ...* screaming for the final knockout. But Kong toyed with them as he danced around the ring. *TEN ... TEN ... TEN.* He winked at the ringmaster in Friday orange who had once gotten him out of a jam that favored sleight of hand over brute force. Electrified the crowd with his trademark blood curdling roar then unleashed a flurry of punishing body blows followed a thunderous right to the jaw that knocked number ten through the ropes. You could hear bones break as he landed as a gift on the cement at Jimmy Dot's feet.

"I came through with my end of the deal," said Hard Bernard, his grating voice loud enough to be heard over the riotous crowd as the fallen boxer was tended to by the medical staff. "Now, where's Bond?"

"His hair is different. He had plastic surgery to bend his nose and make his face fatter, but you'll recognize him by the eyes. You can't change the eyes."

"Where is he?"

"Working in the casino, where he'll be a sitting duck until eight o'clock. All you have to do is walk in, flash your tin star and take him."

THREE JACKS MOTEL. BOULDER HIGHWAY.
FRIDAY 3:37 PM

Boulder Highway was a mostly white trash thoroughfare that cut a diagonal line along the east side of the Las Vegas valley all the way to Hoover Dam. Trailer parks and used car lots. Strip joints that would never be confused for gentlemen's clubs. Seedy motels, many of which were long closed, like the Three Jacks.

Had the owner of the motel held three jacks when he won the place in a poker game? Why not? Embracing a colorful past was what gave Las Vegas enduring character, enriched by tales that grew a lot taller with generations of telling. And who knows, someday they might be spinning yarns about the black Town Car with the rental sticker on the windshield that kicked up gravel as it pulled into the lot that chilly early spring afternoon and parked out of sight at the rear of the shuttered motel.

Most kidnap victims were blindfolded and listened for the sounds of playgrounds or train whistles. Guestimated mileage and counted the minutes in their head, hoping to later give police a vague idea of where they had been taken. But these kidnappers had the destination programmed into the car's GPS and did not seem to care that not only did Jenny know where they were, she had seen their faces.

"Get out of the car."

Jenny did as she was told. Sizing up the has-been motel that suffered the indignities of graffiti, broken windows and an empty swimming pool ankle-deep in dead leaves and trash. Slipping on loose gravel as a push in the back propelled her toward what had once been room twenty-five. Wondering how Brown Jacket and Guido, two goons obviously from out of town, had ever found this place.

Brown inserted a key that had undoubtedly been obtained without the knowledge of anyone named Jack. Opened the door and shoved her inside. Made sure the curtains were closed tight then switched on battery operated camping lights that had been placed there earlier in the day.

"Sit down."

The cleanest thing she could see was a straight-back wooden chair.

"Give me your phone."

"My husband will pay whatever you ask," Jenny assured the kidnappers. Then nervously wondered if he would, as that morning she had told Dot that she was leaving him. This time for good.

"We don't want money, Mrs. Dot," Guido told her as she slid the phone from the front pocket of her jeans and handed it to him. He scrolled through the contacts and found no one named Jimmy. "You have him listed under a pet name or a nickname?"

"Jimmy doesn't have a cell phone."

"Quit stalling."

"No e-mail, no computer, nothing. You'll have to call his room at The Fabulous."

The call was placed. Connected to suite 7402. Busy signal.

If not money, Jenny thought, what did they want? And more importantly, would Jimmy give it to them? And what if they couldn't reach him? What were these two gorillas capable of? Unanswered questions that scared the crap out of her.

Rented black Lincoln Town Car, license plate beginning with the numbers three eight. Details. Remember the details. Just in case. Room twenty-five at the old Three Jacks Motel on Boulder Highway. Half-eaten tacos, used condoms and broken bottles that had missed the trash can by the dresser. No heat and no running water. A faded desert landscape print above a bed that had not been made since the last time a girl had been escorted there. A girl who probably took care of business and was back on the stroll in half an hour. Jenny wondered if she would be alive in half an hour.

"Still busy."

"If you don't want money, what do you want?" asked Jenny, trying to reason with her abductors without showing panic. "Whatever you ask for, he'll get it for you."

Brown ogled her tight sweater as he popped open his switchblade. Pressed the cold steel flat against her cheek, the razor sharp point of the knife a blink away from her eye as Guido gave her an ultimatum.

"You will explain to your husband that if he spreads lies about ZeeFil to one more reporter or politician or anybody else, my partner will violate that long hot body of yours in ways far more disgusting than you could ever imagine."

"Little stabs, just enough to break the skin. Then deeper and deeper until the torture is too much for you," smiled Brown as he caressed the crotch of her jeans with the sharp blade. "And then we have some real fun."

Jenny trembled as she saw the vulgar blood lust in his eyes.

"I hope you like sex toys," added Guido as he picked a broken beer bottle off the floor beside the trash can. "Because we want your husband to know you had a good time when he watches the video of my partner raping you with this, then getting his rocks off while you bleed out."

He let her fear fester and take root.

"But if your husband keeps his mouth shut until the drug goes on sale to the public Monday morning, we'll drop you off at the hotel unharmed," promised Guido. "Tell him exactly that. No more and no less. Do you understand?"

"Yes."

He dialed the number again. This time it rang.

"Thank God," whispered Jenny under her breath.

And rang. And rang.

"Please try again. Maybe he's in the shower. Maybe he went down the hall to get some ice. Please keep trying. He has to be there."

Again, no answer.

"Can I call one of his friends?" Brown had backed off, but Jenny was still frantic as she looked at the blue steel automatic in Guido's shoulder holster. "Somebody will know where he is and get a message to him."

"No messages and no tricks."

THE FABULOUS. FLOAT LOUNGE.
FRIDAY 4:41 PM

White cygnet dinghies that appeared to swim through mid-air ferried guests to the colossal inflatable swan that floated a hundred feet above the swimming pool. A lounge ringed with tables in the shape of pool toys, a whimsical vibe that contrasted sharply with the stodgy assemblage of wealthy men and women attending the private EcoGreen-hosted reception to celebrate becoming even wealthier. The biggest winners in Las Vegas, yet most had an air about them as if starch had been poured on their bran flakes that morning.

"Excuse me," an old man said to a bald rosy-cheeked fellow in a brown suit and bow tie. "I believe you dropped this."

"My God!" said the man whose round hazel eyes dominated his face as he accepted the wallet, checked the contents and placed it into the same inside jacket pocket where Frank Ballinger had lifted it moments earlier. "I don't know how I could have lost it, but thank you. My name is Reynolds Cabot."

This Ballinger already knew as the men shook hands. Reynolds Ford Cabot IV, the sixty-year-old scion of a founding family who possessed one of the largest privately held blocks

of EcoGreen stock. A man whose criticism of the way Randy
Leeds ran the company was well documented.

"Dr. Frank Ballinger. Thoracic surgeon, retired."

Each man held a glass of whiskey. Cabot's with ice,
Ballinger's neat. They toasted the introduction.

"Where did you practice, Doctor?"

"I was at Mass General, then chief of surgery at Cedars in
L.A. But that was all more years ago than I care to remember."

"Some doctors retire to the golf course while others remain
involved with medicine. Which are you?"

"Medicine has been my life's calling since I received my first
aid merit badge from the Boy Scouts. I lecture and I volunteer. Stay in contact with some of my colleagues still in the
trenches." The old man in the newly pressed but still woefully
out of style gray suit had not lost his ability to gain acceptance
as whatever he masqueraded himself to be. "What do you say
we step over to the bar and freshen these?"

"Capital idea, Doctor."

Fast friends, these two cocktail enthusiasts settled in com-
fortably on adjoining barstools.

"This is supposed to be a party, though you'd never know it
by looking at these stiffs," remarked Ballinger as he perused
the activity inside the whimsical lounge. Noting that though
the booze was undoubtedly higher quality, the guests seemed
to compare quite unfavorably to the clientele of the Top Hat,
as at least on Skid Row people knew how to have a good time.

"It's only new money that lets its hair down in public,"
explained Cabot. "Social position dictates that old money

cut loose behind closed doors. And misbehave behind locked doors."

"Misbehave? This group?"

"See that man over there in the chalk-striped blue suit? Rumor has it he put four of his cocaine dealer's children through college." Cabot signaled to the bartender dressed like Daffy Duck for two more. "For most it's just the usual social vices, though some of these degenerates have been known to push the envelope as far as incest and even murder, because generally old money is immune from moral or legal judgment."

"If I may be so bold?" queried Ballinger.

"Myself?" laughed Cabot. "I'm afraid I am rather boring in that regard."

"No vices at all?"

"Good whiskey, a trashy novel and early to bed."

"Which allows you a clear head for business."

"A man must keep an eye on his portfolio, or risk one day residing in the guest house instead of the main house."

"What's your opinion of the risk associated with ZeeFil?"

"There is no risk, Doctor. That's why we're here celebrating."

"You don't feel the side effect constitutes an unacceptable health concern?"

"What exactly do you know that the rest of us don't?"

"A researcher who worked on the formula told a former colleague of mine at Mass General about a substantial risk of pancreatic cancer."

"Cancer?" Cabot choked on his drink. "ZeeFil causes cancer?"

"When I tried to get confirmation from the company all I got was the run around. You would think that as a shareholder of some standing I would be entitled to the truth. That we would all be entitled to the truth."

"Can this researcher provide proof?"

"I'm told it can be easily proven if the FDA will retest the drug, but Randy Leeds says there's nothing to indicate it falls outside the risk-benefit paradigm. And who knows? Maybe the cancer risk is so negligible that Leeds is right to stand in the way of retesting it." Ballinger was on cruise control. Enjoyed another sip of the good stuff, and then punctuated his point. "But as a medical man, I'd like to know for sure."

"If any of this were true, why would the FDA grant its approval?"

Ballinger sipped his drink. "I hear rumors of bribery."

"That seems more than a bit far fetched."

"That's what I've been told. What other explanation could there be?"

"I always said that cocky bastard would run this company into the ground one day. A company that was founded as C&K Laboratories in my grandfather's garage, so for me there is much more at stake here than just money." Cabot stated it with noble conviction as if giving a speech. Then saw Randy Leeds walking in their direction. "Leeds. What's this I hear about ..."

"Forgive the intrusion, Cabot." The CEO grabbed the old man by the arm. "There are some people I want Dr. Ballinger to meet."

As Leeds spirited the old man away from the conversation and toward the tail of the swan, Ballinger gasped and bent over.

"My heart."

"Shut up and keep moving."

"Pills." Ballinger's breath was short and he had difficulty getting the words out. "In my jacket pocket."

"Move, you fucking rummy," commanded Leeds as he pulled the old man's arm behind his back and shoved him forward.

"Help me," he begged. "Please."

"Your friend Jimmy Dot is about to learn the hard way to stop meddling in my affairs." Leeds jerked the arm hard, inciting a cry of pain as the bone snapped. Pushed Ballinger into an inflatable baby swan floating in the air at the exit of the lounge. "And if I hear that you have told that libelous story about ZeeFil to anyone else, you won't live to have your next drink."

"Call him again. Please!"

"Shut up," barked Guido who lit a cigarette then turned back to his partner. "Dasher."

"Prancer."

"Jimmy and the others hang out in the dressing room before every show. Please let me call one of them. When he gets there they'll have him call me. No tricks, I promise."

"Maybe later. Now shut up."

"Blitzen."

The room was cold and Jenny's ass hurt from two hours on the hard wooden chair. She stood up and rubbed her arms, trying to revive her circulation.

"Sit down."

"I need to stretch my legs."

"Sit down."

The chair was only a few feet away from the door, and she wondered how quickly she could get it open and sprint to the busy street. An extra-tall woman in a tight sweater, she figured it would be easy to attract attention and flag a ride before they got to her. And even if they did catch up to her, would they grab her in front of witnesses? Would people in passing cars even notice two men with guns? Would any of them even care? Regardless, getting hit by a car was probably more favorable than getting hit by a bullet and Jenny would slalom through traffic until someone stopped. But before she could get into traffic, she would have to get out of the room.

She was closer to the door than her captors, one of whom relaxed on a creaky wicker chair while the other sat on the dresser smoking a cigarette. But to get out the door she would have to beat them to the door. Unlock it, turn the knob and pull it open in one quick fluid motion, then hit the pavement running before they got to their feet. It seemed her only chance and she talked herself into thinking it was a good chance.

"Donner."

"Comet," countered Guido.

Brown thought for a moment, and then seemed stumped for an answer.

"Vixen," Jenny called out, seeing her opportunity.

"I told you to shut up."

"Come on, let me play."

"For the last time, keep your fucking mouth shut!"

"Why?" Jenny knew it was now or never. Got off her chair and walked toward them. "Afraid of getting beaten by a girl?"

Guido raised his hand as if to strike her. "Sit the fuck down before I knock you down."

"Vixen," said Brown.

"You can't use an answer the broad gave you."

"Show me in the rules where it says I can't."

"What rules? You just fucking can't."

Jenny made her way slowly back toward her chair. It was now or never as her bickering captors were distracted. Her only chance, so she had to make it count. Kept walking past the chair and in one quick fluid motion unlocked the door, turned the knob and pulled it open ready to run.

"Going somewhere?"

The muscular man who blocked the doorway slapped her hard across the face and shoved her back inside room twenty-five.

"I know you."

He hit her harder, the force of the blow knocking her backward onto the pecker-tracked sheets of the unmade bed.

Jenny didn't really know him, but she had seen his face before. Had seen it that day. But where?

He slugged her again to knock that thought out of her head. Then again to make sure.

OFFICE OF SENATOR MALVIN WILLIAMS. SUBURBAN HENDERSON.
FRIDAY 5:51 PM

Jimmy Dot toked the driver a twenty and climbed out of the taxi in front of a strip mall, which at a glance seemed no different than the thousand other strip malls stamped across the map of the Las Vegas valley. Nail salon, dog groomer, tacos, pizza, Starbucks. Only the pylon sign fronting this particular strip mall also boasted the office of United States Senator Malvin W. Williams.

A man of the people, the door to the senator's unassuming office was open to everyone. Dot delighted the gray haired receptionist in the outer office with a couple of jokes and a magic trick as he cooled his heels waiting for Williams to finish a call. Checked out a wall of framed certificates of appreciation and honorary degrees. Photos of the cowboy senator with presidents and kings, Sammy, Sinatra and a dozen other legendary Las Vegas headliners. And as he awaited the expected news that further testing had been ordered that would save countless lives by exposing ZeeFil's fatal flaw, Dot wondered if such heroics might lead to his photographic inclusion on this wall of honor.

At first he had been annoyed that such great responsibility had fallen upon his shoulders, but at this moment he swelled with the pride of accomplishing in less than twenty-four hours what an insider had been unable to in months. And other than maybe his picture on the wall in the company of greatness, personal pride was the only acknowledgement Dot required as he waited to hear confirmation from the senator so he could get back to dealing with the pressing tribulations of his own life.

"You can go in now," the receptionist told him.

"Hope you don't mind coming out to Henderson twice in one day, but I didn't want to tell you this over the phone." The senator leaned forward in his well-worn desk chair, the leather contoured to his backside like a favorite saddle. He pushed back the brim of his black cowboy hat. "Wanted the satisfaction of saying it to your face."

"For news this good I would have hopped here on a pogo stick," laughed Dot as he pulled up a chair.

"Don't sit down." The senator's folksy tone turned hard. "You used me and I want to know why."

"What are you talking about?"

"Don't bullshit a bullshitter. You're a small time con man who never did anything for anyone unless you were working an angle. You'd make a great politician because that's exactly how government works." The senator pounded his fist on the desk then yelled. "But this isn't Washington, and if you don't tell me what in blazes you've got up your sleeve, I'll squash you like a goddamn cockroach."

"On the square, Mal ..."

"Senator Williams."

"I'm not working an angle, Senator. Every word I told you is the truth."

"You wouldn't know the truth if it walked up and spit in your eye."

"I may not always be honest, Senator, but you can bet that silver rodeo buckle that I am very much an honorable man." Dot resented being put in the position of having to justify himself. "And I give you my word that all I'm trying to do is prevent ZeeFil from killing people."

"You think all I do is sit around all day eating pie and ice cream? I'm the second most powerful man in the United States of America and you wasted an entire afternoon of my time. Not to mention making me look like a goddamn jackass to the commissioner of the Food and Drug Administration."

"They won't retest it?"

"Which formula? The one submitted by EcoGreen or the one Bill Revson gave them?"

"They're different?"

"As a lightening bug and a new-born colt. One is for ZeeFil and the other is a chemical formula for chocolate chip cookies, meaning that your pal Revson was even more insane than everybody says he was."

"Cookies? Really? How gullible are you? How did you get to be such a big shot if you fall for simple misdirection that wouldn't fool any half-ripe Cub Scout?"

"Your conspiracy theory plays like a broken record. Baseless accusations without a lick of proof to substantiate any of it."

"Then why was Bill Revson murdered?"

'Police say it was suicide."

"It wasn't."

"Says you."

"Says logic. Randy Leeds and his company will lose billions if the truth comes out, and Revson was very close to exposing it."

"Where's the proof?"

"Test the drug and you'll have that proof."

"The FDA says it's safe."

"That's what they're paid to say."

"Are you actually trying to make me believe that the commissioner of the Food and Drug Administration took a bribe to allow a drug to go on the market that will kill the people who take it?"

"Somebody over there did. Did you even bother to check out all the supervisors who worked on each step of the approval process?"

"You've wasted enough of my time. Now hit the trail before I have you thrown in the hoosegow for being a public nuisance."

Dot was out of ideas and out of time. Kicked back to square one by an obstinate cowboy senator who had gone out of his way to ignore the obvious truth.

"Everyone knows politicians are whores, Malvin. How much did Leeds pay you?"

THE FABULOUS. WHITE BAR.
FRIDAY 7:21 PM

A statuesque mademoiselle clothed only in white body paint stood at the end of the bar, a studded dog collar around her neck attached to a leash held by a chimpanzee in a white tuxedo. Eye-catching mod cuties in white mini-dresses topping white go-go boots. Pretty men in white jeans and white suits. Danish twin sisters in form-fitting white Nehru jackets. Every one of them focused on a cement-faced man wearing a brown checked sports jacket.

While everyone in the room stared at the hulking man who had badged his way past the seven-foot albino gatekeeper, Hard Bernard stared at the bartender. Crooked nose and fat face, just as he had been told. He was about the right height and had the trademark baby blues, but he had to be sure as there was too much at stake not to be sure. He needed to hear him speak. Popped two bennies and stepped to the bar.

"What can I get for you," asked the bartender.

Hard Bernard needed to hear the voice again.

"Do you have the time?"

"No clocks in the casino."

It wasn't exactly the voice from the movies, but it was close enough as he figured that the timbre had probably dulled a bit from a couple years in the dry desert air. Add that to the face, the eyes and a detective's instinct and he knew he had his man. Again flashed his badge.

"I need you to come with me."

"I'm too busy for practical jokes. What do you want to drink?"

"Listen, wiseass. I know who you are and you're coming with me. Right now!"

"You listen, asshole." The bartender had no patience for this. "I don't know how you got past the door but I don't have to serve you. So get the fuck lost."

Hard Bernard grabbed the bartender by the arms, knocking over bottles and glasses as he yanked him up and over the bar. Cuffed his hands behind his back.

"Preston Bond. You're under arrest for resisting an officer."

"Are you crazy?"

"Shut your mouth and let's go."

"I'm not going anywhere with you, you fucking lunatic."

Hard Bernard punched him in the gut so hard that the handcuffed bartender collapsed like a melting snowman.

"Now get up. We've got business in the penthouse."

It defied logic that surreal people in a surreal bar could be astonished by anything, but every last one of them was stunned by the absurd scene they were witnessing.

"It's Preston Bond!"

"He doesn't look anything like Bond."

"The cop says he's Bond."

The gatekeeper, who was a head taller and strong as a bull, grabbed Hard Bernard from behind but the enraged ex-cop broke free and slammed the albino's head on the bar, knocking him out.

"I get it. This is performance art."

"No way. These guys are hurt bad."

"Nobody's hurt. It's like professional wrestling."

Two patrons with more sense tackled Hard Bernard while the chimpanzee pounded a bongo beat on his rock-hard skull.

"*Interactive* performance art."

"Then what are we waiting for?"

"Let's go!"

In the riot that ensued, Hard Bernard grappled with his attackers, as most of the men in the bar spiritedly joined in what they thought was a live action video game of cocktail Armageddon. Their women cheering the action from the sidelines, while Hard Bernard brawled like a wild man as he single-handedly bloodied the white haberdashery of a dozen assailants. Then broke free and seized the handcuffed bartender by the feet and dragged him toward the exit.

Hotel security officers rushed in to restore order but were unable to subdue Hard Bernard who came at them in a rage, swinging the bartender like a weapon. It took multiple Taser shots to finally slow him down enough for the officers to take him into custody.

"We found Preston Bond!" yelled a delusional hipster in a white fedora, who rushed over and took a selfie with the unconscious bartender. "Dude, this is epic!"

THE FABULOUS. POONTANG JOHNSON'S DRESSING ROOM.
FRIDAY 7:57 PM

Sparkle and Swanky drank beer on the couch while Zazzo stood in front of a full length mirror, fussing with an insubordinate lock of hair that refused to stay tucked beneath his turban. Poontang sat at the dressing table, her phone ringing as she attached the matching earrings that accompanied her dazzling diamond and sapphire necklace.

"Hey, Jenny."

Poontang listened as she checked herself out in the mirror.

"No, he's already backstage."

One last look and she proclaimed herself magnificent.

"Calm down, girl. What's the matter?"

"Two minutes," the stage manager called through the door.

"Gotta run. Call me after the show."

Poontang ended the call, tossed her phone on the dressing table and followed the others out the door.

FOUNTAIN TOWERS. ROTURBO'S CANTINA.
FRIDAY 10:19 PM

The drinks were powerful and the food wicked spicy at this popular Tex-Mex cantina on the street level of a steel and glass condominium high rise a block off the Strip. Zazzo wore a V-neck sweater and jeans as he sat in a corner booth sipping a margarita with a pretty blonde in a tight blue dress that matched her eyes. She was twenty-four and petite, wore her hair in a bob and had skin so perfect she looked like a porcelain doll. And that's what everyone called her, Doll. She could not have weighed more than 105 pounds with her shoes on, hardly believable as she finished a Texas-sized bowl of fiery-hot habanero chili then scarfed down half a dozen jalapeno poppers.

"We okay on time?" she asked him.

"Keep eating."

Of all the women who had revolving-doored in and out of his life, Doll was the only one Zazzo had ever cared enough about to remember her name. And in the months he had known her had become comfortable enough to let his guard down, as much as a tight-lipped loner like Zazzo was capable.

"I hear they have some new games at the Pinball Hall Of Fame," Doll told him. "Maybe tomorrow we can check it out."

"Can't tomorrow." He would be otherwise engaged putting the snatch on a necklace of imperial jade while seducing the girl whose daddy owned ten thousand acres of money in Texas. He watched Doll attack a Frito pie. "Or maybe I can."

What? Why the hell had he said that? Why would he ever pass up a sure thing parlay of fleecing and fucking to play pinball? Why would anybody? Yet at that moment, stung by a strange sensation he could not quite identify, the thought very much appealed to him.

Zazzo and Doll were best friends who hung out a lot. Square stuff like going to the movies and playing afternoon bingo with blue-haired old ladies. Maybe they enjoyed it because it was the polar opposite of who they were. A girl who made her money the easy way and a charming cat burglar who got his rocks off tempting fate. But as he watched Doll devour the Frito pie, Zazzo began to wonder if maybe Squaresville was exactly where they were meant to be.

"Have you ever been on a date?" he asked her.

"I go on dates every night. You know that."

"I mean a real date. Flowers and a nice restaurant. Goodnight kiss at the door."

"Are you asking me out on a real date?"

Please say yes. Please say yes, she silently urged.

The word yes made it as far as his tongue but refused to roll off. Men asked women out every day, and he could not understand why one simple word tied his stomach in knots like it would a nervous fifteen-year-old. Which was beyond ironic, as when Zazzo was fifteen he was already screwing showgirls. Just not dating them.

Doll had been in love with Zazzo since the day they met last October while waiting in line for pumpkin spice lattes. A crush actually, but it quickly blossomed. She saw him as daring and fun. Spontaneous enough to keep things fresh and handsome enough to marry, though Doll had always figured they could never be anything more than fuck buddies, as she lived as dangerously close to the edge as he did. But was all that about to change? Was this the day he finally fell in love with her? She was probably the only person ever to get close enough to him to understand that Zazzo's bold and cocksure exterior masked a deep-rooted shyness. She also knew that shy men often needed a nudge to express their true feelings.

"So? Are you asking me out on a real date?"

"I was just curious," replied Zazzo, not making eye contact.

"Odd time to be curious about dating considering what we're about to do," she mumbled disappointedly through a mouthful of spicy beef and onions and corn chips.

"This is important, baby. I'm counting on you."

Doll got the tingles when he called her baby.

"Don't worry." She polished off the last bite of Frito pie and washed it down with the rest of Zazzo's margarita. "I won't let you down."

"This will help," Zazzo assured her as he unwrapped a bite-sized square of chocolate.

"Give me two."

"That's my girl."

Abbie Leeds looked beyond stunning in a strapless green cocktail dress, billionaire at her side and a priceless diamond on her finger. Sipping champagne as her husband played high stakes baccarat as if he had not a care in the world. And he didn't, as men like Randy Leeds did not become men like Randy Leeds without making sure all the bases were covered. The FDA was in his pocket, Bill Revson was dead, and Jimmy Dot was being neutralized, meaning that absolutely nothing was left to stand in the way of ZeeFil becoming the goose that shit Faberge eggs. Only Dot wasn't neutralized just yet, and as the ringmaster watched surreptitiously from his seat at a slot machine outside the high limit salon, he wondered what enjoyment a control freak like Randy Leeds got from playing in an honest game.

Dot had always relished the challenge of beating impossible odds, but in trying to stop ZeeFil it appeared that he was on the losing end of a game that was more than likely over. If only on Wednesday he had done the crossword puzzles at Max E's Delicatessen instead of the sports book, he would never have met Bill Revson. Would never have become preoccupied with a bet that had done little except get in the way of proving himself to his wife by quitting The Fabulous and reclaiming life and love in their cozy apartment at the Ambassador. But what was the point of dwelling on what-ifs? None of it mattered as, not only had he become involved with Revson, Jenny was probably a thousand miles away by now, having made it perfectly clear that she was never coming back.

"You've had a busy day, Jimmy."

Dot swiveled his stool and looked up at the arrogant billionaire.

"Politicians, publishers, celebrity crackpots. You even tried to subvert one of my largest shareholders. Was I not clear when I told you on the golf course what would happen if you didn't stop meddling in my affairs?"

"You couldn't even kill an eighty-year-old man with a bum ticker."

"Make no mistake that I *will* kill you. But first I'll kill your wife, letting your guilt pluck at raw nerves like a cheap banjo, knowing it was your fault."

Just because Jenny had flown the coop did not mean that Dot had stopped loving her. He would find her and he would do whatever it took to win her back. But at the moment he was glad his Jenny was a thousand miles away. At least he hoped she was.

"Then on to the featured attraction." Leeds spoke slowly, stabbing Dot with every word. "You won't know when or how, because torturing you will be my own personal amusement. Foreplay, if you will, swelling to the powerful orgasm of your final breath. A death you can be certain will be far more excruciating than hurtling toward the pavement from twenty-six stories up."

Dot struck a match on the bottom of his stool and breathed life into a fresh Robusto. Blew a perfect smoke ring that dissolved as it met Leeds' smug grin.

"I suggest you enjoy that cigar as if it's your last. Now, if you will excuse me, my champagne is getting warm."

As Dot watched Leeds walk back to the baccarat table, he thought about Frank Ballinger and the great skill it had taken to sell the Pacific Ocean. But talent alone had not been enough for his mentor to get the Arab prince to buy it a second and third time. With the sucker skeptical of his every move, Ballinger used a shill. An accomplice who blindsided the prince with such a dazzling distraction that he was easily influenced into believing that it was his own idea to buy the ocean again. And yet again. Making Dot realize he had been overthinking everything and that the obvious answer had been right in front of him all along.

No trades. No tricks, and he did not have to con the arrogant billionaire into anything. Nothing disingenuous at all. Just manipulate him into an honest game. A straightforward transaction. He would sell Randy Leeds the Pacific Ocean.

THREE JACKS MOTEL. BOULDER HIGHWAY.
FRIDAY 10:46 PM

"It's freezing in here," complained Jenny, her face bruised and swollen as she sat on the bed. Her back against the headboard, clutching her knees to her chest.

"Then get under the covers and quit your bitching," Brown shot back.

"You slide under these spooge-stained sheets and get eaten alive by crotch crickets. Let me have your jacket, or at least go out and get me some hot coffee."

Ballsy words from a woman who knew she was up against it, and Brown made no secret that he was turned on.

"Down boy," ordered the third man, who was obviously in charge. Using her phone, he rang The Fabulous and asked for Suite 7402, then softened his tone as he smiled at Jenny. "Once you speak with your husband, I'll see to it that you won't have to worry about the cold."

The smile. THAT SMILE. Jenny remembered where she had seen him, frightening her to the core as suddenly everything made sense. No wonder her captors didn't care if she could identify them. This wasn't a kidnapping. It was to be an execution, with her being killed the minute Jimmy picked up the phone and she relayed the captors' instructions. And if she refused? They would tell him themselves and kill her anyway. Her murder the catalyst that would set into motion an explosive chain of events where Jimmy would also die, no matter how it played out.

She had been promised a torturous end but her mind refused to picture the horrid perversities described by these sickos, and the unimaginable pain that would accompany her final moments. But death itself did not frighten her as much as knowing that the last words her husband had heard her say to him were in anger. That she would face eternity with the man she loved so dearly thinking that she did not love him at all. Cruel truths she had no choice but to accept. Or did she? It was still possible for Jimmy to escape with his life if she could warn him, and to do that she would have to play along and allow her captors to think that she believed their promise to set her free after the message was delivered and ZeeFil was available to the public.

Two or three seconds, four at the most, would be all the time she would have to make herself understood before they ripped the phone away from her. Economize the words as she would have precious few, every syllable of vital importance as she mentally prepared for what would be her only chance to alert and save the man who was her everything. Not enough time to apologize for walking out on him. Not enough time to take back the hurtful words she had said to him. Not even enough time to tell him she loved him. Just a few crucial seconds to warn him of the danger he faced so that he could escape with his life.

Again there was no answer.

Brown and Guido played cards. The third man sat on the wooden chair in front of the door, taking no chances as he waited to call again. Dice, dope, depravity. Girls, booze, all night pizzerias. There was a lot in Las Vegas that might keep a man from going straight home after work, and they braced themselves for what might be a long night. Jenny's last night.

Jenny was able to slow her countdown to the inevitable as she relived her first date with Jimmy. Their first kiss by the condiment stand at Hot Dog Buddy Buddy. The night at Hop Louie's when he first told her he loved her. Conversely, her remaining time passed quickly as she braced herself for death. Never would she explore the magical alleyways of Tokyo or drink rum on a black sand beach in Tahiti. Never again would she delight an audience or make an old lady laugh. Never again would she wake up in the arms of the man who electrified her with his touch.

BULLSHIT. No fucking way was Jenny going to go down without a fight. What? How? She didn't know. But she wasn't just going to sit there and let these goons steal twenty thousand tomorrows.

She sneezed.

"Will one of you pass me a Kleenex?"

Brown tossed her the box. She pulled one free, the last one, and then blew her nose.

She sneezed again. And again.

"Are there any more Kleenex?"

"Nope."

"Then toss me a roll of toilet paper."

Brown grudgingly got the roll from the bathroom and threw it at her. She unwound several sheets and blew her nose. Then again. And again. Stuffing the used snot rags under the bedspread.

"It's no fun playing two handed poker," Jenny called across the room.

"Gin rummy."

"Can three play?"

"Shut up."

"Then how about something all four of us can play?"

"Shut up."

Jenny blew her nose twice more. And twice more she crumpled the used toilet paper and stuffed it under the bedspread.

She asked Guido for a cigarette. He ignored her.

"Come on. A smoke will warm me up."

"Give her one. At least it'll shut her up," said Brown, undressing Jenny with his eyes as he started his own countdown to her viciously degrading and violent end. The clock not ticking fast enough to suit his sexual blood lust.

Annoyed, as now both of them kept him from concentrating on his cards, Guido pulled a cigarette from the pack and threw it at Jenny.

"Should I eat it, or are you going to toss me a light?"

"No tricks." Guido walked over to the bed and lit her smoke, then put the lighter back in his pocket. "Now shut your fucking trap and enjoy it. It's the only one you're gonna get."

Jenny was not a smoker, so even without inhaling she coughed while breathing life into the cigarette. Three quick puffs sparking a glowing ember that she held to the expanding wad of used Kleenex and toilet paper, trying to spark a flame. But it quickly burned out. Three more puffs and she tried again. No dice. Only a fool would attempt the same thing again and again hoping for a different result. But whether it was launching a flaming projectile or sparking a Kleenex, Jenny knew fire and would make it work. She had to, as there was no other way out. If she didn't escape that room she would be killed and if she didn't figure out a way to warn Jimmy, one way or another he would be killed as well. One final try as the cigarette had burned almost down to the butt. This time, one piece of crumpled toilet paper ignited another, but it was a crawling burn and not a flame. She gently blew on it. Just hard enough to give it a boost but not so hard as to blow it out. Come on. Come on, she silently urged. Willing the smoldering paper to ignite into flame.

"What the fuck!"

Guido smelled the smoke and rushed over just as the bedspread caught fire. Jenny threw it over his head while quickly grabbing the gun from his shoulder holster, then kicked him to the floor as he thrashed frantically to free himself from the flames. She got to her feet and aimed at Brown.

"Put your knife on the floor and kick it over here."

Brown gave up his weapon, then dove toward the fiery cocoon in an attempt to smother the flames. Jenny wheeled toward the door, finding herself face to face with the third man. Each with a gun pointed at the other.

"You want to die, tough guy?" Jenny was in the zone and nothing was going to stop her from getting out of that room. "Pull the trigger and I'll pull mine. Is all this bullshit really worth dying for?"

He cocked his pistol and aimed it at her head.

"You think I'm bluffing, tough guy? Pull that trigger and it will be the last thing you ever do."

Brown and Guido had become a screaming ball of fire that crashed into the wall, igniting the drapes. In a blink, half the room was engulfed in flames. Jenny used the distraction to run for the door, losing her gun as she was tackled by the third man. As the putrid reek of burning flesh permeated the smoke-filled room she jerked her head away from a thundering left that still stunned as it caught her ear. A second punch landed squarely, her face bloodied as he now stood over her. As his boot came crashing down toward her head she grabbed his foot and pulled him to the floor, the impact jarring his gun from his grasp.

As fire raged all around them, Jenny smashed the wooden chair over his head, only stunning him. He slammed her into the wall but she came back at him kicking and clawing, again dropping him hard to the floor. Fitness training in a boxing gym does not prepare a person for a street fight, but twice a week for ten years had taught Jenny how to land a solid punch. He was more powerful but she was quicker with a longer reach and seemed to have the upper hand, until he rolled over on the gun that had earlier been knocked from his grasp. As he fumbled for it, Jenny raced for the door. Unlocked it, turned the knob and pulled it open in one fluid motion, then hit the parking lot running toward the safety of the traffic on Boulder Highway.

Brown and Guido were burned to a crisp as room twenty-five had become a raging inferno. The third man stood in the doorway, aiming his gun at Jenny. He fired. The shot dropped her face first onto the gravel.

POONTANG JOHNSON'S HOME. LAS VEGAS COUNTRY CLUB.
FRIDAY 10:58 PM

Deputy Chief Sig Samuels. Average size and average features and dressed like any other average forty-two year-old man you might see in line at the grocery store. An educated man who had earned his success within the police department by using his brains, who at this moment snuggled on the couch with his girlfriend waiting for the local news to come on.

"Ready for a drink?" offered Poontang as she walked to the bar to make one for herself.

"Not yet, baby."

Poontang wore a slinky red and gold Chinese dressing gown and a simple wig of long straight blue-black hair. No makeup and no jewelry. As flamboyant as she was in public, at home she was just an average woman relaxing after work with her man in the living room of her mid-century modern home overlooking the seventeenth fairway.

"You think the department pressured the news people into whitewashing the story?"

"No chance." Sig was not gay. But love was love and he and his exotic lady man were very much in love. "There were too many injuries and too many witnesses."

Sig turned up the sound.

Our top story ... After a series of events that can only be described as bizarre, a retired Las Vegas Metro Police officer is in jail tonight accused of inciting a bloody riot earlier this evening at The Fabulous.

They watched casino surveillance video as the newscaster gave voice over play-by-play of Hard Bernard destroying the White Bar.

Eleven people, including the bartender and one other employee, suffered serious injuries and were taken to area hospitals. Metro Police spokesman Lieutenant Harry Kagel would not comment, other than to say the former officer, Lewis Bernard, was in custody pending arraignment. Eyewitness News will bring you more information on this horrific attack as it becomes available.

In other news, a valley shopkeeper was ...

Sig turned off the television.

"How come they let a guy like that stay on the force for so long?" asked Poontang as she poured her man's favorite

Japanese whiskey over ice. "Everybody at The Fabulous knows he's nothing more than a thug and a rapist."

"He had something on the sheriff. Something big. There was no other explanation for why he was allowed to get away with the things he did. Then when the sheriff finally lost an election, Bernard was smart enough to retire before the new administration could fire him." Samuels was disgusted by the whole thing, but a sip of his drink calmed him a bit. "Even in retirement, he's got enough dirt on so many people, judges included, that it's possible he could be released on his own recognizance."

"So he just gets away with it?"

"Not a chance. Bernard will eventually have to stand before a jury of twelve hard-working people who will find him and everything he stands for reprehensible. He's a goner."

"And you're a keeper."

Poontang opened her dressing gown and let it fall to the floor. Sig Samuels may not have been gay, but he sure was in love.

The bedroom lights were off, but the glare of neighboring casino neon penetrated the windows with a rich prismatic glow. Jackie Fink lay naked on the bed, coupled with a pretty young woman whose skin was smooth as brand new.

Fink had always liked his girls young, but it was a pleasure he was rarely able to enjoy even when he was young. Too short. Too ugly. Too much to overcome. Even during his showbiz years on the comedy circuit he was usually too broke to afford prostitutes, instead finding release with beat-off mags like *Asian Fever* and *Barely Legal*. But now that he was in the money he could pluck young talent from his own stable, sampling his 31 flavors of world-class merchandise whenever he wanted. Life was good for Jackie Fink, a complete turnaround from his days in Cleveland and the struggles of the road, and he voraciously made up for lost time by lapping up every drop of pleasure he could.

Beneath her in a sixty-nine position, Fink devoured Doll's pussy then licked upward toward her asshole, which had been bleached clean as if it had never been used. Waiting for her to wrap her mouth around his cock. Take his load like she always did on nights when he summoned her, only this night it was she who had suggested the tryst. Just like it was she who for once was setting the pace, prolonging climax for just the right moment, as she could not allow him come too quickly or it would ruin everything.

"Come on, baby. This dick isn't gonna suck itself."

"Not yet," she cooed. "Not yet."

"I'm almost there. I'm ready to explode."

But Doll would keep him on the edge until she was ready to explode, which would not be long as he continued to tongue her asshole. She could feel it build. Feel it swell. Coming. Coming. NOW!

She shit liquid mud all over his face. He tried to escape the eruption but she kept him pinned down. The chocolate laxative working full force as she unloaded more and more still, until finally the petite porcelain doll was empty.

As Fink struggled to free himself, the lights were switched on.

"Don't move!" commanded Everest in full voice as he entered the bedroom with Zazzo and Sparkle.

Doll climbed off and hurried to the bathroom as Fink laid helpless, his face and head covered with chili-fueled diarrhea. Spitting, then spitting again and again. Frantically blowing dripping feces away from his mouth so he could breathe as he groped blindly for the sheet to wipe his face.

"I said don't move."

Fink let go of the sheet, obeying the rich baritone voice he recognized.

"What the fuck, Everest! What the hell do you want?"

"Revenge, you low-life cocksucker," demanded a different voice.

Shit yielded like warm chocolate around his eyes as he eased them open and saw Sparkle. Then Zazzo coming out of the bathroom, where he had turned on the shower for Doll. Zazzo knew what she did every night but it was something else altogether to actually see it, stinging him with yet another foreign emotion. Jealousy.

"Revenge for what? What did I do? You guys are fucking crazy!"

"Shut up and listen," commanded Everest. Then said to Sparkle, "Go ahead. Tell him."

The midget pulled up an image on his phone.

"Three people were murdered at the Erie Motel in Cleveland on May 4, 1989 in a dope deal gone bad. This is a copy of the witness report the cops took from a couple who'd been banging on hot sheets in the room next to where it went down. Says here these two people were August Boyloygan and Elizabeth Dotoski." Sparkle glared hatefully at Fink. "You were the one having the affair with Jimmy's mother that caused his old man to croak himself."

"No! That's not how it was." The man covered in shit was terrified. "You have to believe me. I can explain."

"You couldn't be more responsible if you would have pulled the trigger on the old man yourself," snapped Zazzo. "Then you left town, leaving Jimmy's mother alone to die from the shame. All while pretending to be his friend. Taking his charity for years while he beat himself up inside, trying to figure out who the man was so he could finally have some closure. Lying to his face that you had no clue when the whole time it was you, you two-faced Judas prick motherfucker."

"Please don't tell Jimmy." Two days earlier, Fink had experienced Dot's rage at the delicatessen. "He'll kill me."

"Don't worry," assured Zazzo as he assessed Fink's pasty torso and white chest hair spattered with the foul runoff. "All we're going to do is make you the biggest star on YouTube by dumping your naked shit-stained carcass in the middle of Las Vegas Boulevard."

Fink breathed an inner sigh of relief, as humiliation beat the hell out of being dead.

"And *then* we're going to tell Jimmy."

"You can't, Zazzo. Please," begged Fink. "It would be murder."

"An eye for an eye."

"Give me a chance to make it right."

"How?"

"Fuller also has a copy of that witness report."

"We know," said Everest. "How is that going to make things right?"

"Because he's using it to blackmail me into feeding him information about what Jimmy is up to."

"Why does Fuller care about what Jimmy does, as long as the show keeps steering suckers into the casino every night?"

"That's just it. Jimmy's trying to break his contract and quit the show."

Sparkle and Zazzo shared a look of surprise.

"How do you know that?" demanded Everest.

From behind the mask Fink's eyes showed fear.

"Because you're a rat," continued Everest as a lot of things began to make sense. "You're the one who spilled to Fuller and monkey-wrenched Jimmy's play with Leeds at the Top Hat."

"It wasn't me. I swear it wasn't me!'"

"And later, Jimmy was suspicious of how I knew that Leeds had called his bluff, and how I knew that Fuller was threatening him with something when that immigration agent came around. But it was you, you rat cocksucker. You were in the chair right before he showed up, and you told me."

"You gotta understand." Fink was terrified as the huge man towered over him. "Fuller had me by the balls."

"He thinks I'm the one who crossed him, you rat prick." Everest looked hatefully at Fink. "I ought to rip those hair plugs out of your head, but I'm going to save that pleasure for Jimmy."

"No!" Fink looked desperately at Sparkle and Zazzo. "You two need to make sure that I stay alive to keep tipping off Fuller, or the show will close and you'll be back robbing piggy banks."

"It would be worth losing the gig to watch Jimmy tear you apart," said Zazzo honestly.

"Fuckin-A right," agreed the midget.

"Only we're not going to tell Jimmy anything," said Everest.

"We're not?" Sparkle and Zazzo called out in unison.

"No matter how much fun it might be to watch Jimmy beat the life out of this creep, telling him would not provide closure. Just the opposite. It would open an even deeper wound of betrayal, and we all know he doesn't deserve that."

"What's the catch?" Fink knew he wasn't getting out of it that easily.

"You're going to continue to let Fuller think he has you by the balls, and keep feeding him information," explained Everest, seizing fresh opportunity. "But from now on you're only going to tell him what we want you to tell him."

"No way. If Fuller finds out I'm crossing him, he'll tell Jimmy and I'll be dead."

"Then you had better not let Fuller find out."

"It's too dangerous. I can't take that chance."

"Stand up and go look at yourself in the mirror, you fucking rat," Zazzo ordered the naked geezer whose face was sealed inside a mask of hardened shit. "Now tell me who you're more afraid of, Blake Fuller or us?"

THE FABULOUS. JIMMY DOT'S SUITE.
SATURDAY 12:04 AM

She opened the door and flipped the wall switch. Beaten and weary. Jeans ripped at the knee. Road rash on Jenny's hands and face from when she had stumbled and fallen an instant before the shot sailed over her head. Thankful for loose gravel or the bullet would have smashed into the back of her skull rather than the fender of a passing Ford pickup.

A quick check of the bedroom and bathroom. No Jimmy. She needed to find him. To warn him that he was being set up. Brown and Guido were toast, but number three had more than likely escaped the flames and she had to find Jimmy before it was too late. She needed to call Poontang, Zazzo, Everest and anybody else who might know where he was, but she had no one's number as her phone was somewhere in the smoldering rubble of the Three Jacks Motel.

Jenny sat on the bed then popped quickly to her feet, knowing that if she didn't she would conk out from exhaustion. Went into the bathroom and splashed cold water on her face, gently patting herself dry with a hand towel. Cleaned her wounds with Listerine, figuring that if the mouth gargle killed bad breath germs it must have enough antiseptic in it to disinfect her cuts and scrapes.

She chugged a Red Bull from the bar. Left a note on the bed and another by the phone on the desk just in case, then went out into the night looking for her husband.

BLAKE FULLER'S HOME. SUBURBAN SUMMERLIN.
SATURDAY 1:25 AM

"**C**an you open it?" asked Dot, standing in the dark as he aimed a flashlight at the safe bolted to the floor in Blake Fuller's bedroom closet.

"Piece of cake," replied Zazzo as he looked up the basic specs of the lock on his phone. "This cracker box isn't even fireproof."

Zazzo turned the dial clockwise several times so that the wheels of the lock would disengage. Then opened a leather bag and took out a stethoscope, holding it to the door of the safe to amplify the sound of the tumblers, listening for clicks as he very slowly turned the dial in the other direction. And even though he looked like a yegg in an old gangster movie, Dot had no reason to doubt the antiquated method of his friend who had already picked the front door lock and bypassed the alarm.

Ten minutes passed. Twenty.

Dot smiled as he envisioned the look on Blake Fuller's face when he would march into the boss' office in the morning and announce that he had the kiddie porn laptop. Fuller would undoubtedly claim it to be a Mexican standoff, but a thousand years in prison trumped a one-way ticket to Athens any day of the week. Meaning that Fuller would have no choice but to release him from all obligation to The Fabulous and send that Nazi immigration agent back on the street to harass people not named Dotoski.

"How much longer?" asked Dot as he watched Zazzo's skilled hands slowly manipulate the dial.

"Few minutes. Maybe an hour."

"Another hour?"

"If you keep talking. I need complete silence if this is going to work."

"What if it doesn't work?"

"Then I'll drill the box and use the borescope. Lets me look through an eyepiece and see the wear marks on the wheel pad so I can figure out the combination from the inside. Have it open in no time."

"Then why didn't you just do it that way to begin with?"

"Any two-bit ham snatcher can drill a safe. This way I get to feel the pride of a job well done."

"Just drill the damn thing and let's get the hell out of here."

Zazzo took a drill from his bag and went to work, the sound of steel cutting into steel filling the late night stillness. The carbide bit would get the job done quickly, but there was more on his mind than popping the safe. Remorse, another emotion he had yet to feel but was beginning to quickly understand, as he felt terrible about the disgusting thing he had asked Doll to do earlier.

"Were you ever in love before you met Jenny?"

"Nope."

"Then how did you know? I mean, how did you know it was love and not just your cock talking?"

"All your cock wants is to get its rocks off and move on. Real love makes you want to give and keep on giving until you have nothing left to give, then give some more. So believe me, you'll know, as it's a stronger emotion than anything else you've ever felt." It made him happy to think of his love for Jenny, but only for a moment until the sucker punch of reality reminded him that she was gone, this time maybe forever. "The only emotion stronger than love is the anguish when she breaks your heart."

"No matter how hard I try, I can't think of anything but her. Everything I see makes me think of her. I can smell her, touch her and taste her like she's right here. Is that love?"

"Probably just gas."

"Come on, Jimmy. I'm serious."

"I figured you as the last guy who would ever fall for a broad," laughed Dot. "She must have a lot of money."

"Nope."

"Then her family must."

"Not a cent. She's just a nice girl who likes pinball and going to the movies."

So was Jenny. And Dot hoped that once she found out that he had broken the contract and officially quit The Fabulous, maybe they would have another chance at happily ever after.

"On the square, Jimmy. Is it love?"

"It's love, Zazzo. That's why you couldn't manipulate the tumblers," Dot told him as he again aimed the flashlight at the safe. "So keep making with that drill and let's grab what we came here for, then get the fuck out of this creep joint so you can get back to your girl."

The drill did its job and Zazzo inserted the borescope, but his attention was elsewhere. He could envision Doll in the bath, soaking off the aftermath of the disgusting thing he had asked her to do. Could smell her bath soap as he put his eye to the lens of the borescope. His mind racing with ways he would make it up to her. New territory. Exciting territory, as he knew that he was one hundred percent full blown in love, and would race to her the minute he cracked open the box and gave Jimmy what they had come for. He looked for certain landmarks on the combination lock's wheel pad, and within moments he was able to unlock the safe as easily as if it was his own.

The room flooded with light.

"Impressive," said Blake Fuller as he flipped the switch, a gun pointed at them. "But as you can see, it was a wasted effort."

No laptop. No nothing. Just an empty safe.

"Do you really think I look at kiddie porn?"

"I wouldn't put anything past a creep like you," Dot told him.

"And if I did, do you really think I would be stupid enough to have it on a computer I keep in my own house?"

"Why not? You never struck me as being very smart."

"As opposed to you, who let Bernard play you just like you played him," laughed Fuller. "A double cross that left him in jail and you looking down the barrel of a gun. I can't believe you fell for that gorilla's line of bullshit."

Neither could Dot. He believed it was true simply because he wanted to believe it was true, and he felt like the prize sucker of all time.

"Did you think I didn't know? That bent ex-cop works for me, remember? Or at least he did until you convinced him that a fat-faced bartender was a dead movie star. He's even dumber than you are, if that's possible," laughed Fuller as he enjoyed rubbing it in. Then with his free hand removed his phone from the pocket of his suit jacket.

"Are you going to tell the cops you caught two trespassers?" asked Dot. "Because we haven't taken anything, so that's all this is."

"You have burglar tools. You vandalized my safe and stole everything that was inside."

"There was nothing inside and you can't prove there was. So put down that cap pistol before you hurt yourself. If it's even loaded."

"Your contract extension is on the dresser," Fuller told his headliner. "Sign it and I won't call the police."

"Come on, Zazzo. Grab your stuff and let's get out of here."

With his foot, Fuller nudged a gym bag from under the bed then kicked it in the air toward Dot who caught it out of reflex.

"That bag contains the cash and jewelry you stole. Your fingerprints are on it and your accomplice's prints are on the safe you broke into. Now sign the contract."

"Fuck you, Fuller."

"I have every legal right to shoot burglars inside my own house."

"Fuck you."

"Sign it, or I'll shoot you where you stand."

"You don't have the balls," said Zazzo as he picked up his leather bag and started toward the door. "We're leaving."

Fuller shot Zazzo.

He dropped to the floor. A hole in his chest and his head twisted at a grotesque angle. Dot knelt down and cradled him in his arms. Blood soaking his shirt as he urged his friend to hold on.

"Stay with me, Zazzo! Stay with me," Dot pleaded, then screamed at Fuller. "Get help! Call 911!"

Dot held his friend close. Tried to stabilize him, but the light was leaving Zazzo's eyes.

"Sign the contract extension, or you're next," demanded Fuller.

As Zazzo bled out, Dot felt his own life slipping away as well. Nothing left as he had lost the only things that mattered to him. His wife had left him for good. Halfway across the country by now for all he knew. Resigning him to live out his days with her foremost in his mind, yet unable to touch her ever again. And now he was about to lose his freedom, forced to continue living under a public spotlight so invasive it burned away almost all chance to ply his trade and take pride in just being himself. Forced to hang out at The Fabulous a certain number of hours every day and pose for photos with obnoxious tourists who thought they had the right to butt into his business in the sports book, the barber shop and even when he took a leak.

Two men dead. One cold on the floor, and one who might just as well have been. Jimmy Dot signed the contract.

COLONEL CLUCK'S FRIED CHICKEN. NORTHTOWN.
SATURDAY 3:11 AM

"**H**oly shit, girl!" said the white-haired cluck monger who looked like Fred Sanford wearing a Latin American military officer's parade finest. An old horn dog who worked nights because a free basket of wings placed on the right table in the wee hours could get him laid. "What the hell happened to your face?"

"Never mind that, Colonel." Jenny's voice was steady but borderline frantic. "Have you seen Jimmy tonight?"

"Sorry, Jenn. Haven't seen him all week."

The scuzzy all night chicken joint was not in the worst part of North Las Vegas but was certainly downwind from the best, catering mostly to drunks and night crawlers attracted by cheap eats and the wafting aphrodisiac of week old fryer oil. The heavy aroma didn't do much for Jenny's appetite, but it had always revved Jimmy's engine to maximum torque. She once kicked around the idea of dabbing a bit of the greasy oil behind each ear to see what effect it would have on her man, but decided against it as the explosive sex it might inspire probably would have killed them both.

The Colonel poured black coffee into a mug and set it on the counter with Jenny's favorite, homemade biscuits with strawberry jam. "Sit down a minute and catch hold of yourself."

Jenny sat. Steadied herself with a sip of hot coffee. Then realizing she had not eaten since before being snatched off the street that afternoon, scarfed the biscuits while using the Colonel's Wi-Fi to upload her contacts onto a burner phone she had just picked up at Walgreen's. Had a taxi waiting outside that had already taken her to check out some of Jimmy's other late night haunts, and would take her to however many more it took until she found him. Unless the third man found him first. But that was a thought she would not allow to fester.

Upload finally complete, she gave the Colonel her new number and made him promise to call if Jimmy showed up. Walked outside to her taxi and told the driver to head toward Max E's Delicatessen, and then called Poontang. No answer, so she left a message. Called Zazzo, Sparkle, Fink and Everest. Knowing it was a long shot that any of them would answer a late night call from a number they did not recognize, her hopes hung on the fact that eventually one of them would check their voicemail and call back. But eventually was not soon enough, as she had to find Jimmy. Had to warn her husband that he was in the crosshairs of an enemy unknown to him. She called the suite at The Fabulous. No answer.

Outside Max E's two alley hags fought over a half-eaten sandwich they found in the trash. Inside Max E's a debate raged over whether or not the pork chops were kosher. Jenny pulled the counter man aside and asked if he had seen Jimmy.

Nope. She wrote her new number on a hundred dollar bill. Would he please tell Jimmy to call if he came in? Yep.

She left a hundred dollar note at Hop Louie's, texting instead of calling as she sat on the opposite side of the bar from ancient Chinese men with wispy white whiskers who gambled on games of chance not found in any casino. Left a hundred dollar note at Buddy Bomar's Bowlarama, where she dispatched another round of voicemails amid crashing pins exacerbating the pounding in her head from the beating it had taken at the Three Jacks. She left a hundred dollars at John John's, the Plush Horse and Frankie's Tiki Room. Becoming more frightened each time she struck out. More frantic with every passing minute that her phone didn't ring. At the Double Down Saloon she spotted a friendly face behind the bar.

"Kelcy." Her frantic tone had given way to pointed determination. "Have you seen Jimmy tonight?"

"You okay?" asked the punk rock bartender as he wiped down the hardwood and tossed a couple dead soldiers into the trash. "What happened to your face?"

"Later, Kelcy. Have you seen him?"

"I just came on. Hang on a minute and I'll ask Elmer. He's in the back counting his tips."

Jenny looked at the pool table where Jimmy had once spent an entire day and night teaching her how to perfect a three-cushion bank shot. The booth by the stage where he showed her how tasty Cheetos were when dipped in French's yellow.

"Sorry, Jenn. He hasn't been in tonight," reported Kelcy as he came back behind the bar. "Can I get you something to drink?"

A shot of Irish calmed her nerves, but only for a moment.

"If Jimmy comes in, tell him to meet me at The Fabulous ASAP. It's urgent."

Jenny was out of places to look as she walked back out into the night and climbed inside the taxi, nothing left to do except go back to the hotel and wait for her man to call or come home.

The taxi breezed down Paradise Road parallel to the Strip, and as Jenny fired off a round of texts her phone rang.

"Jimmy!"

She listened a moment.

"Sparkle." Her enthusiasm cut short, but at least she had made contact with someone. "Do you know where Jimmy is?"

Jenny listened, then turned white as a ghost. Dropped the phone.

"No. NO!"

THE FABULOUS. JIMMY DOT'S SUITE.
SATURDAY 4:46 AM

Jenny opened the door and switched on the light, her note still by the telephone where she had left it. Weary and dragging and her body demanding sleep, her feet shuffled on the carpet as she walked toward the bedroom.

"Jimmy!" she cried out as she saw her husband sitting on the edge of the bed in the dark. Staring at nothing, his face empty of expression. "I've been looking everywhere for you."

"Zazzo's dead."

"I know." She grimaced as she noticed his blood soaked shirt. "Sparkle told me."

"And I signed the new contract. So you may as well just turn around and leave."

"I don't care about the contract." The strong woman who had not cried since being taunted by cruel classmates in the fourth grade lost control with tears of sorrow for Zazzo, mixed with an outpouring of joy that she had survived the day to be with the man she worried she would never see again. She sat beside him on the bed. "Please forgive me for not believing in you, Jimmy. And forgive me for saying that I never loved you. You know that's not true."

A glint of life appeared in Dot's eyes as he drew his wife closer and kissed her gently. Wiped tears from her cheek, then quickly pulled his hand away and reached for the lamp on the nightstand that illuminated the bruises on her face that had begun to turn hideous shades of purple and yellow.

"What the hell happened?"

Jenny told him about being grabbed by the two goons outside the Dead End Bar & Grill. About being held captive at the Three Jacks Motel and the dozens of unsuccessful calls in attempt to convey the message for him to lay off ZeeFil. She chose her words carefully as not to lose his attention to revenge. Went behind the bar and poured them each a double before continuing about the fight, the fire and her escape. But it would have taken a lot more than whiskey to temper her husband's swelling rage.

"I'll murder that motherfucker!" yelled Dot as he got up and stormed toward the door.

Jenny stepped in his way

"Killing Randy Leeds won't keep ZeeFil from killing innocent people."

"But it'll keep him from killing you and me."

"I'm safe, Jimmy. I got away."

"Which has probably made that asshole more determined than ever." He told her Leeds' threat word for word. "For him it's not just about ZeeFil anymore, it's personal. This guy's off his nut and won't stop until we're both dead."

"So what do we do?"

"I kill the psycho son of a bitch, that's what we do."

"No, Jimmy."

"I'm not going to just sit around here and wait for him to murder us."

"There's a lot more to it than that."

"Kill him before he kills us. Seems pretty simple to me."

"Will you shut up for a minute and listen." She massaged his neck and shoulders until eventually he began to soften. "The situation has changed and you need to understand exactly what's going on."

"Okay, baby. You've got my undivided attention." Dot composed himself with a deep breath, but could not avert his eyes from the scrapes and bruises on his wife's face. "Right after I rip his fucking ears off!"

"God damn it, Jimmy. That's exactly what they want you to do," Jenny told him as she again was forced to block his path to the door.

"He tried to kill you and he's going to try again. He sent Ballinger to the hospital."

"And you've got to let all that go, at least for now. Because they've got it rigged where whatever happens to Leeds will happen to you."

"Again with *they*. Who the hell are *they*?"

Jenny pushed him backward onto the bed. Unbuttoned the blood stained orange Hawaiian and playfully wove her fingertips through the thicket of hair on her husband's barrel chest. Finished undressing him and worked her tongue south until his mind was powerless to think beyond the pleasure until eventually the pleasure made him explode. Calming him enough to listen rationally as Jenny explained the details of the puzzle she had begun to piece together in the burned-out motel room. Eventually making Dot understand that the game had indeed changed, and in order to have any chance of stopping Leeds and his deadly pill, they first needed to prevent the billionaire from being murdered.

"Why the hell would we do that?"

"Because the third kidnapper from the motel is going to try to kill him, and set it up to make it look like you did it. And because you have such a strong motive, the cops will believe it. So in order to save you, we have to warn Leeds."

"By telling him what?" Dot didn't like this at all, but he saw her point. "Without the kidnapper's name, he'll accuse me of feeding him just another line of bullshit."

Early morning sunlight had just begun to penetrate the room as Jenny propped up the pillows, then on her burner phone began searching the Internet for the missing piece of the puzzle. School records gave her a dozen possible names and frustratingly little else, and Googling people who had done nothing remarkable with their lives led only to Facebook, where scores of Jay Bradshaws and hundreds of Joe Drapers indicated it would be a waste of time searching the other names. So armed with only rudimentary information and a credit card, Jenny registered on a website that conducted basic background checks. Has your new boyfriend ever been in jail? Is your kid's teacher a pedophile? Your doctor ever been sued for malpractice? Nestled safely in the arms of her husband, Jenny carefully researched the names on her list one by one, looking for a killer.

Nope. Nope. Nope. Christ, these people were boring. Nope.

"There he is!" she called out, seeing that unmistakable smile that had sent a horrific chill down her spine at the Three Jacks Motel. "His name is Tommy Casterlee."

Dot looked at the photo on the tiny screen of her cheap mobile phone. "That's Owen Howard."

"The journalist? Look again."

Dot squinted as he took a closer look. "That's Owen Howard."

Jenny Googled the journalist and showed Dot a picture of the real McCoy. "Casterlee doesn't even look like Owen Howard."

"With bleached hair and colored contacts he does. At least enough to fool Revson," reasoned Dot, as he looked closer at the image on her phone. "No wonder he refused to help me tie Leeds to the murder. That phony's in this up to his ass."

"We have to stop him, Jimmy."

"Bet on it," Dot assured his wife. "And I guarantee I can put the kibosh on both Leeds and ZeeFil at the same time. All I have to do is go upstairs for a face to face."

"Leeds wants to kill you, and Casterlee wants to hang a hundred year frame on you. You can't go anywhere near that penthouse."

"For this plan to work, I have to look Leeds in the eye." Dot's confidence was beginning to surge. "He'll be expecting me to try to con him, so I'll knock him off-balance with a dazzling dose of the truth. With everything you just told me, I can get him into an honest game where he will have no option but to believe every word I say."

"And what if he doesn't?"

"Trust me, Jenny. I'll make him believe."

She did trust him, just not the odds.

"But before I confront Leeds, I need some more information. Go to the FDA website and make a list of every name you can find who has any kind of authority. Then cross reference the names with the Departments of Motor Vehicles in Maryland, D.C. and Virginia."

Jenny was proud that her man was willing to put his life on the line to do the right thing, but at the same time, his fearlessness scared the crap out of her. That fear, plus a double espresso, kept her focused as she squinted through page after page of information on the tiny screen of the burner phone. Finally, after about an hour, she found what she was looking for. Handed the phone to her husband.

"It's not circumstantial anymore." Dot smiled. All of a sudden very positive about the way the rest of the day was going to play out. "Finally, the proof everybody's been yammering about."

"It proves that ZeeFil causes cancer, but there's no proof of any connection to Leeds."

"By the time I'm through with that egomaniac, he'll be begging to make that connection himself."

"If he doesn't kill you first, or if he's even still alive," warned Jenny, worried that her man was letting his own ego get in the way. "Confront Leeds, if you must. But there's no way I'm going to let you walk into that penthouse with Casterlee still on the loose."

She started to dial 911, but Dot snatched the phone from her hand.

"No cops. It goes against everything I've ever stood for."

Jenny softened her husband with a kiss. "How about just one cop?"

"What if he doesn't believe us? I'll blow my cork if one more square calls me a loser, or tells me I should write for the movies." Dot checked the clock on the nightstand. "Besides, they won't be up yet."

"We'll bring breakfast. And we'll make him believe us."

Husband and wife took a quick shower that ended up being not such a quick shower, then looked cautiously both ways more than once before getting in and out of the elevator that delivered them downstairs to the casino. Dot buying coffee and pastries to go, while Jenny made a quick swap of ripped jeans for a jaunty floral print dress at one of the stylish boutiques. They reconnected beneath the porte cochere where a doorman assisted them into a taxi.

"Take us to the Las Vegas Country Club."

FOUNTAIN TOWERS. JACKIE FINK'S APARTMENT.
SATURDAY 9:06 AM

Fink's eyes popped open as his ringtone woke him from an uncomfortable sleep under a scratchy blanket on a bare mattress, as his soiled bed linen was nine floors below in the dumpster. He tensed as he saw the name displayed on the Caller ID.

"You sure didn't waste any time. What do you want me to tell him?"

Fink listened.

"Of course I'll keep my end of the deal. I'm not likely to cross you after it took me three long showers to get that ..." Fink stopped short of an unfortunate choice of words. "To get clean. And you had better keep your end of the deal, because I'm not worth anything to you if Jimmy finds out the truth."

Fink pulled open the curtains, his mind unable to shake the frightening thought of Dot's violent revenge should the details of his mother's affair become known. He opened the window to air out the room.

"I said I'd tell Fuller whatever you want me to, but why do I have to meet you downtown? Why can't you just tell me now?"

THE FABULOUS. CASINO.
SATURDAY 9:19 AM

"We've got a monster afternoon ahead of us," said Dot, invigorated by a successful mission at the country club. Keeping an eye out for trouble as he and Jenny made their way quickly through the early morning casino action toward the elevators.

"And we have a show to do tonight."

"We?" Dot gave her a look.

Jenny reached her arms around her husband's neck and kissed him. "Remember all the fun we used to have doing the warehouse shows?"

"Nobody tried to kill us when we did those shows," Dot reminded her, as his gaze remained vigilant. Casterlee could be anywhere. Leeds could be anywhere. His goons could be anywhere. "Besides, it's not the same here. It's no fun being on stage when you have to trade your soul for the privilege."

"Together we'll make the most of a bad situation."

"I love you for trying to put a positive spin on it, but we can't live our lives like this. We can't be slaves to this place."

"What about the contract you signed?"

"I'll do a monkey act. Take a big steamy shit on stage and throw it at the audience. And if that isn't enough to get me fired, I'll quit and let the lawyers sort it out. They can take away the money and the fame, but they can't put me in jail for breaking a contract."

Jenny was proud of her man as they walked hand in hand past an already crowded casino bar and through a maze of slot machines, giving a starstruck tourist and his wife an opportunity to see up close what real love looked like. The Love Dots, as Gladys liked to call them, pushed the elevator call button and waited to be whisked skyward to prepare for the day of reckoning.

"No sudden moves," came a familiar voice from behind. "Turn around slowly and keep your hands where I can see them."

Jenny and Dot turned around to find themselves face to face with immigration agent Harry Gunther.

"Jennal Alexis Dotoski. I have a warrant for your arrest, pending an order of deportation."

Jenny was scared. At least at the Three Jacks there was a sliver of hope that she could make it out the door. But from Homeland Security there was no possible escape.

"Get lost, Gunther."

"Stay out of this, Dotoski."

A furious Dot stepped threateningly between Jenny and the agent. "You're not taking my wife anywhere."

"You want to do this the hard way?" Gunther fed off the confrontation. "Okay by me."

"You touch her and I'll drop you where you stand."

As the agent produced a pair of handcuffs, the starstruck tourist, oblivious to what was happening, walked right into the middle of it.

"Jimmy! I'm a huge fan. Can I get a picture?"

"Hell yes," Dot called out. "Come on up close."

As the over-anxious fan pushed his way into the mix, Dot slugged Gunther and grabbed the handcuffs. Locked one cuff on the agent's wrist then shackled him to the tourist, shoving them through the open elevator doors and launching the car toward the upper floors of the tower.

Dot wasted no time in whisking his wife back through the casino toward the front entrance of the hotel.

"You need to stay off the radar for a few hours. Don't come back to the hotel, don't go near the apartment and don't use any credit cards until I can straighten this out. And turn off that phone."

"It's a burner phone. They can't trace it to me."

"Unless they work backwards from the numbers you called."

"That seems a bit extreme."

"Gunther is a pissed off Fed with all the resources of Homeland Security. Who knows what he'll do."

Jenny removed the battery from her phone.

"Be careful, Jimmy."

"I'll be fine," he assured her as they walked outside and had the doorman whistle for a taxi. "Go to Caesars, then walk next door to the Mirage and get another cab to the Top Hat. I'll meet you there as soon as I can."

"Be careful."

"You already said that."

"I wanted to say it again."

THE FABULOUS. BLAKE FULLER'S OFFICE.
SATURDAY 9:47 AM

"**C**all him off!" yelled Dot as he grabbed Fuller and slammed him hard against the one-way glass behind his desk.

"Don't you love the poetic irony?" smirked Fuller. "You laughing on stage every night, knowing that halfway around the world your wife is choking on sweaty Greek cock."

"I signed the fucking contract, now call him off!" Dot threw Fuller onto the desk chair so hard that two of the support screws Sparkle had loosened the day before fell out, tumbling him ass first onto the silver shag carpet. "Tell that asshole Gunther to tear up the warrant and leave Jenny alone."

"You probably thought you were pretty smart the way you got away from him downstairs," said Fuller as he stood up. Nonplussed. In the zone, as he had his employee right where he wanted him. "But you made a big mistake in making Gunther look like a fool. I couldn't call him off now even if I wanted to, and he'll have your precious Jenny in custody before the end of the day if he has to use a squad of agents to track her down and make the arrest."

"So a woman who has never hurt anyone in her entire life is hunted down like public enemy number one, while a murderer gets a pass."

"I didn't murder anyone."

"You killed Zazzo in cold blood. And when I'm done dealing with your stooge Gunther, I'm going to kill you."

"No, you won't, because I still hold all the cards."

"You're playing a dead hand, Fuller. And no cheap bluff is going to change the fact that you're a murderer."

"The police don't see it that way. I was protecting myself and my property against a burglar."

"There were two burglars. Why did you wait until after I was gone to call it in?"

"To protect the hotel's investment in you," said Fuller as he leaned his rear end on the edge of the desk, proud that his bold move had put the twenty million dollar bonus within his reach. The contract extension had been signed, but to ensure this monster payday he still needed to keep Dot in line. Knew the time had come to pull the last ace from his sleeve and hit his star attraction where it hurt the most. "When you were a kid, your father committed suicide because of your mother's infidelity."

"How could you possibly know that?" Anger in Dot's voice as his privacy had yet again been violated at The Fabulous, and he put two and two together quickly. "So I guess it wasn't just a line of bullshit when that asshole Gunther said he knew everything there was to know about me and my parents."

"Including documented proof in the file he gave me of the one thing that's been eating at your guts since you were ten years old. The name of your mother's lover."

Dot was stunned. Replayed the words in his head to make sure he had heard right.

"I know every last detail, from who he is to where he took her for those afternoon delights. And you know the best part, Jimmy? Not only is that geriatric Romeo still alive, but I know where he is."

"Who the fuck is he?" raged Dot as he grabbed Fuller roughly by the lapels of his dark blue suit. "Tell me right now, or I swear to fucking Christ I will throw you through that window!"

"Violence is the mark of a small man," laughed Fuller as he pushed back, then smoothed out his lapels. "Your only chance of ever finding out his name is if you continue to pack my showroom every night."

McCARRAN AIRPORT. TERMINAL THREE.
SATURDAY 11:22 AM

Tommy Casterlee washed down a bag of pretzels with a cold Budweiser, half-heartedly watching the White Sox pummel the Red Sox on the bar TV, while keeping an eye on his flight that was getting ready to pre-board. The airport was always hopping on Saturdays with people from here, there, and everywhere scurrying from their arrival gates to baggage claim so they could kick-start their weekend of Vegas fun. Departure gates were not so busy. Neither were the bars.

"Who's winning?" asked an average looking man in a pressed sport shirt who gestured toward the TV as he sat on the stool beside him.

"Sox," answered Casterlee as he watched fellow outbound travelers chase good money after bad on concourse slot machines that anybody with an ounce of sense knew offered the worst odds of any in town. Then stiffened as a man in a blue windbreaker took the stool on his other side.

Cops. Casterlee could smell them a mile away, but when they boxed him in at an almost empty bar, the stench was unmistakable. But so what? They had nothing on him. Revson had committed suicide and any evidence of kidnapping had been burned in the motel fire. He reached for the carry on bag beneath his stool but Sig Samuels beat him to it.

"Easy, Casterlee," cautioned the policeman as he passed the bag to the other officer, and then identified himself with his badge. "I'm Deputy Chief Samuels and this is Detective Hogenson. We'd like to ask you a few questions."

"Then hurry up and ask. They're calling my flight."

"Do you know a man named Bill Revson?"

"Nope."

"Kind of a mousy middle-aged guy. Thinning hair and glasses."

"Nope."

"That's interesting, because surveillance video at The Fabulous shows you talking with him on two separate occasions."

"I'm a friendly guy. I talk to a lot of people." Casterlee took a sip of beer. He was cocky. Knew the cops had squat. "Now if there's nothing else, I've got a plane to catch."

"Just a couple more things, Mr. Casterlee. Then you can go."

"What am I supposed to know about some schmuck I met in passing?"

"Maybe you can explain to us why right after you met him the second time, that schmuck flew out of a twenty-sixth floor window."

"The jumper?"

"Then you do remember him."

"Nope. But there was talk all over the hotel and it was on the news." He finished his beer. "So that was the guy, huh?"

"That was the guy. Only he didn't jump, he was pushed. And there's video of you getting onto the elevator from Revson's floor minutes after the murder."

"Just a coincidence. I went up there with a girl I met at the bar."

"Which bar?"

"The White Bar."

"You were wearing a blue blazer and blue jeans."

"Maybe it was another bar. There are a lot of them in that casino."

"What was the girl's name?"

"Just some pick up. Who gets names?"

"Mind if we look inside your bag?"

"You have a warrant?"

Deputy Chief Samuels produced the document.

"Make it quick, will ya," said Casterlee as Detective Hogenson sifted through the contents of the carry on bag. "They're almost finished boarding my flight."

Hogenson rummaged through standard carry on items then fished out a pair of black leather gloves. Held them upside down and shook out a class ring from Dartmouth College.

"Why you guys take souvenirs is beyond me," laughed Samuels as he stepped between his suspect and the concourse.

"That doesn't prove anything."

"You have the dead man's ring and were on his floor at the time of the murder."

"But not in his room. Did you find my fingerprints in his room?"

"There wouldn't be any if you wore these gloves."

Casterlee didn't even try to contain his thin smile.

"But what happens when we find your DNA on the empty Budweiser bottle that was in Revson's trash?"

"You've got nothing."

"Pay your check."

Casterlee put down a twenty to cover a $17 tab.

"This is Vegas, leave another five," Samuels told him, then added, "Thomas Casterlee, you are under arrest for the murder of William Revson."

"Good luck, cop," laughed Casterlee, armed with the knowledge that even with a DNA match, the person who orchestrated the whole thing had enough money to buy him out of a thousand murder raps. "I'll be back here in time to catch the next flight out."

"**B**ottle of Ketel One, eight ball of coke and a pint of dark chocolate ice cream." Seated at his regular corner booth Jackie Fink made a quick calculation in his head and, as usual, rounded up the total. "It comes to eight hundred even. Be at your door in a half hour to forty-five minutes."

"Looking sharp," remarked Everest as he eyeballed Fink's custom suit, then squeezed his super-sized frame into the booth across the table. "You'd never know that twelve hours ago your head looked like a malted milk ball. Good thing we have pictures."

"You don't really, do you?" Fink suddenly lost interest in his lox and cream cheese bagel. "Please tell me you don't."

"Video too, of you with shit dripping from your face while you cried like a whiny little bitch."

"I'll buy them. How much do you want?"

"Not for sale. Just a little insurance in case we find it necessary to remind you where your loyalty lies."

"So is that why you made me come all the way down here, so you could try to blackmail me with disgusting pictures and videos? Let me remind you that I'm not some rube who's going to sit back and let you gouge him six ways to Sunday."

"You've got a little piece of something in your left ear."

Fink dug around with his finger. Flicked a dried fleck of something onto the floor.

"Doesn't matter how many showers you take, you'll never be clean until you Q-Tip that shit out of every nook and cranny."

"Fuck you, Everest." Fink spit on the finger and wiped it on his napkin.

"You see, it's that kind of attitude that concerns me. Last night you begged for mercy and promised to do whatever you were told, and today you sit here cursing at me and telling me what you won't do."

"Don't worry. I'll keep my end of the bargain." Fink's aggravation continued to fester as Everest ordered a Dr. Brown's celery soda with no ice. "But I won't forget what you did to me."

"That's the point," said the big man as out the window he saw Jimmy Dot exit a taxi. "Since Zazzo's murder last night a lot of things have changed. Priorities have shifted and it's no longer important that you double cross Fuller. What is important is that every man needs to know who his friends are. Who he can trust and who he can't."

Fink turned white as a sheet as Dot slid into the booth beside him.

"I can explain," groveled Fink, trapped between Dot and the wall. "Please, Jimmy. You wouldn't hurt me in front of all these people."

"Why wouldn't he?" said Everest as he surveyed the restaurant to see that most potential witnesses were criminals and social deviants. "Most of these muzzlers have wanted to rip you a new one for years."

"What the hell are you guys talking about?" demanded Dot, irritated as he looked across the table at Everest, whose betrayal had cut him to the quick. "And you had better have a damn good reason for getting me down here on this day of all days."

The waitress brought the celery soda and the usual Orange Crush for Dot.

"Please, Jimmy," Fink begged. His brain scrambling for a way out, before figuring that the only possible chance he had to escape with his life would be to come clean and beg for mercy. "She was lonely and it just happened. With your dad at the store day and night she needed companionship. It just got out of hand."

Dot narrowed his eyes, not needing a map to see where this unsolicited confession was going.

Fink pissed his pants as he realized that Dot had not known, and that he had just ratted himself out.

"You destroyed my family." A lifetime of anger surged into focus as Dot twisted in his seat and faced Fink. "Betrayed me. Took money and played me for a fool."

"Jimmy, please don't. I'm begging you not to," pleaded Fink, trembling with fear as he watched Dot squeeze the thick glass of the Orange Crush bottle with all his strength. Knowing that if it broke he would use it to cut him and if it didn't he would smash his face with it.

"And Fuller knows," added Dot, his fist gripping the bottle even harder as the big picture became clear to him. "That's why you've been tipping that asshole to every move I made. That's how Leeds knew about my bet with Revson. How Everest knew almost before it happened that Fuller had me on the spot with Immigration."

"I'd take it back in a second if I could. Please don't hurt me."

"This rat isn't worth it, Jimmy," said Everest, attempting to let some air out of his friend's fury. "Do you think I wanted to spend the last forty years of my life with shoe polish under my fingernails? But it was either that or do something stupid that would have landed me back in prison. Be smart. Think of Jenny. You've got too much to live for."

"You've had my back ever since I was a smartass kid, and I almost threw our friendship away by jumping to a conclusion without knowing the facts. I believed the worst rather than listen to what you had to say." Dot eased his grip on the bottle and took a cooling sip of orange soda. "Will you ever be able to forgive me?"

Everest smiled. Reached across the table and shook his friend's hand.

"I promise I'll make it up to you," Dot told Everest as he got up from the table. "But right now I've got something to take care of that won't wait."

"Then we're okay?" uttered Fink meekly.

"I'm not going to hurt you, if that's what you mean." Dot's temper and propensity toward violence had been born out of the hurt and frustration of not knowing the name of the man responsible for the deaths of his mother and father. And fittingly, all these years later, that violent streak was about to fizzle out now that he knew the answer. "But if you ever see me coming, you had better cross the street."

"Thanks, Jimmy. Thank you," blubbered Fink, his trousers sopped in a puddle of his own urine. "I owe you."

"You made me think that Everest was the one who crossed me. You owe him."

Dot walked out of the delicatessen. Had let Fink off the hook because he knew Everest wouldn't. Knew now that Fuller really was playing a dead hand and that killing him would be the final violent act of a once violent man.

"He's right, Everest. What will it be?" offered Fink, pulling a wad of napkins out the dispenser and wiping the perspiration of fear from his face. Not sure why or how, but he was still breathing and not about to question it. "How about a matinee with a smokin' hot blonde right off the plane from Paris? Or even better, how about the blonde and a big titted redhead? Or a kinky Chinese broad. Anything you want. On the house."

Everest reached across the table and grabbed Fink by the hair. Pulled it hard.

"Stop it!" Fink screamed through excruciating pain. "Stop!"

Everest pulled harder. Then harder still until the man whose strength had earned him two Super Bowl rings, ripped a handful of transplanted hair out of Fink's scalp and jammed the bloody tuft into his mouth.

Villains and lowlifes crowded around the table to watch, busting their guts laughing as Fink howled for mercy.

"Swallow that hair, you fucking rat."

Fink tried to spit out the disgusting mouthful, but the hair was too dry and bits of scalp stuck in his teeth. Tried to remove it with his fingers but Everest reached across the table and slammed his head against the back of the booth.

"I said swallow it! Every ugly fucking hair!" roared the big man as he pushed his celery soda across the table. "Wash it down with this."

Fink shook his head violently from side to side.

"Do it!"

Fink gagged and swallowed. Again and again and again. Coughed as his oral passage finally began to clear.

"Squeeze in closer, fellas," Everest told the amused group crowded around the table as he removed his phone from the watch pocket of his paisley vest. "You think this was funny, I'm gonna show you a video our pal Fink starred in last night."

A bbie Leeds, looking smart in a pink sweater and matching slacks, was shocked as she pulled open one of the double doors and saw Jimmy Dot standing at the threshold holding a plate of cookies.

"Are you out of your mind coming here?"

"Just a neighborly visit."

"It's your funeral," she shrugged, and then led him through an opulent maze of art and style until they reached the oak-paneled library where Randy Leeds relaxed on a burnt orange leather sofa, enjoying a Perrier with lemon as he thumbed through a book on the history of golf.

"You've got a lot of balls showing your face here."

"Come on, Randy. You're not really going to kill me."

"I am absolutely going to kill you."

"I'm here with a peace offering."

Dot was not invited to sit and the billionaire scoffed as he placed the plate of chocolate chip cookies in front of him on the zebrawood coffee table. "You try every trick in the book to ruin me and my company, then think you can commute a death sentence with cookies?"

"Not just any cookies. I stopped by Bobby Flay's and had him bake these just for you. Try one. They're still warm from the oven."

"Why the hell are you here?"

"To propose a truce. Lay off me and my wife and, in exchange, I'll arrange that photo-op you came to Las Vegas for."

"Cut the crap, Jimmy. If you could do that you would have brought Preston Bond with you instead of a plate of fucking cookies. Now get your ass out of here. Abbie and I have to get ready for my shareholders meeting."

"I know I've caused you a lot of aggravation, Randy, and I'm here to apologize. Please find it in your heart to allow Jenny and I to enjoy the life we used to have before The Fabulous and ZeeFil turned everything inside out."

"Very touching. And I might be inclined to find that plea sincere, if I didn't know you so well."

"Trust me, Randy. All I want is my life back. Agree to a truce, and I guarantee that before the afternoon is over you'll have that photo you want so badly."

"You're a professional liar who has spent the past few days trying to con me, and now all of a sudden I'm supposed to trust you?"

"Your ghost busters came up empty, Fuller won't help you, and Hard Bernard is locked in jail. What other option do you have, Randy? You know as well as I do that I'm the only one who can get you face to face with Preston Bond."

"I'm telling you for the last time to leave."

"A lot has changed for me since yesterday, especially since I found out that ZeeFil really is safe after all."

"And what made you suddenly come to that conclusion?"

"I went to see Senator Williams who gave me the straight dope he got from the commissioner of the FDA. Then gave me a good old fashioned cowboy ass kicking for wasting his time."

"You deserved that boot up your ass for even thinking that the Food & Drug Administration would give the go ahead to a medicine that was going to kill people. How you could have been so gullible is beyond me."

"Revson believed it too, and he worked on developing that medicine."

"Revson was insane. So far off his rocker that he gave the FDA a formula to test that, you obviously now know, is a chemical formula for chocolate chip cookies," said Leeds as he picked up one of the warm cookies from the plate and took a bite. "These are delicious. Flay really bake them?"

"Just for you," smiled Dot. "I'm sorry I doubted you, Randy. Please accept my apology."

"You accused me of bribing the FDA, murdering Revson and attempting to kill half the population. All without a lick of proof. And you think a few cookies and that half-assed apology is enough to make things right? If you would have listened to me in the first place, you would have saved us both a lot of bother."

"Then why did you let me keep thinking the drug was dangerous?"

"I told you it wasn't."

"Not very convincingly. Did you get a kick out of watching me chase my tail?"

"I did," admitted Leeds."

"Just as you did with Revson."

"Until he started shooting off his mouth to the media."

"You can thank your wife for that." Dot was focused. Making his play. "She and her goon squad worked for months to fuel Revson's fears and prod him to go public with the cancer scare. She made him believe it was real, and that you were covering it up."

"Her goon squad?"

"She drove Revson out of his gourd by convincing the poor schmuck that you were the one who kept having him beaten up."

"Throw him out, Randy. You said yourself that this guy is nothing but a professional liar who has spent the past few days trying to con you."

"She's right, Jimmy. You're nothing but a second rate con man trying to sell a third rate line of bullshit."

"Is it a third rate line of bullshit that the two of you don't get along as well behind closed doors as you do in public? And that Abbie can't split because she was naïve enough to sign a crazy prenup that gives her practically nothing if she tries to get a divorce."

"Damn it, Randy. Throw this guy out."

"And she can't kill you for the life insurance money because, as everyone knows, the spouse is always the prime suspect. So she hatched the clever idea of killing Bill Revson and hanging a frame on you."

"Enough!" Leeds slammed his golf book hard on the coffee table. "It's just another wild story you can't prove. I don't know what your game is this time, Jimmy, but it's over. I'm going to kill your wife, and then take my own sweet time killing you. Now get the fuck out while you can still walk!"

"Can't you see I'm trying to do you a favor?"

Leeds bolted up off the sofa and slugged Dot hard in the jaw.

Dot absorbed the punch.

"Hit him again, Randy!" provoked Abbie. "Shut this clown up once and for all."

Leeds rocked him with another. Then another.

Dot kept his footing, but dropped his hands to his side and did not fight back.

"Hit him back, you fucking coward!" Abbie yelled at Dot. "Hit him!"

Leeds relaxed his fist, confused as he looked at his wife.

"Don't you get it, Randy?" explained Dot, rolling his tongue around his mouth to make sure he still had all his teeth. "If you kill me you'll go to prison, which will probably void the prenup and let her collect a fat divorce settlement, and if I kill you she's a rich widow. Either way she hits the jackpot. That's why she doesn't care who wins as long as it's a fight to the finish."

"You're insane!" she yelled at him.

"Give it up, Abbie. It's over," said Dot calmly. "Everybody knew that Revson had been accusing Randy of all sorts of horrible things, so you figured you'd have Tommy Casterlee pose as a sympathetic journalist. You called Revson anonymously and told him the journalist was at the White Bar, hoping Casterlee could gain the schmuck's trust so he'd turn over whatever lab notes he might have had."

"Who is Tommy Casterlee?" demanded Leeds.

"Your wife's boyfriend."

Leeds slugged Dot again, and when he again failed to defend himself, the billionaire began to believe. He sat down.

So did Dot, rubbing his sore jaw as he went on with his story.

"Casterlee is the one who threw Revson out the window, and because you had both motive and opportunity, it was easy for them to hang the frame on you. He left one of your monogrammed cuff links on the floor as evidence, and then gave the poor chump's journal to Abbie, who put it in your sock drawer or under your mattress or some other obvious place where the police would easily find it. Then all that remained was for them to wait for the coppers to come and arrest you, then pocket a big divorce settlement while you rotted in the can."

"If any of this is true," demanded Abbie, "why hasn't Randy been arrested?"

"Because your whole plan went to shit when the cops found what they thought was Revson's suicide note. No murder, no fall guy. So you had to find another way, and came up with Plan B, where you had my wife snatched up by the two goons you imported from Pennsylvania, and tried to make me think Randy did it. But it wasn't actually a kidnapping, was it Abbie? The plan was to murder Jenny, figuring I would go into a rage and kill Randy, which would give you a clean double indemnity claim on his gigantic life insurance policy."

"You're insane."

"And on top of that, you would have inherited enough to keep you and your boyfriend farting through silk for the rest of your lives. Or at least that's how you sold it to Casterlee. And the plan might have worked even after Jenny escaped, because you still could pretty much count on me coming after Randy. That's why you were so surprised when I showed up at the door with cookies in my hand, instead of in a gun."

"You know he's lying, Randy. Throw him out."

"Come on, Abbie. You don't want me to leave before I get to the part of the story where you had sex with the burglar who stole your diamond ring."

"That's a lie!" The Stepford polish was gone from her voice. "A d-dirty lie!"

Leeds knew his wife was scared. Knew that she was lying. But he still demanded proof.

"It didn't take much of an Internet search for Jenny to find Abbie Anderson's La Crosse, Wisconsin high school yearbook." Dot's voice was even and convincing as he continued to fill in the blanks for Leeds. "Then cross reference to connect her with the thug who beat her to a pulp at the Three Jacks Motel. The same thug who convinced Bill Revson that he was an investigative journalist named Owen Howard."

"Tell me about this Casterlee."

"Abbie's high school sweetheart. A wannabe wise guy she tricked into thinking that the two of them would take your money and live happily ever after. And he's such a fucktard he believed her, though you and I both know she's had a sense of entitlement ever since she was old enough to grow tits, and was not about to share a dollar of this blood money with Casterlee or anybody."

Leeds rose from the sofa and slapped his wife's face with such force that she dropped to the floor. Scared shitless as she knew from experience that the next blow would be harder, and Dot wished upon all he held dear that Abbie was as frightened of her husband as Jenny had been facing execution at the motel.

"So her plan must have been to tie it all up in a neat package by killing Casterlee too, but she'll never get the chance because right now the cops have him downtown, where he's getting ready to sing like a stage-struck canary."

"Bullshit," yelled Abbie, abandoning all denials as she picked herself up off the floor and became aggressive. "Tommy C would never sell me out. Besides, he's on a flight back to Chicago."

"You told him to lam out of here and lay low, then you'd meet up with him when everything blew over. But the dipshit got himself arrested at the airport an hour ago with Bill Revson's ring in his carry on bag, and a long record of calls and texts from you on his phone. How long do you think it will be before he takes a deal and gives you up?"

"He won't say a word."

"How long until he realizes he's in so far over his head that you can't help him? So don't kid yourself into thinking that he's going to take this rap alone."

"You fucking slut!" exploded Leeds, hammering his wife hard into a wall of first editions. "I give you everything, and you repay me by spreading your legs for burglars and small timers and who knows what other trash. Try to undermine the biggest medical miracle since the polio vaccine, then have me killed! You're dead! You are fucking dead!"

Leeds smashed his fist into his wife's face, blood gushing from a nose that was no longer centered between her eyes. But before he could deliver the knockout punch, Dot jumped out of his chair and got between them.

"Don't do it, Randy."

"Why?" Leeds propped his wife up by the neck. "You want her for yourself? Crack her skull for what she did to Jenny."

"Fortunately, my Jenny is safe, so I'm content to let the law take its course. And if you're smart, you'll do the same," cautioned Dot. "If Casterlee hasn't cracked yet he will soon, meaning that the cops will be busting in here before long to haul her ass to jail. And if you don't back off, you'll be in jail with her instead of at your shareholders meeting."

Leeds belted his wife once more for good measure and she collapsed to the floor like wet spaghetti. Then he cooled himself with a sip of Perrier. Sank into the sofa and took a moment to regain his composure.

"There is nothing more dangerous than an enemy attacking from within, and you risked a lot to come up here and set me straight. I'm grateful, Jimmy."

"Thanks, Randy." Dot extended his hand across the zebra-wood table. "Friends?"

"Friends," replied Leeds with an easy smile as the men shook hands. "And sorry I had to smack you around, but under the circumstances ... well, you understand."

"No hard feelings, Randy."

"Does that mean you're still willing to arrange my celebrity photo-op?"

"Absolutely."

I've been scared out of my mind," said Jenny, wrapping her arms tightly around her husband as he slid onto the stool beside her at the busy bar full of day drunks. "Tell me everything that happened."

"Casterlee is in jail and Abbie's on her way," smiled Dot as he took a sip of her beer. "Not to mention that Leeds has kindly agreed not to murder us."

"He took the bait?"

"Hook, line and sinker." Dot was focused. Confident as he neared the finish line. "And in an hour he'll announce to the world that ZeeFil causes cancer."

"You're positive of that?"

"Absolutely."

Dot had been rolling sevens all day as, not only was he about to accomplish the impossible, he had finally achieved closure about the deaths of his parents. He dropped the big news on his wife.

"Jackie Fink was the one who had the affair with my mother."

Jenny was stunned, then after thinking for a moment about what a creep Fink was, she was suddenly not surprised at all.

"How did you find out?"

"It's a long story."

"You can tell me all about it in the cab back to The Fabulous," she said as she got off her barstool.

"Sorry, Jenn. You need to keep out of sight a while longer," said Dot, as he looked up at the woman who was his everything. Bruises on her face concealed with makeup. Contusions that had started to scab. "Leeds may have erased the bulls-eye, but Gunther has a squad of immigration agents all over the hotel looking for you."

"After what I've been through, there's no way I'm not going to be front and center to watch Leeds crash and burn."

"And there's no way I'm going to let that crooked Fed jeopardize our future together." Dot would not concede the point, though he did soften his tone. "I need you to pick up Ballinger from the hospital and make sure he gets home okay. Then I've arranged for you to hang out at Swanky's. Nobody would ever think to look there."

"One room above a Laundromat?" Jenny did not like the idea one bit, but knew he was right. "Does it even have cable?"

"No. But it doesn't have a view of the Acropolis either."

Jenny sat down and ordered another beer.

"While I was cooling my heels, Klubs lent me his phone so I could Google that asshole Fed."

"Anything we can use against him?"

"A few job related hits, but other than that our pal Agent Gunther is as boring as wheat toast. Facebook says he bowls every other Thursday, and on his days off schleps a twelve-foot catamaran out to Lake Mead. Not much of a life."

"Hey, Klubs. Can I use your cellphone a minute?" Dot called down the bar, then smiled to Jenny. "Just a couple more things to take care of and we're home free."

The bartender slid him the phone and went on about his business of propping up the elite of Skid Row society. Dot dialed a number from memory.

"It's me, Jimmy. You all set? ... Yeah, I'm on my way to the event center now. Make your entrance at exactly three o'clock. Not a minute later ... Thanks, man. See you there."

Dot ended the call then handed the phone to Jenny, "Will you pull up the want ads on this thing?"

"Want ads?" She cut loose with a natural, carefree laugh. Her first in a long time.

"Okay, wisenheimer." Dot smiled, sharing his wife's amusement. "Type in Greg's List. I want to buy something really expensive."

THE FABULOUS. CASINO.
SATURDAY 2:43 PM

Jimmy Dot kept his head down to avoid eye contact, determination in his stride as he cut a sharp swath through the afternoon casino crowd. Past dreamers gathered around the Rocket Billionaire slot machine that had no clue that money could not buy happiness. Past enticing aromas wafting from PizzaPalooza and Bacon&Beer, wishing he had the time. Past Naked Lunch where a hand from behind grabbed his shoulder and spun him around.

"Fuck off, Gunther," growled Dot as he pushed back, creating separation as the two angry men faced off.

"Don't try my patience, Dotoski," threatened Agent Gunther. "You'll regret it."

"You don't give two shits about Jenny's immigration status. How much is Fuller paying you?"

"It stopped being about money when you pulled that stunt in the elevator this morning. Now it's personal."

"It's always about money with guys like you. Did that peanut-sized brain of yours ever consider that I have a lot more of it than Fuller does?"

"Not interested."

"Maybe I have something else that might soothe your bruised ego."

"You've got ten seconds."

"I hear that on days off you enjoy sailing your little catamaran around Lake Mead."

"Five seconds."

"How would you like to trade that bathtub toy for a sixty foot racing sloop I have docked in San Diego?"

Dot got a quick answer as Agent Gunther cuffed his hands behind his back.

"James Dotoski. You are under arrest for attempting to bribe a federal officer. You have the right to remain silent. Anything you say can and will be used against you in a court of law," recited Gunther as he pushed his prisoner through an unmarked door, down a fluorescently lit hallway toward the hotel security office.

Dot spun around and karate kicked Gunther into the wall. Tried to head butt him, but without the use of his hands he was quickly subdued and shoved into a detention cell.

"You have the right to speak with an attorney and to have that attorney present during questioning. If you cannot afford to hire an attorney, one will be appointed to represent you at no cost before any questioning," Gunther told him through the bars. "Do you understand each of these rights I have explained to you?"

"Tell me, asshole. What happens when I tell the judge that you took money from Fuller to roust my wife?"

"First of all, you can't prove that any money changed hands. Secondly, the warrant is legitimate because, in case you forget, your wife is in this country illegally. And most importantly, by the time you get face to face with a judge, or even a lawyer for that matter, she will already be on the other side of the world."

"What makes Fuller's money greener than mine? Why short change yourself by doing business on just one side of the street?"

"I told you, it's not about money anymore."

"You're a putz, Gunther. You might have me but you'll never find Jenny."

"She's at the Top Hat Ballroom."

Time stopped. A collision of moments when Gunther first saw Dot nervous and Dot first saw Gunther smile.

"The agents I have on your tail saw you leave there twenty minutes ago."

"Have they arrested her?"

"That pleasure will belong to me, then I'll take you both in together. Perp walk, news cameras and probably a promotion."

"Stuff it, Gunther. This has nothing to do with you making yourself out to be a hero, because a desk job and an extra C-note a week wouldn't satisfy a greedy prick like you. This is still about money. Real money." Dot was up against it, and dancing as fast as he could. "The reason you picked me up alone, and have me in this cell alone, is so you can shake me down and play both ends against the middle. So cut to the chase. What's it gonna cost me?"

"Don't you see that it's over, Dotoski?" Gunther enjoyed having total control over peoples' lives. Tossing Mexicans back across the border was fun, but taking down a big fish was what really got his rocks off. "You could have saved your wife if you would have signed the contract that Fuller eventually got you to sign anyway. But instead, she's being deported to a place where unemployment is so high that the only job she'll be able to get will be on her back. While you rot in prison, counting the days until you get out and can finally go to her. But by then she'll hate your guts, knowing that you could have prevented the whole thing."

THE FABULOUS. MILKY WAY EVENT CENTER.
SATURDAY 2:59 PM

U sually just a couple hundred people with nothing better to do on an early spring afternoon would gather in western Pennsylvania for the EcoGreen Pharmaceuticals annual meeting. No frills, no refreshments and out the door in less than ninety minutes. But not this year, as almost two thousand shareholders made the trip to Las Vegas to bask in the glow of record profits and help themselves to gift bags overflowing with samples of ZeeFil and corporate logoed swag. In full party mode as they enjoyed a buffet luncheon and open bar under a gigantic backlit 3-D mural of a squadron of UFOs screaming through the Milky Way galaxy. And then there was the lone party pooper, Reynolds Ford Cabot IV.

Cabot had long contended that, despite all the checks and balances in place to keep a publicly traded company honest, Chief Executive Officer Randy Leeds ran EcoGreen to suit his own purposes. He listened as it was announced that all twelve of Leeds' hand picked corporate directors had been almost unanimously re-elected. Watched his nemesis bask in adulation as the hero who had developed a miracle drug that was about to make the company billions upon billions of dollars while padding the bank account of each and every person in the room, and knew that any opinions he might attempt to express supporting claims of malfeasance would most certainly fall upon deaf ears.

Cabot cast a pained look at the smug directors on the dais as resolution after resolution was virtually rubber stamped, wondering what he was even doing there, when he could just as easily have watched the webcast of this glorified circle jerk from the comfort of his favorite chair back in Connecticut. Then wondered no longer as a rumble began to roll through the gathering. The shareholders awestruck. Gawking in startled amazement. Camera phones recording shots of a lifetime as the rumble exploded into cheers, as the man who was larger than life made his way through the venue toward the stage.

THE FABULOUS. DETENTION CELL.
SATURDAY 3:01 PM

Dot was screwed and he knew it. His ass on a cold steel bench with his hands still locked behind his back. No way out, and not enough left in the tank to muster a proper fuck you through the bars of the cell to the asshole agent yakking on his phone. Then he saw Gunther's expression sour. And from the information Dot was able to piece together from eavesdropping one side of the conversation, he smiled as it became clear that the situation had fishtailed a quick U-turn.

"Jenny got away, didn't she?"

"She won't get far."

"Forget it, Gunther. She's already in the wind and you'll never find her."

"Tell me where she's going and I'll drop the charge against you."

"A bullshit bribery charge?" laughed Dot, his swagger surging back as he got off the bench and faced Gunther through the bars. "Were you wearing a wire? Because I sure wasn't, which means you have no proof that I said anything. And no money changed hands so unlock this fucking cell."

"I've seen the way your wife looks at you. She'll turn herself in if it keeps you from spending even one day in prison."

"I would never let Jenny make that trade."

"With a warrant out for her arrest, how is she going to get a job? A bank account or a driver's license? She can't live her life totally off the grid, Dotoski. Eventually she'll be caught."

"Give it up, Gunther. It's over. There's nothing left for you to gain by being a hard ass, so tear up the warrant and let me out of here."

"Not on your life."

"Then I'll get a busload of underage Mexican girls to go to the District Attorney and say you made them have sex with you in exchange for leaving their illegal relatives alone."

"It isn't true."

"Doesn't matter. You're so despised in the Mexican community that people will be lined up around the block to testify against you. And even if you somehow manage to beat the rap, by the time it all gets sorted out, the best you can hope for is working the graveyard shift in a guard shack at some border crossing in the Arctic Circle."

Harry Gunther's record showed that he had performed his duties with honor on every rung of the law enforcement ladder. Decorated for both valor and exemplary service. Had shaken hands with two presidents. And he knew there was no way an agent of his stature could ever be railroaded by the best justice system in the world. Or could he? Twelve people not smart enough to get out of jury duty might be swayed by witness after witness telling the same lie. And what if the judge was Latino? He figured all the possible scenarios, finally realizing that there was only one surefire way to guarantee justice.

Agent Gunther unlocked the cell and stepped inside. Lowered his voice as he removed the handcuffs and stood face to face with Jimmy Dot.

"Tell me more about the boat in San Diego."

THE FABULOUS. MILKY WAY EVENT CENTER.
SATURDAY 3:17 PM

The crowd cheered wildly as Randy Leeds stood at the podium beside one of the most famous men in the world. It was not Preston Bond, but the surprise appearance by Killer Kong served the CEO's self-promotion purposes almost as well, as media photogs snapped images of the pinstriped executive embracing the popular fighter in the Grim Reaper T-shirt like he was his best bro.

Kong ripped off the shirt and rattled the walls with his trademark roar. Flexed powerful biceps and flaunted his necklace made from the teeth of fallen opponents. Twisted the legs of a metal chair into a knot then pretended to spar with Leeds. The boxer was a master showman. The ultimate black hat. The villain of all villains who even sweet little old ladies loved to root for, and the crowd went berserk as cellphone video captured every second of it.

In all the commotion, Jimmy Dot was able to enter the packed event center unnoticed. Was shocked to see Jenny seated with Swanky at the end of a row near the front. Knelt in the aisle beside her.

"I saw the Feds lurking outside the Top Hat and ducked out the back," Jenny told him. "I know I'm taking a big chance being here, but nothing was going to keep me from watching that asshole Leeds go down in flames."

"Gunther won't be bothering us anymore. You're safe, baby. It's all over." Dot kissed his wife, and then smiled. "Enjoy the fireworks."

As the cheering finally died down, Leeds adjusted the microphone and fed the shareholders a heaping dose of what they wanted to hear, then turned the floor over to the boxer for more of the same.

Kong had the revved-up crowd eating out of the palm of his hand, then suddenly dropped out of character. No longer the bravado of a vicious fighter who had once killed in the ring and vowed to do it again, Kong's words were now heartfelt and believable as if being delivered by young Ernie Congalosi before he punched his way out of Queens. Sticking to the script as Jimmy Dot had outlined it for him. Saying it in his own words, but saying it. A laundry list of truths that could be boiled down to the simple fact that the miracle drug they were all there to celebrate would probably kill them, along with millions of other men, women and children if it was allowed to go on sale to the public.

"Liar!"

"Bullshit!"

"Get off the stage!"

The shareholders weren't buying any of it. Showering the boxer with boos and catcalls as they found it impossible to believe Kong's assertion that Randy Leeds and EcoGreen would put profits ahead of human lives.

All day the dice had been coming up sevens but on his most important roll Dot crapped out, helplessly watching his can't-miss plan implode as the crowd shouted down one of the most popular celebrities on earth. His mind racing furiously in attempt to find another way, only to realize there was no other way. And then, as if by divine intervention, a final chance to convince the shareholders miraculously appeared in the most unlikely form as rosy-cheeked Reynolds Ford Cabot IV climbed onto the stage. Pushed past Killer Kong with the determination of a poodle believing he could take down a Doberman. Grabbed the microphone and settled the restless gathering who demanded facts from someone other than a bloodthirsty fighter.

"As many of you know, my grandfather co-founded the company that evolved into EcoGreen Pharmaceuticals. And as many of you also know, I am an outspoken critic of the way Randy Leeds manages our interests to suit his own personal greed, and I now have the proof to back up my accusations of malfeasance. Dr. Frank Ballinger can attest ..."

"Ballinger is nothing but a Skid Row drunk," interrupted Leeds as he tried unsuccessfully to push the determined man away from the microphone.

"Your arrogance and lack of knowledge is an embarrassment to both yourself and to the company you represent," charged Cabot, who then told the shareholders, "Dr. Ballinger is the well-respected former chief of surgery at both Massachusetts General Hospital and Cedars Sinai in Los Angeles. Dr.

Ballinger can attest through sources within the Food & Drug Administration that there were indeed irregularities in the expedited ZeeFil approval process. And these sources will confirm that further in-depth testing will prove that ZeeFil does indeed cause pancreatic cancer in a significant percentage of the people who take it."

"Six percent," shouted Leeds, as smartphones throughout the room captured the confession on video. "That's all. Just six percent."

"And yet that fact does not appear anywhere in the final FDA analysis," Cabot told the crowd, who at this point did not know who or what to believe. "Explain that to the shareholders, Randy."

"ZeeFil does NOT cause cancer." Leeds knew how to work a crowd. Especially this crowd. "Only symptoms. And out of the six percent who develop these symptoms of early stage pancreatic cancer, most can expect a normal life expectancy by using proven EcoGreen cancer inhibitors, dropping that percentage to well within the acceptable risk-benefit paradigm."

Great save as the gathering responded to their leader with a rousing ovation, and as Dot watched Cabot implode, he knew that his only chance now was to wing it. Manipulate the situation, then orchestrate the chaos. He jumped onto the stage, flashed his trademark smile, and emphatically shook hands with the CEO as he crashed the party and joined him at the podium. Leeds knew that Dot had set him up. That he was the puppet master behind the spectacle of Kong and the anarchy of Cabot, but had no choice other than to momentarily feign public solidarity with the popular funnyman.

"Thanks for stopping by to help us celebrate, Jimmy," said Leeds through a stage smile, then to the crowd. "Come on, everyone. Let's have a big EcoGreen round of applause for Jimmy Dot, ringmaster of the most popular show on the Las Vegas Strip."

"Thanks, Randy," he responded as the applause died down. "But before I go, can you tell me what time it is?"

"If it will get you off this stage any faster, you fucking retard," seethed Leeds under his breath, then gasped in horror as he caught sight of his bare wrist. "My watch!"

"You lost your watch?" asked Dot. "Don't worry, Randy. I'm sure everybody will help you look for it."

"It's irreplaceable. It's one-of-a-kind."

"Come on, everybody," Dot urged the shareholders. "Let's help the boss find his watch. Check under your seats. What does it look like, Randy?"

"Vintage Patek Philippe. Eighteen karat rose gold with twenty-eight precious jewels," Leeds uttered in a panic as the crowd checked around their seats. "It's worth ten million dollars!"

"Just a regular fella. Aren't you, Randy."

"Shut up and help me find it."

"Have you looked in your pocket?" asked Dot.

"It's not in my pocket, you idiot!"

"How can you expect your loyal shareholders to look for your watch if you won't even check your own pockets?"

The shareholders watching, Leeds grudgingly checked. Nothing.

"How about your inside jacket pocket?"

Leeds reached inside his jacket, hatred burning in his eyes as he pulled out the ten million dollar ticker.

Dot's face exploded with laughter. He took an exaggerated bow as the crowd roared its approval of the watch trick, then grinned at the pissed off billionaire.

"Now, who's the retard?"

"I should have killed you back at the hotel," snarled Leeds, as he was forced to cede the spotlight to the popular funnyman, who now had the delighted shareholders rolling in the aisles as he cracked jokes in rapid-fire succession. Then Jimmy Dot did a quick one-eighty and got to the point.

"I think it's great that by using other EcoGreen drugs, the percentage of people who will get cancer from taking ZeeFil will drop to an acceptable number," Dot told the crowd, then looked at Leeds. "But people will still die, right Randy?"

It took every ounce of his self-control for Leeds not to murder Dot in front of two thousand witnesses.

"How many people will die, Randy?" Dot was not to be denied. "How much death is acceptable?"

"There is risk attached to everything each of us does in this life, even crossing the street," justified Leeds, grinding his teeth as he was forced to go toe to toe with Dot. "And in this case, that risk falls well within government guidelines."

"On paper. But what happens when ZeeFil goes on sale and those statistics become real people?" Dot turned to the shareholders. "Bill Revson was the research chemist who discovered the fatal side effect. And when he tried to come forward with this information, your CEO fired him, blackballed him in the scientific community and ruined his credibility with the media. But nothing would stop Revson from trying to do the right thing, and when he got too close to exposing the cover-up he was killed."

"Get this lunatic off the stage," Leeds commanded hotel security, who made a move toward Dot only to retreat when Killer Kong blocked their path.

"Less than an hour ago, the police arrested your wife for the murder of Bill Revson. Come on, Randy. Are you going to insult the intelligence of these good people by saying that you had nothing to do with it?"

The word *murder* took the air out of the room.

"For once, do the right thing and put public safety above corporate greed," shouted Dot as he turned away from the microphone and faced the Board of Directors, his bullish voice still loud enough to be heard throughout the event center. "Recall ZeeFil before it's too late to stop all the suffering and death."

"Why should we approve a massive recall that will cost the company a fortune in lost revenue?" called out one of the board members.

"Lost revenue will be the least of your problems when people start to die. The devastating loss of public confidence will cause your stock price to fall so far that it would more than likely put the company out of business." Dot pointed to random shareholders. "You and you and you. Where would any of you be if the money you invested in EcoGreen was suddenly gone? Because that's exactly what's going to happen when doctors discover the link between ZeeFil and pancreatic cancer. Not only that, Leeds and his Board of Directors are about to make you all accomplices to their crime by misusing your hard-earned money to endanger the lives of *your* family and *your* friends and *your* neighbors."

A few angry investors shouted obscenities and pelted the stage with sample packs of ZeeFil and bound copies of the annual report as Jimmy Dot climbed on top of the podium and towered over the proceedings. Never more a ringmaster than he was at that moment, he pointed an accusing finger at the Board of Directors seated behind him then further incited the crowd.

"You don't need these greedy bastards to agree to do anything. You have the power to stop ZeeFil. You have the power to save lives. Post the videos you're taking. Send them to the media and everybody you know. Leeds' cancer confession will go viral and nobody will buy his killer pill. You will all be heroes, each and every one of you. Post your videos and save the world!"

Jim-my Dot ... Jim-my Dot ... Jim-my Dot ....

Dot kept his foot on the gas. "Are you ready to show these stuffed shirts who owns this company?"

YES!

"Who *really* owns this company?"

YES!

With the amped up crowd on its feet, Dot yelled *CHARGE* into the microphone and the doors of the event center burst open. Riding on the back of a Great Dane, Sparkle galloped like a warrior down the center aisle toward the stage, firing a water cannon at the Board of Directors as he yelled for the enraged crowd to follow him.

Scores of normally mild mannered men and women stormed the stage. Metro police and agents in FBI windbreakers rushed in, but were overmatched as angry shareholders threw chairs and bottles at the people who valued money over human life.

Jim-my Dot ... Jim-my Dot ... Jim-my Dot ....

With no way to escape, the EcoGreen brass was at the mercy of the violent mob. Some of the directors were held down while samples of ZeeFil were forced down their throats. Two old ladies went Full Kong on another until his bloody face bore little resemblance to his smirking photo in the annual reports that were strewn about the stage. Leeds was pummeled mercilessly by angry investors until two of the FBI agents finally broke through the melee and came to his rescue.

"Do your fucking job," Leeds screamed as he pointed at Dot. "Arrest that son of a bitch."

The agents assisted the embattled CEO to his feet.

"Randy Leeds. You're under arrest on charges of bribery and attempted murder."

"Me?" he screamed. "Are you fucking insane? I'll have your badges for this. I didn't bribe anybody and I did not kill that idiot Revson."

"The charge is *attempted* murder."

"Who the hell did I try to kill?"

"Everybody."

Feeling his world of wealth and entitlement crumbling, Leeds grabbed an agent's service revolver and pointed it up at Jimmy Dot, who continued to orchestrate the riot from atop the podium.

"You ruined me for a motherfucking hot dog?"

Nowhere to run. Nowhere to hide. No talking his way out of it as Jimmy Dot stared down the barrel of finality.

"You're dead!" screamed Leeds as he steadied himself. No way he could miss at this distance, but he still kept both hands on the gun as he took aim. "You are fucking dead!"

"Wrong, asshole! You're the one who's dead!"

The words hit Leeds an instant before he was blasted at point blank range by a gusher from Sparkle's water cannon.

Dot flew off the podium and tackled the sopping wet CEO who fired a shot that whizzed past his ear. They wrestled on the stage for control of the gun, the barrel inches from Dot's face. Leeds' finger within a whisker of the trigger. Dot struggled to push the gun away but an enraged Leeds matched his strength. Both men giving it everything they had until Dot's wet hand caused his grip on the weapon to slip. A shot rang out. Then another. The second bullet burning a furrow into Dot's fuzzy scalp as he managed to grab Leeds by the arm. Jerked it behind his back until the bone snapped and the gun fell from his grasp.

Dot smashed him in the face with the gun. "That's for Jenny." He smashed his face again. "That's for Ballinger." Again even harder. "And that's for trying to kill half the fucking world."

Jim-my Dot ... Jim-my Dot ... Jim-my Dot ....

Bloodied, broken, but still unbowed, Leeds looked up, as Dot stood over him ready to dish out more of the same. "I've got the best lawyers money can buy, and I guarantee you I will be acquitted of whatever trumped-up charges the Feds throw at me."

"Maybe you are slick enough to beat the rap in court," Dot told him as emergency medical personnel scaled the stage. "But even if you do you'll be broke and disgraced, serving twenty-five to life selling floor tile in Catoosa, Oklahoma."

"Never in a million years," snarled Leeds as he coughed up blood. Remained defiant through excruciating pain as he struggled to get words out through broken teeth. "You may have talked me out of killing Abbie, but when this is all over I am sure as hell going to kill you."

"I wouldn't try it, asshole," said Jenny, who kicked Leeds in the balls as hard as she could. Emergency medical personnel stepped aside in case she wanted to kick him again, but she had made her point.

"Nice of you to finally show up with the cavalry," said Dot, his scalp wound being attended to as Malvin Williams joined them on the stage. "But I had the situation under control."

"I can see that," chuckled the most powerful man in the United States Senate as he watched police and FBI try to calm the riot still raging around them.

"I told you that arrogant prick overplayed his hand with that chocolate chip cookie bullshit," gloated Dot as they watched the EMTs cart Leeds away. "Good to see that you finally believed me."

"I never believed you for a second. But I know dang well that whether a con man holds elected office or wears orange polka dot under-britches, his lies are supposed to be believable, and

I could not for one second figure out why you would try to hornswoggle me with such a steaming pile of horse manure."

"Even this morning after I called you with the name of the FDA supervisor who just bought his and hers Escalades?"

"Nothing illegal in a federal employee buying a couple of expensive cars. But your tip did turn out to be good as gold, because when the FBI checked further they found out that not only did he pay cash for those Escalades, he paid off the mortgage on his house as well. It took all of five minutes for investigators to get him to spill his guts about everything, which put them on the trail of a large off shore deposit made by the Deputy Commissioner, who in turn gave up Randy Leeds."

With the help of Killer Kong, law enforcement was finally able to restore order as the senator tipped his cowboy hat to Jenny.

"I have some very good news for you, Mrs. Dotoski," he smiled. "I'm Mal Williams, and I've figured a way to quash the warrant and take care of your immigration problem."

"I already took care of it," Dot told him.

"How, Jimmy? You pay that sidewinder off?"

"Doesn't matter how. It's over."

"For now, maybe. But what happens when your wife's alien status shows up on some other agent's radar?"

"Please, Senator," interrupted Jenny.

"My friends call me Mal."

"Please, Mal. Tell us how we can take care of this legally."

"Sit tight a minute, gal. Got a little business to take care of first," he told Jenny as he saw television news crews arrive, then looked at Dot. "You saved millions of lives, Jimmy. Let's go tell the world about it."

"You go, Mr. President."

The senator smiled, and then excused himself to crow to an audience a lot more far reaching than the Silver State's six electoral votes.

Jenny picked up an overturned chair and sat down. Looked at her husband, eyes pleading for the answer she so desperately needed. "Is it over, Jimmy? Is it finally over so we can go home?"

"As soon as I settle the score with Blake Fuller."

"Let it go, Jimmy," she urged. "I'm safe from deportation, which means the worst that prick can do is sue you for breach of contract. And good luck to him collecting anything because you just spent all the money you have on a sixty foot racing sloop."

"He killed Zazzo. I can't let him get away with that."

"He won't," interrupted Swanky as he gave each of them a beer he had snatched out of the ice when the bartenders ran for cover.

"Stay out of it, Swank."

"You helped me when I literally had nowhere to go. Staked me to some groceries and a place to sleep. Gave me a job and a new look. There was nothing in it for you, yet you not only kept my secret you gave me a new life."

"And I'm not going to let you throw it away."

"And I'm not going to let you throw yours away. Everybody knows there's bad blood between you and Fuller, and you'd never get away with it." For the first time in the two years he had known Dot, Swanky was asserting himself. "It's time I stopped hiding from the world and hit Fuller with something that will hurt him a lot more than dying."

Swanky took his phone from his pocket and made a call.

"Hello, Anderson. This is Preston Bond."

THE FABULOUS. JIMMY DOT'S SUITE.
SATURDAY 6:16 PM

The Love Dots snuggled on the sofa, waiting for the CNN special report they were watching to return from a commercial break. Audi. Charles Schwab. Promos for The *Situation Room* and *Parts Unknown*. Cue Anderson Cooper.

> COOPER: *For those of you just joining us, CNN has pre-empted our regular programming so that we can bring you exclusive coverage of the news bombshell of the year. Preston Bond is alive. And the biggest movie star in the world when he was reported killed in a plane crash two years ago, is on the phone with us right now.*

Sharing the screen with the newsman was a photo of the reincarnated movie star, with a graphic beneath it that read: PRESTON BOND – LIVE VIA TELEPHONE. Dot's thoughts took him back two years, noting that the photograph looked nothing like the bearded drifter he had found sleeping in an all night movie. Certainly nothing like post-surgery Swanky LaBeef.

COOPER: *And for any of you who might be skeptical of the call's authenticity, two independent audio experts have confirmed that the voice on the phone is indeed that of Preston Bond .... So tell us, Preston, where have you been and why have you let the world think you were dead these past two years?*

Dot turned up the volume. He and Jenny leaned closer.

BOND: *I was thrown from the wreckage and knocked unconscious. I came to sometime the next day and climbed down the rocky mountainside and made my way to the nearest town to get help. Then the strangest thing happened: nobody recognized me. Probably because my clothes were torn and I was filthy underneath a week's worth of whiskers. Then I saw a newspaper and realized that the world thought I was dead.*

COOPER: *That must have been quite a shock. How did it make you feel?*

BOND: *Free, Anderson. Suddenly I felt free. No longer the prisoner of a celebrity spotlight so invasive that I couldn't use a public men's room. Couldn't skinny dip in my own backyard pool without a drone video showing up on TMZ.*

COOPER: *Most people would say that's the price of fame and fortune.*

BOND: *Why should I have to pay that price, Anderson? I have a background in legitimate theatre and went to Hollywood be an actor, not a movie star. From a small town in Missouri where folks respect each other's privacy and don't find it necessary to lock their doors at night.*

COOPER: *Are you in Missouri right now?*

SHADOW CREEK GOLF COURSE.
NORTH LAS VEGAS.
SATURDAY 6:19 PM

Cy Watson was a clean-cut man of fifty. Not a drop of perspiration on his powder blue Izod shirt, not one salt and pepper hair out of place, as the CEO of the company that owned The Fabulous enjoyed a cold beer in the clubhouse with the members of his foursome after an invigorating eighteen holes. Watching golf on television, because that's what golfers do, when a waitress quickly came behind the bar and changed the channel to CNN.

COOPER: *You won't tell us where you are, and you won't even tell us where you aren't. Preferring to remain in hiding rather than go back to your life of superstardom. Why?*

BOND: *I'm not hiding. I just prefer to live my life privately.*

COOPER: *If that's the case, why you have come forward to let the world know that you're alive? And why now?*

BOND: *You know, Anderson, I think the tabloid head-lines about people spotting me at a bowling alley or flipping burgers at a roadside diner are fun, as they give folks an escape from all the serious news headlines. But when white collar criminals exploit my name to swindle these same people out of their hard-earned money, it's time to come forward and take a stand.*

COOPER: *Again, for those of you just tuning in, Preston Bond, Hollywood's biggest box office draw when he was reportedly killed in a plane crash two years ago is alive. Preston Bond is alive, and he is on the phone with us right now .... Preston, tell us who exactly is using your name to swindle the public.*

The golfers and bar staff hung on Preston Bond's every word. Cy Watson signaled the bartender to turn up the volume.

BOND: *It's come to my attention that a man named Blake Fuller, president of The Fabulous hotel in Las Vegas, got his job by starting a rumor that I secretly lived in the hotel and roamed the casino in disguise late at night. He makes more than a million dollars a year plus bonuses by continuing to exploit the rumor that I am somewhere inside that hotel. And over the past two years The Fabulous has cashed in on this fraud by tripling room rates.*

THE FABULOUS. BLAKE FULLER'S OFFICE.
SATURDAY 6:22 PM

Blake Fuller was steaming as sat at his desk, watching on his computer as Preston Bond ratted him out to Anderson Cooper on CNN.

COOPER: *So you're saying you're not in Las Vegas?*

BOND: *No, Anderson. I haven't been in Las Vegas since CinemaCon five years ago. And I urge each and every person watching this show not to set foot inside The Fabulous as long as Blake Fuller is still employed there.*

Fuller blew his top as he saw Everest walk uninvited into his office.

"What the fuck do you want?"

"I came to kill you so that Jimmy Dot wouldn't have to," Everest told him matter-of-factly. Then laughed, a very satisfied laugh as he nodded toward the computer screen. "But it looks like Preston Bond beat me to it."

THE FABULOUS. POONTANG JOHNSON'S DRESSING ROOM.
SATURDAY 7:27 PM

Though the news was not unexpected, Jimmy Dot's announcement moments earlier that this show would be their last had taken the air out of the room. Sparkle sat on the sofa with Swanky drinking beer and munching sliders while Poontang analyzed her reflection in the makeup mirror, wondering if it was possible to improve on perfection. Each knowing that Dot had no choice but to pull the plug on the show if he wanted to reclaim his life. And each of them cool with it, as they would not have had their moment in the spotlight in the first place if it weren't for him. An understanding reaction that took Dot by surprise, but he still felt guilty at the fame and fortune he was taking away from them and left the dressing room to be by himself.

Jenny, wearing a stunning red and black sorcerer's cloak, and Gladys in her orange unitard and orange beehive wig, sat by themselves, locked in serious conversation.

"It's a government program called EB-5 that offers visas to foreigners who invest over half a million in a project that creates jobs," Jenny told her. "Senator Williams said that if I make the investment he can fast track my permanent green card."

"How is me selling you the Ambassador going to create jobs?"

"That's what I wanted to know, but the senator said he would show us how to sidestep all that job creation red tape."

"It sounds great, Jenny, but I don't want your money. I'll give you the building."

"I have to prove I paid for it in order to qualify for the program."

"Do you have half a million dollars?"

"We will as soon as Jimmy backs out of the deal to buy that asshole Gunther a boat."

"You keep that money. I can't take it."

"You have to, Glad. For me to get a green card, this whole process has to be on the square."

Time had robbed the old lady of a marble or two and, though she very much wanted to help, was adamant that she would not accept any money from the Love Dots.

"Then give it to those starving kids on TV," suggested Jenny.

"I've got a better idea," returned Gladys. "I'll keep the money and leave it to you in my will. I was going to leave you the building anyway."

"Then I'll give it to the starving kids."

Gladys popped with another light bulb moment. "Or better yet. I'll take the money and use it to keep that nice Dr. Ballinger and his friends at the Top Hat Ballroom on Cloud Nine for years."

"Done."

Both smiled, and then shook hands like seasoned business-women closing a deal.

Down the hall Dot sat quietly, alone in his own dressing room. Reflecting on everything that had transpired over the past few days. Zazzo and Revson were dead. Fink confessed to the ultimate betrayal. Everest had taken nobility to a new level. Then there was Poontang, Sparkle and Swanky, all of whom had proven great loyalty that transcended great friendship. And how was he repaying that loyalty? By putting his own happiness ahead of theirs and kicking them to the curb. He felt like a shit heel.

There was a polite knock at the door.

"Excuse me for barging in, Mr. Dotoski. My name is Cy Watson."

The boss of all bosses pertaining to all things Fabulous, still sporting golf togs in his rush to initiate damage control, apologized for everything he had so far been made aware of, as well as the landslide of offenses he was sure would soon come to light.

"First of all, let me tell you that Blake Fuller has been fired."

"A bit late with that one, don't you think?"

"Point taken, Jimmy. May I call you Jimmy?"

"Knock yourself out."

"And given the public relations disaster Fuller has created, it is vital that The Fabulous right the ship quickly so that we can earn back public trust."

"That's your problem." Dot could give two shits about The Fabulous. Guilt gnawing at his guts that he would never earn back the trust of his friends. "I already quit. Tonight is my last show."

"That's why I'm here, Jimmy." No negotiating. He cut to the chase. "Your show brings five thousand people through the door every night, creating huge ancillary revenue for the casino. What would it take to keep the Jimmy Dot Circus at The Fabulous? How much more money?"

"What guys like you don't understand is that this has never been about money," replied Dot, his brain kicking around an idea.

"What then?" asked Watson anxiously. "Tell me what it's going to take to keep your circus in my showroom."

THE FABULOUS. BLAKE FULLER'S OFFICE.
SATURDAY 8:39 PM

Blake Fuller hated Cy Watson for firing him after his genius had made the company a fortune, and was doubly angry that the untimely ax had screwed him out of his huge bonus. If only Jimmy Dot had kept his fat nose out of things. If only Preston Bond had stayed dead another couple of weeks. But smart men knew that *if only* was a sucker's lament. Smart men knew that when one door closed another opened. And Fuller was well aware of the fact that he was a smart man as he took down the Corralez and other artwork from his personal collection that hung in the office. For him The Fabulous had never been more than the means to an end, and during his two years at the helm he had been able to bank enough cash to make himself a player in the art world. Not a serious player with a gigantic bankroll. Not yet anyway. But he would get there. He couldn't miss. He had the eye. It said so in the latest issue of *Zoom Bop*.

A pretty girl with blond hair stood quietly in the doorway as he removed personal items from desk drawers and placed them into a file box. After a few moments he noticed her.

"Whatever you're selling, I don't work here anymore."

After all that had happened, Fuller felt surprisingly good saying that. Invigorated. Excited about the new world of opportunity in front of him.

Doll entered the office. Only the desk between them.

"Why did you murder my boyfriend?"

"Just because a guy steals your jewelry doesn't make him your boyfriend."

"I'm not a mark."

"Then you must be a hooker. Because from what I hear, all that bullshit swami ever fucked were marks and hookers."

Doll removed a .44 magnum revolver from her purse and aimed it at him.

"You're not going to shoot me," he laughed. "Way too much gun for a tiny girl like you to handle."

Doll gripped the weapon tightly with both hands and pulled the trigger six times. Each bullet hitting the target and knocking Fuller backwards through the one-way glass, crashing him into the middle of a crap-out roll on a dice table two floors below.

THE FABULOUS.
JIMMY DOT THEATRE.
SATURDAY 9:42 PM

Crossbow archer The Great Moretti thrilled the crowd as his blindfolded triple ricochet shot pierced an apple on Jimmy Dot's head. The ringmaster took a bite of the skewered Golden Delicious, then attempted a feat of skill almost as difficult as he tried to calm down an audience that had spent the past ninety minutes cheering from the edge of their seats.

"Just before tonight's show, I agreed to a new contract that will keep the Jimmy Dot Circus and all your favorite performers here at The Fabulous to entertain you for many years to come!"

Sparkle and Poontang's faces lit up at the surprise announcement as the crowd screamed its approval.

"But the show will go on without Jimmy Dot, because I decided I would rather spend every night in bed with my beautiful wife eating pizza and watching movies." A spotlight hit Jenny as Dot flashed his mischievous smile. "What do you say, fellas? Which would you rather do?"

The crowd cheered their answer, then whistled as Jimmy and Jenny kissed center stage.

"And never fear, because I'm turning the polka dot boxer shorts over to a man who was born with legitimate show business in his blood. A man who risked everything just to be on this stage. Your new ringmaster, SWANKY LaBEEF!"

The normally shy and reserved chubby-faced man in the ruffled orange tuxedo shirt exploded into a performing dynamo as he danced a nifty soft shoe, then in a polished showbiz move grabbed a microphone and engaged the capacity crowd.

"You want more?"

Swanky cupped his hand around his ear as the crowd yelled its approval.

"I can't hear you," he teased, and then smiled as he sang out, "Well, you ain't seen nothin' yet!"

Jimmy Dot let the future ringmaster soak up the adulation, and then told the crowd, "And one last thing before me and my gal ride off into the sunset. We want to thank the man without whose help the circus would never have made it to The Fabulous in the first place. He's here in the audience tonight."

A spotlight hit a rooster-haired Englishman seated fourth row center.

"Mr. Rod Stewart! Come on, Rod. Stand up and take a bow."

As the smiling Stewart stood and waved to the audience, Sparkle popped up out of nowhere and smashed him in the face with a pie. The crowd screamed with laughter as Stewart stumbled blindly about, finally removing his suit jacket to wipe the banana cream out of his eyes.

"Take it away, Swanky!" yelled Jimmy Dot as the new ring-master pressed the button on his cassette player that ignited *Viva Las Vegas.* Balloons and streamers cascaded from the rafters as the wheelchair dancers came to life and rolled tightly choreographed figure eights. Jenny blew a stream of fire that burned the ropes binding a wooden crate suspended above the stage and a dozen monkeys tumbled out wearing orange bikinis and orange beehive wigs, jumping on unicycles and turning figure eights opposite the dancers. Poontang cast a fishing line and reeled in a merman, while bare chested Santas swallowed strands of Christmas lights and lit themselves up from the inside. Sparkle chased the six hundred pound bearded lady with a giant dildo while one-armed acrobats juggled live chickens.

The noise in the theatre was deafening as Jimmy Dot threw Twinkies as he led his cast of oddballs and misfits on a victory lap through the revved-up audience toward the gift shop where, one final time, he would shake the hand of each and every one of them.

Promise kept. A couple hundred heart-shaped balloons tied to bags of Cheetos filled the modest apartment as Jimmy and Jenny relaxed in their own bed, reading the Sunday comics with a pizza on the way. Jenny's favorites were Blondie and Bizarro, which she always read last, then finally gave in to the inevitable and checked out the front page.

"You really did a number on that place," she laughed, showing her husband a photo of the demolished post-riot event center.

"Well, if you're gonna make an omelet."

Then Jenny's mood turned somber as she looked at a photo of Bill Revson's wife and children mourning the loss of a hero who had sacrificed his life to do the right thing.

"Those assholes turned their backs on him when he needed them the most. Called him an embarrassment and refused to even speak to him," grumbled Dot as he got up and went into the kitchen. Opened the freezer and took some cash from an empty ice cream carton. Counted out $10,000 and dropped the bills on Jenny's nightstand.

"What's this for?"

"Pay off the bet."

"You won the bet. You got Leeds to admit in public that his drug causes cancer."

"No, I didn't. Cabot and Kong did," he told her. "Revson had a nine-year-old granddaughter who risked thirty days in the cooler every time she texted him. She was the only family he had who understood unconditional love. We need to find out where she is and send her this cash."

"Unconditional love, huh?"

"Unconditionally," smiled Dot as he kissed his wife.

There was a knock at the door.

"Pizza!" they yelled in unison.

Dot pulled on his boxers and batted his way through a swarm of heart-shaped balloons. As he reached for the door it was kicked in with such force that Dot was knocked backwards as Hard Bernard burst into the apartment, roaring like a madman. Wearing the same clothes he'd had on two days before when he had destroyed the White Bar. A fierce boner fueled by revenge straining at the fabric of his trousers as he launched himself like an attack missile, but Dot sidestepped the assault and subdued the savage gorilla with a wrestling hold. Hard Bernard stomped Dot's bare foot with a heavy boot and broke free, then pummeled him with a flurry of punches until Dot was finally able to duck for cover amid the red mylar balloons.

He jumped on Hard Bernard's back and pounded his cement head until the ferocious ex-cop tossed him off. Each smashing the other with chairs, lamps, vases. Whatever was within reach. Hard Bernard's boner continued to rage as both men were now on their feet, squaring off face to face. Dot connected with an uppercut that Hard Bernard answered with the swing of a fireplace poker. Again he swung it. Again and again. Dot bobbing and weaving. Backpedaling until he was trapped against the wall. As the madman wound up for his home run swing, Jenny came up from behind and smashed Hard Bernard's ears with the sharp corners of DVD box sets of *Racket Squad* and *Johnny Staccato.*

As Hard Bernard screamed from excruciating inner ear pain and lost his equilibrium, Dot staggered him with a right to the jaw. Then another and another until the raging maniac was as defenseless as a dented tomato can. Dot measured him for the big one, and then smashed his fist into Hard Bernard's face with such force that the big man finally went down. Flat on his back. Not moving a muscle. Still breathing, but out cold.

Dot and Jenny got dressed and dragged Hard Bernard, not so gently, by his feet around the pool and toward the towering palms that fronted the Ambassador. All the way to the street where they rolled him into the gutter. Then Dot had an idea. Ran back to the apartment and returned a moment later with a red balloon. Rolled Hard Bernard onto his back and pulled down his pants, then tied the heart-shaped helium-filled balloon to the madman's still raging hard on.

Dot admired his work, and then walked arm-in-arm with the woman he loved unconditionally forever and always. Stuck their heads inside the open door of apartment number one, where Gladys was busy preparing for that evening's welcome home party.

"Knock, knock," called Dot as they entered the apartment.

The old lady beamed from ear to ear and then wrapped her arms around them both, happy that her family was at last together again.

"Can I use your phone?" asked Dot.

"I hope you're calling that nice Dr. Ballinger to invite him to the party."

"Already did, Glad. He said he's feeling better and wouldn't miss it for the world."

Dot then picked up the telephone and dialed 911. Told the operator that some pervert was in front of the building bothering the neighborhood kids.

As Jimmy Dot kept an eye out for the pizza man, Gladys opened the refrigerator and popped the top on some liquid refreshment. Handed him an icy-cold bottle of Orange Crush while Jenny helped her with the pineapple upside down cake.

ACKNOWLEDGMENTS

Thanks to my wonderful wife Katie for her unconditional support. To my brilliant editor Scott Dickensheets and to Andrew Kiraly for his unwavering encouragement. To Sue Campbell for so much more than another great book design. To James P. Reza, the original Jimmy Dot. To the one and only Jenn O. Cide. To Harry Fagel for pushing Hard Bernard into retirement. To Drew and Scott at the Writer's Block. To fellow author and bandmate Dirk Vermin. To Amy Prenner, Lance Corralez, Chris Andrasfay, Louie Thomas, Staci Linklater, Ally Carter, Mark T. Zeilman, Ryan Reason, Jenn Burkart, Jennifer Danger, Carolyn Uber, Geoff Schumacher, Jarrett Keene, Dayvid Figler, Geoff Carter, Annie B, Steve Fahlsing, Hossy Von Bloodcock, Jay and Star, the Yorkshire Mob, Donald Frazer, Porkpie, Richie Rock, Rob Gelardi, Reverend Timmy Bloodcock, the irrepressible Willie K. Vanderbilt and especially Allan Carter for making everything possible.

ABOUT THE AUTHOR

P Moss is a longtime Las Vegan whose short fiction has appeared in several magazines and anthologies. He is a musician and songwriter whose band Bloodcocks UK, the only American band never to play in America, recently completed a rollicking fifth tour of Japan. He is a film noir and pulp fiction enthusiast, and an avid booster of the Scunthorpe United Football Club. A member of the Mystery Writers of America, *Vegas Tabloid* is the final book of his Las Vegas trilogy.